Maximus

THE IMMORTAL HIGHLAND CENTURIONS
BOOK ONE

JAYNE CASTEL

WINTER MIST
PRESS

A Roman centurion doomed to an immortal life. A courageous Scottish widow with an uncertain future. One night of passion that changes everything. High adventure and epic love in Medieval Scotland—with a touch of fantasy.

Maximus Flavius Cato should have died in 118 AD—the year the Ninth legion was lost forever in the wilds of Caledonia. Instead, a Pict druidess curses him and two others with immortality. Over a thousand years later, as he struggles to solve the riddle that holds the key to breaking the curse, Maximus has an encounter with a comely tavern wench. His immortal life will never be the same again.

Heather De Keith has made a lot of mistakes—but marrying a bad man was her greatest. After her husband never returns from battle, she's forced to take up work serving ale in a local tavern. Stubborn pride prevents her from returning to her kin at Dunnottar Castle. But when an enigmatic stranger comes to her aid one evening in the tavern, Heather lets attraction overrule good sense. The night they spend together spurs her to make the decision she's put off for too long. It's time to go home.

Pursued by a vengeful laird's son, Maximus and Heather flee north to Dunnottar. However, once on the road, they soon realize that neither of them will finish this journey with their hearts unscathed.

Historical Romances
by Jayne Castel

DARK AGES BRITAIN

The Kingdom of the East Angles series
Night Shadows (prequel novella)
Dark Under the Cover of Night (Book One)
Nightfall till Daybreak (Book Two)
The Deepening Night (Book Three)
The Kingdom of the East Angles: The Complete Series

The Kingdom of Mercia series
The Breaking Dawn (Book One)
Darkest before Dawn (Book Two)
Dawn of Wolves (Book Three)
The Kingdom of Mercia: The Complete Series

The Kingdom of Northumbria series
The Whispering Wind (Book One)
Wind Song (Book Two)
Lord of the North Wind (Book Three)
The Kingdom of Northumbria: The Complete Series

DARK AGES SCOTLAND

The Warrior Brothers of Skye series
Blood Feud (Book One)
Barbarian Slave (Book Two)
Battle Eagle (Book Three)
The Warrior Brothers of Skye: The Complete Series

The Pict Wars series
Warrior's Heart (Book One)
Warrior's Secret (Book Two)
Warrior's Wrath (Book Three)
The Pict Wars: The Complete Series

Novellas
Winter's Promise

MEDIEVAL SCOTLAND

The Brides of Skye series
The Beast's Bride (Book One)
The Outlaw's Bride (Book Two)
The Rogue's Bride (Book Three)
The Brides of Skye: The Complete Series

The Sisters of Kilbride series
Unforgotten (Book One)
Awoken (Book Two)
Fallen (Book Three)
Claimed (Epilogue novella)

The Immortal Highland Centurions series
Maximus (Book One)

Epic Fantasy Romances
by Jayne Castel

Light and Darkness series
Ruled by Shadows (Book One)
The Lost Swallow (Book Two)
Path of the Dark (Book Three)
Light and Darkness: The Complete Series

All characters and situations in this publication are fictitious, and any resemblance to living persons is purely coincidental.

Maximus, by Jayne Castel

Published by Winter Mist Press

ISBN: 978-0-473-53293-2 (paperback)

Edited by Tim Burton
Cover design by Winter Mist Press
Cover photography courtesy of www.shutterstock.com
Roman Imperial image courtesy of www.shutterstock.com

Visit Jayne's website: www.jaynecastel.com

***

To wee Max—may you have a life worthy of great stories!

***

Contents

"Every man dies, not every man really lives."
—William Wallace

PROLOGUE

INGLORIOUS

The Roman Fort of Pinnata Castra
Northern Caledonia (Scotland)

Winter, 118 AD

HE NEVER THOUGHT his death would be inglorious.

Knee-deep in gore, splattered in mud, and surrounded by clinging mist, with the howling of Pict warriors in his ears—Maximus Flavius Cato railed against his fate. Rage, hot and blistering, rose within him. He wasn't ready to go yet. He had a future serving Rome—and these barbarians were about to rip it from him.

He'd envisaged his end would come as he fought under clear, blue skies, shouting the emperor's name while he led his men to glory.

Not here in this forgotten, frozen shit-hole, brought down by savages.

The Picts surrounded him now, their eyes wild upon their blue-painted faces. Maximus's belly cramped, an ice-cold knot tightening under his ribcage.

It's over.

Five thousand soldiers had marched north into the wilds of Caledonia, and when they made their last stand that morning, only two centuries of his cohort remained: barely one hundred and sixty men to stand against the wrath of the northern tribes.

Thuds, grunts, and cries of battle filled the damp air. The mist curled in like steam drifting from hot baths. What was left of the Ninth had made their stand before the crumbling walls of Pinnata Castra—the fort Agricola had built many years earlier. High upon a ridge, surrounded by a dark pine wood, it felt like the end of the earth.

It *was* the end of the earth.

Maximus surged forward, slashing at the swarm of bodies clad in fur and leather, their limbs streaked in woad.

"Die!" He bellowed so loudly that it ripped his throat raw. It was the cry of a doomed man. But he was the pilus prior—the commander of what remained of the first cohort of the Ninth—and he wouldn't crumble in front of his men.

The legate was no use to them now. That craven was hiding up in the watchtower behind them, cowering with his standard-bearers.

The legate—this legion's imperial general—had pushed them into the wild north and argued with any who dared question him. He'd had deserters hunted down and stoned. But when the final stand came, where was he?

The fury within Maximus pulsed like a stoked ember. It made him feel invincible—as if nothing, not even a sharp Pict blade, could touch him.

The light was fading now, making visibility even more difficult through the tendrils of snaking mist. There was barely room to swing his sword, yet Maximus fought on, jaw clenched in iron determination. He slashed a Picti warrior across the throat. Blood gushed, coating them both, but he barely noticed. Raw anger turned him savage. If he was going to die today, he'd bring as many of these blue-painted bastards down with him as he could.

Maximus slashed and stabbed at any warrior who came within reach of his sword, aware then that he now stood alone. The men who'd fought at his shoulder were all dead. He brought down a woman who lunged at him with an iron-tipped pike—impaling her through the throat with his blade—before glancing behind him at the walls of the old fort. Had it been overrun yet?

There, above the lichen-encrusted walls, he saw the proud golden Eagle standard rising into the foggy gloaming. But as he watched, the Eagle listed and went down, disappearing from view.

Maximus's belly clenched. With the Eagle went the hope of the Hispana, the empire's mighty Spanish Legion. The Eagle standard was a symbol of honor for each centurion—and if they lost it, they lost everything.

The end had come. For him, and for the Hispana.

Roaring, Maximus whirled to face another attacker. An instant later, something heavy collided with the back of his helmet.

The last thing Maximus Flavius Cato saw before darkness claimed him was the muddy, blood-drenched ground rushing up to meet him.

There was only one thing worse than dying on the end of a Pict blade—and that was to live through the battle, only to be taken captive.

Maximus wasn't alone. Two other centurions sat with him, wrists and ankles bound, slumped up against the wall. All three of them were injured and barely conscious. Maximus's head hurt so badly that he felt sick. The back of his skull pounded in time with his heartbeat.

He was just about to close his eyes and let the pain consume him, when a woman walked into the hut.

Young, tall, and dark-haired, she was also beautiful. However, lust was the last thing on Maximus's mind as he stared at her. Instead, fear slithered through his gut, threatening to overwhelm his outrage at waking up to find himself trussed up like a hog.

Her expression was blank, cold.

It was the same look—one devoid of mercy—he'd witnessed on a cat's face once, right before it bit the head of a mouse clean off. Previously, the spoiled tom cat, his mother's cherished pet, had been toying with the field mouse.

Maximus knew who she was; the interior of this wattle and daub hut had told him. He'd observed the strange hangings made of bones, teeth, and feathers; and the shriveled corpses of animals and birds that swung from the rafters. This woman was a witch—or bandrúi as she was known in this land.

And Maximus knew enough of the Painted People and their ways to realize he should fear her. Yet, arrogant to the last, he glared at the woman. The fury that had consumed him during the Ninth's final stand still smoldered in his gut, seeking a chance to reignite.

The bandrúi had large, ice-blue eyes, rimmed with charcoal. Her face remained expressionless as she crossed the floor toward her three captives. The druidess had a loose-limbed walk. Her bare feet whispered on the dirt floor, her bone jewelry jangling. In one hand, she carried an earthen cup.

Her gaze went to Maximus first, and she dropped to a crouch before him, placing the cup on the ground next to her. He saw that it was full of a dark, viscous liquid.

"Inns dhomh na hainmean agad."

Tell me your names. It was not a request, but a command.

She spoke the Pict tongue with a different, sharper cadence than Maximus was used to hearing. He'd learned the local language from the tribesmen who lived farther south when he'd been stationed at Trimontium for a spell.

For a moment, he considered defying the woman, but something in those empty eyes warned him against doing so. "Maximus." His voice came out in a rasp. He was so thirsty he could barely swallow. His head hurt so badly that he had trouble even thinking. He'd lost all concept of time since the battle.

"And your friends?"

Maximus's lip curled. Still staring the woman down, he nudged the man next to him with his elbow. He was a hulking cohort centurion with close-cropped, brown hair, who kept drifting in and out of consciousness. "She wants to know your names," Maximus croaked.

A heavy pause followed before the centurion raised his battered face, his hazel eyes unfocused. "Cassian," he mumbled.

The woman nodded before her attention shifted to the third prisoner: a tall, lean man with hawkish features and short, curly black hair. Blood encrusted the centurion's chest from the wound he'd taken, but he was still awake and alert enough to snarl at the bandrúi, his white teeth flashing in the gloom. "Draco."

The bandrúi sat back on her heels. "Maximus. Cassian. Draco." She spoke their names slowly, rolling the unfamiliar words across her tongue, and then she shuffled back from them.

Using a blue-stained finger, the woman drew a crescent design upon the dirt floor between them.

"A blood moon rides tonight, and I have sacrificed three crows under it," she announced, her voice as impassive as her face. The woman's gaze snared Maximus's once more. Now that she knew he understood her tongue, she focused upon him. "I drained their blood, burned their hearts, and gained the favor of the Gods ... so that I may take vengeance upon our enemies."

A chill walked down Maximus's spine at these words, cooling the rage in his belly. There was power in this woman's eyes, as if she could strip away his flesh with a word and bare his soul to her.

"What's she muttering about?" the centurion Draco asked. He was glaring at the bandrúi, his face rigid.

Maximus hesitated before replying. He wasn't sure what the witch's words meant—only that death in battle would have been a mercy in comparison to what she had in store for them.

Fear's long fingers clasped around his throat and gently squeezed.

Inglorious, indeed, he thought grimly. *That'll teach me to take a posting in Britannia*. He could have gone anywhere in the empire, and yet he'd chosen its farthest flung, most savage corner. He'd had something to prove—and had once bragged to his younger brothers that he was heading off to 'tame the barbarians'—but now he was paying for his arrogance.

"She's about to kill us," Maximus murmured after a lengthy pause, focusing on his companions properly for the first time since he'd awoken. He recognized both these men, for they'd formed part of his cohort. They were both good fighters from Hispania.

He suddenly wished that, like them, he was ignorant of these people's tongue. Better not to understand this woman's chilling words.

For she wasn't yet finished with them.

"A curse be upon you three," the bandrúi continued, her voice turning harsh. She picked up the cup and dipped her finger into it. Maximus realized then that the dark liquid was congealing blood—crow's blood most likely. She leaned forward and drew a mark upon Maximus's forehead.

Spitting out an oath, he shrank back from the woman's touch. Yet injured and trussed up, there was nowhere to go. Likewise, his two companions endured the same treatment.

Maximus's already pounding heart quickened further when he saw she'd drawn a crescent symbol upon their foreheads. He didn't know the significance of such a mark, but understood that it didn't bode well for any of them.

Some of the priestesses of his homeland wielded dangerous power—but he'd never feared a woman like he did this one. He'd prefer to face down a pike-bearing Picti warrior any day than this cold-eyed druidess.

"I was wrong," he rasped. "The bitch is cursing us ... *before* she kills us."

"Let her," Cassian said. His voice was a rattling wheeze. "Filthy barbarian witch."

"*You three* will endure eternal life," the bandrúi intoned, oblivious to their insults. "Age will never touch you ... but you are doomed to watch everyone you love wither and die. You are forever bound to the borders of these lands, and you will never father children. Eventually, you will live long enough to watch the world end."

A hollow silence followed her words.

Maximus's heart was thundering so violently now he felt ill. Like most of his people, he was superstitious. The witch's words were outrageous, impossible, and yet he found himself believing them.

Another woman, many years earlier, had cursed his legion—Queen Boudicca of the Iceni—and the Hispana had been in decline ever since.

"Enough," he snarled, his hard-won control finally unraveling. "Kill us, woman. Give us warriors' deaths."

The bandrúi's mouth twisted, and she shook her head. "Arrogant man of the Caesars," she snarled. "You march upon our lands with your bright shields, crested helmets, and red cloaks, and demand we kneel before you. You will suffer for your conceit. Death is too kind!"

Maximus stared up at her, at her terrible beauty. His head ached so badly now, he almost groaned out loud with the pain. Still, he didn't break her stare.

Long moments stretched out, while the pair of them watched each other, and then a cold smile curved the bandrúi's lips. It was the first expression to shatter her inscrutable mask, yet it was a terrifying one.

"You are one of their chieftains," she observed finally. "I knew it when I took that strange helmet with a red fan from you." Her gaze raked down over the leather harness, metal breastplate, and crimson cloak he wore, before she inclined her head. "You are brave ... I shall give you that. The warriors said you fought like a cornered wolf before the walls. But it will not save you."

Maximus's mouth twisted. He'd fought with the savagery of a doomed man—there had been no glory in it. History wouldn't remember Maximus Flavius Cato. The Empire had abandoned the Ninth, sacrificed them to the wild.

The woman then rose to her feet, towering above them. She wore a smirk upon her face now. "But, maybe, I will allow you a chance to save yourselves ... a riddle."

Maximus swallowed hard, heat washing over him as his temper flared once more. She was playing with him. *He* was that field mouse, with its tail pinned under the tom cat's paw. His life was worthless to her.

"Remember my words well, Maximus," the druidess continued, her smirk widening into a death's-head grin. "For if you solve it, the curse will be broken."

Maximus stared back at her. He refused to believe that a shred of mercy beat in her savage heart. This woman wasn't really offering him hope. Yet he had no choice in this. All he could do was play her twisted game.

Holding the bandrúi's eye, Maximus clenched his jaw and prepared to listen.

When the Broom-star crosses the sky,
And the Hammer strikes the fort
Upon the Shelving Slope.
When the White Hawk and the Dragon wed,
Only then will the curse be broke.

1, 183 years later …

I

WISH UPON A STAR

*The village of Fintry
Stirlingshire, Scotland*

Spring, 1301 AD

SHE NEVER THOUGHT she'd end up serving ale to
drunks.

Weaving her way through the busy tavern—eyes
stinging from cloying peat smoke, and deafened by the
raucous laughter surrounding her—Heather wondered
how she'd gotten herself into this mess. She'd once had
dreams, but now spent her days scrubbing floors and
emptying privies. Her evenings were taken up serving
food and drink to the rough men who frequented *The
Bogside Tavern*, Fintry's only watering hole.

Heather let out a long sigh and settled the tray of pies
she carried against her hip.

This is my own doing.

Aye, she'd dreamed of being a contented wife to the
village's handsome smithy, of spending her days tending
the garden behind their cottage, cooking hearty stews

and baking oaten bannocks, and bringing up a brood of bairns—but she'd chosen the wrong man.

In the past, she'd blamed her parents for their overbearing ways or Iain for being such a disappointment. Yet in the end, she was responsible for her own choices.

Heather was considering this unpalatable fact, and attempting to squeeze past a group of farmers who were arguing over the price of rams, when a large hand made a grab for her backside.

Batting the offending paw away, with enough force to make the farmer spill the tankard of mead he was sipping, Heather fixed him with a gimlet stare. "Try that again, Murdoc, and I'll break yer fingers," she warned, injecting a falsely cheerful note into her voice.

"Aw, be nice, Heather," the farmer leered. "Can't ye let a lonely man have a feel?"

She elbowed her way past him. "Ye've been warned."

Ignoring the coarse laughter that followed, Heather made her way over to where two elderly men sat in a corner. The common room was the heart of *The Bogside*: a large, rectangular space with two sides lined in booths and a scattering of circular tables in the middle of a sawdust-covered floor. A huge fire roared at one end, and above it loomed a grizzled boar's head. The beast— one that the tavern owner, Aonghus Galbraith, had hunted as a younger man—snarled out at the patrons, its large, yellowed tusks gleaming in the firelight. Heavy oaken beams crisscrossed overhead, trapping a pall of acrid peat smoke.

The two men were regulars who, since they'd lost their wives, spent every eve at *The Bogside* playing at knucklebones.

"Did ye see the star yesterday?" one of them said as he flipped the bones and tried to catch them on the back of his hand.

"What?" His companion grumbled.

"The fire-tailed star ... the one I told ye about."

"What star is this, Fergus?" Heather asked, curiosity replacing the simmering irritation that the farmer with wandering hands had provoked. Every evening was the same. She grew tired of constantly having to fend these letches off.

The old man glanced up as Heather placed a hot pie in front of him. "For the past few days, it's appeared in the night sky," he replied, flashing her a toothless smile. "It's bright silver and has a fiery tail."

Heather inclined her head, ignoring the patron a few tables away who was trying to catch her eye. She'd get to him when she was ready. "Really?" She'd heard that sometimes such stars graced the sky, but had never seen one.

"Aye. When she was alive, my Gran told me about it. She said it heralds change."

His companion snorted, but Fergus ignored him. His gaze remained upon Heather.

She considered his words. Was his gran right—and if so, what change might be coming?

Perhaps we'll finally rid ourselves of the English, she thought, her mouth compressing. *Maybe the Wallace will return and drive every last one of them back over The Wall.*

Dwelling on this thought, Heather set down the second pie before Dougal. "I'll have to search for this star tonight," she said with a smile. "Once I'm done here."

Dougal gave another snort. "Don't encourage him, lass."

Ignoring his grumpy friend, Fergus grinned, his eyes bright in a spider web of wrinkles. "Aye, see that ye do ... such sights only come once in a lifetime, if we're lucky."

Considering this, Heather turned and made her way back to the kitchen. The patron who'd been trying to catch her eye gave an angry shout, but she ignored him. She knew he was waiting for his pie. She hoped he choked on it.

I wish the star heralded change for my life, she thought. *Maybe if I wish upon it, my lot will improve.* The heaviness that had dogged her steps all day increased at the frivolous thought. It felt as if she carried a sack of oats upon her back today. Wishing upon a star wouldn't undo the mistakes she'd made.

Moments later, Heather entered the kitchen to find a tall, thin woman awaiting her, hands on hips. Aonghus was away for the night and had left his wife in charge.

"There ye are!" Morag greeted her with a scowl. "Move yer arse, lass. We're run off our feet tonight. Get those pies served before they go cold."

Heather inhaled sharply and forced down the irritated response that rose within her. It was hard not to talk back to the woman. A steward's daughter, she'd never gotten used to having orders barked at her.

Picking up the tray nearest, she turned and stormed back into the fray. The tavern was filling up even more now, and as Heather worked her way across the floor, batting away more groping hands, she noted that Fergus and Dougal weren't the only ones discussing the fire-tailed star. The strange sight in the night sky was the talk of the common room this evening.

However, Heather paid their conversation little attention. She now had thirsty men shouting for ale in every direction. The urge to tell the lot of them to go to the devil boiled in Heather's gut, and heat rose to her cheeks.

She wasn't cut out for life as a tavern wench. She was too short-tempered, too intolerant.

After her husband's disappearance, she'd been faced with a difficult choice: either return home to her kin and weather their scorn, or look for work locally and endure a life of drudgery. Pride had overruled good sense perhaps, for drudgery had actually seemed the most appealing option at the time.

A year and a half later, she wasn't so sure.

"Two more ales over here, lass!" A man boomed from near the fire. "And hurry yerself about it ... we're thirsty!"

Heather nodded to the customer before she swiveled on her heel and went to do his bidding. On the way back with his drinks, she noted that two tables had just been vacated and were now littered with crumbs and spilled ale.

Thumping the tankards down and hastily side stepping yet another grasping hand, Heather wove her way to the counter, where Aonghus usually presided, and fetched a damp cloth.

Morag would chew her ear off if she didn't wipe down those tables.

She was swishing the cloth across a table top, when the door to the tavern opened, bringing with it a blast of frosty air.

Heather glanced up, her attention traveling to the doorway.

A tall, dark-haired man, clad head-to-toe in black leather, stepped inside. He then pulled the door shut behind him, sealing in the warm, smoky fug.

Heather stilled. This was a new face, and a starkly different one to the regulars inside *The Bogside*.

But she wasn't the only one to notice his entrance. The stranger's arrival caused the roar of conversation inside the tavern to subside—and all gazes swiveled toward him.

II

STRANGER AT THE BOGSIDE

IT WAS DIFFICULT not to stare. Although Fintry was spitting distance from Stirling, it didn't see many strangers—especially ones who looked like him.

In contrast to the locals, who had long hair and thick beards, the newcomer had cropped hair with a short fringe across the brow. He was also clean shaven and had proud, aquiline features, high cheekbones, and skin that was tanned light gold—odd for this time of year, for the last of the winter snow had just melted and the first days of spring were cold and grey.

His swarthy appearance marked him as foreign, and yet he didn't look anything like the English soldiers she'd seen.

Heather straightened up, her gaze narrowing when she saw he carried a knife strapped to his hip. Luckily, Aonghus wasn't here; he wouldn't have liked that. Nonetheless, her attention didn't linger on the knife for long, for the rest of him was too fascinating to ignore.

The stranger carried himself straight and proud, his dark gaze scanning the common room as if he hadn't yet decided whether to linger at the establishment.

Heather's mouth curved. *There isn't any point in being fussy.* These were the only lodgings in Fintry.

Her smile faded then. She didn't like to remind herself that *The Bogside* had been *her* only option as well.

However, the drudgery of her life ceased to matter as Heather continued to observe the newcomer. Since Iain, she'd barely looked at other men. But the sight of this dark-haired stranger sucked the air from her lungs.

For a few moments, she forgot the tyrannical tavern owner and his blade-tongued wife. She ignored her aching back and chapped hands, and the weariness that pulled down at her. She put aside the disappointment that soured her belly, the resentment that gnawed there too, and the underlying sadness that cast a shadow over everything.

Instead, Heather's gaze tracked the tall, lean figure across the sawdust-strewn floor. And heat flooded through her when she realized he was heading in her direction.

Heather tensed as he approached. Now that he focused his attention upon her, she realized he'd caught her staring. Brazening the moment out, she squared her shoulders and held his gaze.

She'd never seen eyes like his—so dark brown that they almost appeared black in the ruddy light of the cressets that burned upon the surrounding stone walls.

"Do you have a room available for the night?" he asked. His voice was as exotic as the rest of him. He spoke her tongue fluently, and yet with a cadence that definitely wasn't local. There was a clipped edge to his words.

"Aye," she replied with a guarded smile. "A penny will get ye a bed, a meal, and a jug of ale."

He nodded, not returning her smile. "Do you have any wine instead?"

"Aye," Heather replied. "There's bramble wine made last autumn. Will that do?"

The stranger nodded again before digging into a pouch at his hip and producing a silver coin, which he placed on the table between them. "Well enough."

"I'll have a room made up for ye then?"

"Thank you. I've stabled my pony already." With that, he turned and strode over to one of the booths lining the nearby wall—which two men had just vacated for a table closer to the hearth.

Heather watched him go. He wasn't the friendliest man she'd ever met, yet now that she'd exchanged a few words with him, she found him even more fascinating than earlier. She was tired of hearing the local men bellow drunkenly at each other night after night, of hearing the same coarse comments.

This man was refreshingly different.

Careful Heather ... ye once thought that about Iain.

The reminder was a sobering one.

"Heather!" Morag's voice lashed through the smoky air. "What are ye doing idling? Finish wiping those tables, and get supper served!"

Fingers clenching around the damp cloth, Heather moved over to the last of the tables before giving it a quick wipe. Not for the first time that evening, hot words bubbled up inside her.

Yer pride will be yer undoing one day, Heather De Keith. Her mother's words came back to her then. Iona De Keith hadn't been wrong. Stubborn pride had landed Heather in a right mess.

With that, she approached the tavern owner's wife and passed her the penny. "I wasn't idling," Heather informed Morag through clenched teeth. "That man I was talking to wants lodgings for the night."

The woman's thin face softened a little. "I'll get Alana to ready a room for him." Morag's gaze then shifted to where the stranger had settled himself into the booth. "Who is he?"

Heather shrugged, feigning a lack of interest. "Speaks with an accent, so he's not from here."

Morag snorted. "Any fool can see that, lass." She jerked her pointy chin toward the kitchen, where more trays of pies were no doubt cooling. "Go on ... get back to work."

Sighing, Maximus leaned against the back of the booth, letting the warmth of the common room seep into his limbs. He tended to avoid taverns and inns—he got tired of the attention he attracted. All these years in this brutal northern land, and still the locals looked upon him with suspicion.

His arrival had literally killed the conversation in the room, although he was relieved to see that most of the patrons had returned to their ales and suppers now that he'd taken a seat.

It was a relief to be indoors. Outside, the weather was damp and frosty, and he'd slept rough for the last few days during his journey up from Dumfries. He only had half a day's travel till his destination—Stirling—but his body ached for a soft bed and a warm meal. He'd just have to put up with the stares.

Maximus tensed at the thought of his destination, and he started to tap his fingers on the polished table top before him. He hoped there would be a message for him in Stirling. It was always a wrench to leave the wilderness behind and re-enter the world—even if he was a man who loved home comforts. It was just easier to spend his days far from other folk and their demands. As such, he didn't want to make the effort to go to Stirling for nothing. If Cassian or Draco hadn't left word for him there, he'd have to wait around until one of them did.

Maximus's attention shifted through the haze that hung underneath the rafters to where the serving lass approached, a jug in one hand, an earthen cup in the other.

His gaze tracked her across the floor toward him.

The women who served in these places seemed to look alike to him: work-worn and put-upon with long-suffering smiles and wary gazes. Yet this tavern wench was different.

She was flustered and pink-cheeked, and wore a thinly veiled look of irritation. But there was something about her—a vibrancy—that made her stand out. She wasn't classically beautiful. Her face was a trifle too round, her features not striking enough. Yet she was comely with an earthiness that made Maximus keenly aware of her. Thick, light brown hair tumbled over her shoulders. Intelligent grey-green eyes watched him steadily. He noted that she had a sensual mouth, with a plump lower lip.

She also had a body that few men could fail to take notice of: full of womanly curves with a bosom that strained against the laces of her moss-green kirtle.

Maximus liked a lass with flesh on her bones, and the ache that spiked through his groin as his gaze raked down the length of her reminded him that he'd been too long without bedding a woman.

How many months had it been now? *Hades ... it's been nearly a year*.

Still, that wasn't why he'd darkened the door of *The Bogside Tavern*, and this woman wasn't a whore. He needed to stop looking at her as if she were part of what his silver penny had paid for.

Maximus knew women found him attractive; he didn't need to pay them to spread their legs for him. Yet he'd learned long ago that doing so made life easier. He avoided emotional entanglements that way—and the unpleasant scenes that always followed as a result.

It was strange really, for so many years had passed since the mess with Evanna, yet he was still wary of women.

Maybe I should visit a brothel in Stirling, he told himself as the lass drew close. Immortal or not, a man still had urges. But, as comely as she was, this serving wench was probably trouble. Most women were.

"Bramble wine for ye," she said, placing the cup and jug down.

Maximus watched her under hooded lids. "Thank you ... what's for supper?"

"Game pie ... pigeon and grouse."

The woman looked boldly down at him, curiosity gleaming in her eyes. She certainly wasn't shy. "What's yer business in Fintry?"

Pouring himself a cup of dark wine, Maximus favored the woman with a cool smile. "Just passing through."

"Heather!"

A thin woman with flushed cheeks appeared in the kitchen door behind them, her shout cutting through the roar of men's voices. "Stop yammering, and move yerself!"

Heather. A bonny Scottish name, and one that suited her.

Huffing an annoyed breath, Heather turned from him and marched off. Maximus watched the sway of her hips and the tantalizing swell of her backside as she did so.

Once she disappeared into the kitchen, he raised the cup to his lips, taking a sip. The bramble wine was good: full-bodied with a pleasing sweetness. It was strange really. All these years away from his homeland and yet wine was still his drink of choice.

It was the taste of a sun-drenched land he'd all but forgotten.

Maximus swallowed, sighing as the liquid slid down his throat and warmed the pit of his belly. The first sip of wine after a long journey always made him forget his cares.

A frigid draft gusted into the common room when the door opened once more, bringing with it three men. They were big and loud, their voices booming across the crowded space. Once again, the tavern's patrons glanced up from their tankards, although they didn't stare as they had when Maximus entered. Instead, a few of them grinned and called out greetings to the newcomers.

The men sauntered across to an occupied table in the center of the space. The group of locals drinking there leaped up and vacated the table.

Not bothering to thank them, one of the three—a hulking young man with wild auburn hair—flung himself down on a chair.

"Ale!" he shouted. "And three of yer biggest pies!"

The man's two friends guffawed, enjoying his self-importance.

A moment later, the serving lass emerged from the kitchen, carrying a platter of food. Ignoring the loud newcomer and his two companions, she circuited their table and headed toward Maximus's booth.

"What's this, Heather?" The big auburn-haired man boomed. "No greeting for me today?"

"I'll greet ye, Cory Galbraith, when ye learn some manners," she replied coolly, still not looking his way. "And when ye can walk in here without shouting the rafters down."

Rough laughter followed this comment, although the man she'd addressed scowled.

Maximus took in the exchange with interest. *Galbraith*. Of course, Fintry sat at the heart of Galbraith lands. The laird himself resided at Culcreuch Castle, a grey stone tower that rose just beyond the village. If Maximus were a betting man, he'd say this loud-mouth was kin to the laird. He'd certainly sauntered into the tavern like he owned the place.

Heather reached Maximus and lowered the tray before him. There was a large wedge of pie, half a loaf of barley and oaten bread, and some cheese. The aroma of the game made Maximus's mouth water, reminding him that he'd hardly eaten today.

He was about to thank the woman, when he noted that the exuberance he'd seen upon her face earlier, the spark in her eyes, was gone. Her jaw was now tense, her gaze shuttered.

"Ye shall greet me when I wish it, woman," Cory Galbraith called out behind her. "Come here, and show me a real welcome."

III

HELL WILL FREEZE OVER

HEATHER RESISTED THE urge to snarl. Cory Galbraith had started to pester her in earnest of late—but he'd gone too far this evening. She'd had enough.

Swiveling to face him, she bestowed the laird's son with a withering look. "I'd not let Aonghus catch ye saying such things. He doesn't like it when ye pester me and Alana."

Cory snorted, before turning in his chair and spreading his legs in a gesture of male dominance that made Heather's jaw clench.

God's teeth, he reminded her of Iain.

Whatever did I see in that man?

How many times over the past years had she asked herself that? These days, she marveled at just how blind she'd been. Her parents had been against the match, as had her sister. But she'd ignored them all. She still flushed hot with humiliation every time she remembered her mother's final words to her.

Ye are too proud, Heather De Keith. Proud and foolish. Ye are making the biggest mistake of yer life ... and when ye come crawling back to Dunnottar with yer tail tucked between yer legs, I will enjoy telling ye so.

She'd stridden out of that chamber, vowing to never give her mother the chance to crow. But five years on, she had to admit that she'd indeed made the biggest mistake of her life. And every time she set eyes on Iain's cocky cousin, she was reminded of it.

"Aonghus is a Galbraith ... as are ye," Cory drawled, his hot gaze raking the length of her. "And just like him, ye'll do as ye are told ... now come here."

"I'm busy," Heather retorted. She frowned then. "And I'm a *De Keith*, not a Galbraith."

Cory's expression darkened. Like Iain, he had ruggedly handsome good looks. And just like his cousin, he didn't appreciate it when Heather contradicted him. Heather's breathing quickened then at the memory of her husband's blistering temper and the harsh feel of his fists.

"Ye are still wed to Iain," Cory reminded her.

"It's two years since that battle," Heather countered. Heat ignited in her belly, dampening the fear; she knew she shouldn't argue with this man, yet Cory's constant harassment had gotten under her skin. "And he never came home. I think we can safely assume my husband's dead." Heart pumping now, she took a step toward him. "But if he isn't ... I'd like to see him beat ye to a pulp for harassing me."

Cory's green eyes widened, while beside him Diarmid and Brodric sniggered, only to quieten down when their leader cut them a dark look.

"He wouldn't like to see ye serving ale in a tavern," Cory growled. "I think it's *ye* that would get the beating."

He wasn't wrong, but Heather wasn't going to agree with him.

"It was either that or starve," she snarled back, her temper well and truly fraying now. "Yer cousin left me with *nothing*."

"Ye had another choice," he replied, his gaze boring into her now.

Heather clenched her jaw. Of course she'd had. Actually, there had been three options open to her when she'd been forced to shut up her husband's forge: return to her kin in the north, find work locally, or warm Cory Galbraith's bed.

Frankly, none of those choices had appealed. She couldn't face her kin, especially after how they'd parted ways. And the thought of becoming Cory's woman made her skin crawl. Working at *The Bogside* had seemed the best option at the time.

Heather was aware that all the regulars at the nearby tables were staring at them, and she could feel the newcomer's gaze upon her too. She resisted the urge to cast a glance in the direction of the kitchen.

Where was Morag and her adder's tongue when she needed her? And trust Cory to behave this way on the rare occasion when Aonghus was away for the night. He must have known.

Placing her hands upon her hips, Heather stared her harasser down. "Let me make this clear. Hell will freeze over before I let ye touch me, Cory Galbraith."

With that, she stepped to one side and headed toward the kitchen.

She'd only gone two strides when Cory lunged from his chair, grabbed her around the waist, and hauled her back, onto his lap.

"Such a fiery lass!" he growled before his mouth fastened on her neck. "Ye were too much for Iain, but I'd tame ye."

Diarmid and Brodric roared with laughter at that, cheering Cory on while he pulled her hard against his groin.

"Get yer hands off me!" Heather drove her elbow into his chest and made a grab for the edge of the table.

Cory laughed and tightened his grip on her, his hands roving boldly now, squeezing and kneading her breasts. She could feel his arousal, pressed hard against her backside.

Gasping as panic bloomed in her chest, Heather twisted frantically before driving her elbow into his throat this time.

Cory's choking intake of breath told her that she'd hurt him, yet his hold on her didn't slacken. If anything, it tightened further. With one hand, he grabbed hold of her hair and yanked her head back. "I'll have a kiss now."

"Do you mind? Some of us are trying to eat."

A cool voice rumbled over them, and as she continued to struggle, Heather's gaze snapped over to the booth where the newcomer had been eating his supper. He must have been hungry because he was already halfway through his pie. The man put down the knife he'd been using to cut a piece of cheese, his dark gaze settling on Cory's face.

"This doesn't concern ye," Cory snarled. "Go back to yer supper, stranger!" His fingers tightened painfully around Heather's hair.

"I would," the man replied, his handsome face inscrutable, "but the noise you're making is ruining it."

In reply, Cory spat on the floor. "Too bad." He then pulled Heather's head down toward his. Fists and elbows flailing, she fought him, yet he was much stronger than her. His lips grazed hers, before she recoiled, her cry echoing through the common room.

"Morag!" she yelled. Where was the woman?

"She knows her place," Cory leered, "as will ye soon enough."

"I paid good silver for this meal." The newcomer was back, his voice edged with irritation now. "And I tire of listening to your grunting."

Cory went still, Heather momentarily forgotten. "What did ye say?"

The stranger heaved a sigh. "You heard me well enough."

Cory let go of Heather and shoved her off his lap—the movement so sudden that she fell forward onto her knees. However, seizing the opportunity to escape, she scrambled away. Rising to her feet, she then backed toward the kitchen, her gaze upon Cory.

Ignoring her, he rose to his considerable full height, looming over the booth where the newcomer sat. "I think it's time for ye to leave, stranger." Cory flexed his fingers at his sides. "Yer sort aren't welcome in Fintry."

The man raised his chin, meeting Cory's gaze squarely. His dark brows knitted together before his mouth quirked. However, he said nothing.

"Did ye hear me?" Cory took a menacing step toward him. "Get up and leave."

The stranger inclined his head. "Sit back down, lordling. You're making a fool of yourself."

From where she stood, Heather couldn't see the expression on Cory's face—although she imagined he'd turned red by now. His hands had fisted at his sides.

The newcomer appeared to be deliberately baiting Cory. A fight was just moments from erupting.

Cory stepped forward and swept the stranger's meal to the floor with his hand. Wine, cheese, and pie splattered onto the sawdust. "Get up!"

Long moments passed, and then the stranger gave another sigh. It was a weary, long-suffering response. There wasn't a trace of fear in it.

Heather swallowed hard, her fingers clutching at the skirts of her kirtle. Didn't this man have any sense of self-preservation? She'd seen Cory and his friends fight in here before—the trio were brutal.

Slowly, the stranger rose to his feet, and as he did so, Diarmid and Brodric stood up.

"He's carrying a blade, Cory," Diarmid murmured, a warning edge to his voice. Now that the newcomer had gotten up, and stepped out of the booth, his presence seemed to fill the common room. His expression hadn't altered, although his gaze had now veiled in a way that made the fine hair on the back of Heather's neck prickle. It was a look that screamed danger.

Around them, men started to mutter excitedly. Heather's throat closed when she realized they were taking bets.

In response, Cory unsheathed the dirk he carried at his hip. "Aye ... and so am I."

IV

A WASTE OF SILVER

CORY LUNGED FOR the stranger, blade flashing, and
Heather bit back a scream.

He moved fast for such a big man. One moment he'd
been standing there, gripping his dirk while he glared at
the dark-haired man who'd dared interrupt his fun, and
the next he was flying at the newcomer's throat.

The stranger ducked as the blade sailed past his neck,
and drew his own blade. It wasn't like any knife Heather
had ever seen. The dirks her people used were long and
thin whereas this dagger had a large, leaf-shaped blade.

Cory's roar of frustration echoed through the
common room, reverberating against the rafters, and
then he lunged again.

Cory was good with a dirk—the whole village had
heard him boast of his prowess—and Heather saw that
he hadn't been exaggerating his skill. He swiped the dirk,
swift and deadly, and when the stranger twisted to avoid
it, he wasn't quite fast enough.

The long, thin blade sliced into his upper arm.

The newcomer grunted before he kicked out, driving
a booted foot into Cory's knee.

The laird's son roared once more, this time in agony, before he crumpled to the ground.

Diarmid and Brodric lunged for the stranger.

Heather watched, her breath stilling, while the newcomer dealt with them with ruthless efficiency. He head-butted Brodric and sent him crashing over a nearby table where two farmers sat drinking. The patrons reeled back as Brodric collided with them.

Oblivious to the ruckus, the stranger then ducked under Diarmid's swiping blade and punched him in the throat with his left hand. He still gripped that strange-shaped dagger in his right, yet he hadn't used it.

Diarmid dropped to his knees, wheezing. His dirk fell to the sawdust while he grasped at his injured throat.

Meanwhile, the stranger moved to defend himself once more from Cory. Despite the fact that his knee had collapsed, the laird's son lurched to his feet once more, his blade flying toward the stranger's heart.

The newcomer twisted out of range, nimble as an eel, before he ducked under Cory's guard, grabbed him by the hair with one hand, and slammed him face-down on the table where he and his friends had been sitting.

And then, he brought his leaf-shaped blade down, skewering Cory's outstretched hand with a dull, meaty thud.

Silence followed. It echoed through *The Bogside Tavern*. All gazes were riveted upon the knife that now pinned Cory's hand to the table's oaken surface.

Cory inhaled sharply. His face had gone the color of raw liver, veins raised upon his forehead and neck.

Still gripping the hilt of the blade, the stranger leaned forward, his mouth hovering close to the younger man's ear. "It's time for you and your friends to go home now, lordling," he murmured. "Leave the rest of us to enjoy what's left of the evening."

With that, the man yanked the blade free, and Cory Galbraith's howl split the smoky air.

Heart thundering against her ribs, Heather cleared up the spilled food and drink, and carried it into the kitchens. Inside, she found Morag standing behind the large scrubbed table that dominated the space.

The woman's face was the color of milk. She'd heard everything, but not dared to venture out into the common room. She'd left Heather at Cory's mercy.

The two women's gazes met across the table. Heather lowered the tray, and she realized her hands were trembling. Heat once more flared in the pit of her belly.

Shock at what she'd just witnessed vied with outrage that Morag had been such a coward. A well-aimed rolling pin would have put Cory in his place before the situation spiraled out of control, and yet Morag, who was usually so fierce, had hidden away.

As if reading the disgust writ upon Heather's face, Morag's throat bobbed. "Have they gone?"

Heather nodded, not trusting herself to speak. Indeed, Cory, Diarmid, and Brodric had dragged their sorry carcasses from the tavern, wheezing and growling threats as they went. Cory had barely been able to walk, and had required his friends' help. A trail of blood from his wounded hand now stained the sawdust-covered floor.

"And that man—the one who started it—where's he?"

"He didn't start it," Heather replied, surprised at just how cold her voice was. "He stepped in to help when no one else would." She looked down at the ruins of his supper. "He's gone upstairs … he's injured."

The stranger had remained silent until Cory and his friends had disappeared. He'd even held his tongue when Cory had paused on the threshold, fixed Heather with a stare, and said, "It's not over between us, Heather. Now that Iain's gone, I will make ye mine."

However, after their departure, the stranger had turned his dark gaze upon Heather. Blood coated the top of his left arm, but he didn't seem to notice. When he'd spoken, his voice was dispassionate. "Which room is mine?"

Heather felt light-headed and a little queasy in the aftermath of watching that fight, and yet underneath it all, she was awed by what she'd just witnessed.

She'd never seen a man handle himself like that.

"He'd better not bloody our bed linen," Morag sniffed, before turning back to the large iron stove, where a second batch of pies were baking. The remains of the first batch still sat upon the table, getting cold.

"It won't be his fault if he does," Heather snapped. "Is this how Fintry welcomes strangers?"

Maximus stripped off his leather jerkin and inspected the wound on his left bicep. That dirk blade had cut him deep, but the wound was already healing; he could feel the itch as the flesh knitted together.

Letting out a long sigh, Maximus scrubbed a hand through his short hair. Why was it that wherever he went, he never failed to find trouble? Or maybe, trouble was always looking for him—either way, it always ended the same.

What a waste of silver.

He'd been enjoying that pie, the sweet bramble wine, and the warmth of the hearth. The last thing he'd wanted was a brawl—and as comely as that serving lass was, he really hadn't been in the mood to defend her virtue.

Yet he couldn't let that jumped-up laird's son humiliate her.

No one else in the common room had defended the woman, and Maximus had the feeling that Cory Galbraith intimidated them all.

Well done ... you've made an enemy there.

Maximus's mouth curved. Even though he spent most of his time living alone in the wilds these days, he'd made enough enemies over the years not to let this new one bother him.

However, he hadn't missed Galbraith's parting threat. Heather had more to fear than he did.

His smile faded. He'd stepped in to help the serving lass, but perhaps he'd just made things worse for her. Maximus's mouth flattened into a thin line. Enough worrying about a woman he'd only just met. He had his own future to think about.

The Broom-star was once again gracing the heavens. A narrow window of opportunity had opened, and he needed to get to Stirling to see if Cassian and Draco had gotten any closer to solving that damn riddle.

The answer had eluded them all for so long he was beginning to think they'd never solve it. Maybe they'd remain alive till the world's ending, just as the bandrúi had foretold.

The heaviness that dogged his steps these days increased.

It had been a particularly harsh winter, and the months alone hadn't done him much good.

The thought of continuing like this forever made his chest ache.

With a sigh, Maximus sat down upon the narrow bed. Alone in the tiny chamber, on the top floor of the tavern, he took in the freshly white-washed walls and pots of dried flowers decorating the room. The ceiling was so low that the heavy beams nearly brushed the crown of his head when he stood up. Even so, it was a roof over his head after many nights sleeping on frosted ground. A small hearth burned against one wall, warming the damp air.

Maximus sniffed before wrinkling his nose. There was a rank smell in here, and he realized it was coming from him. He was in need of a bath—and fortunately he'd spotted a large bowl of water upon a table by the single shuttered window. A coarse drying cloth and a cracked cake of lye soap sat next to it.

He rose to his feet, stripped off the rest of his clothing, and crossed to the bowl.

The water was cold, and he gritted his teeth against it as he bathed, scrubbing away the blood, sweat, and grime of the past few days. The wash was bracing, yet he enjoyed how his skin tingled in the aftermath.

Finishing his wash, Maximus pulled on his leather leggings and padded barefoot back over to the narrow bed. He then stretched out onto the scratchy woolen blanket, his gaze traveling to the beams above his head.

His belly growled, reminding him that he was still hungry. Those idiots had spoiled the best pie he'd tasted in a long while. He wondered if he could risk a trip down to the kitchen and request more food.

The brawl hadn't been his fault after all.

I could go down and see Heather again.

For a moment, he allowed himself to dwell upon her sensual mouth and winsome smile. He hadn't liked to see Galbraith grope the woman, but he certainly understood why the laird's son lusted after her. She had the body of a goddess. Maximus's groin ached as he recalled the way her lush breasts had heaved in outrage, and he clenched his jaw. He definitely needed to find a brothel once he reached Stirling. The ache for a woman was going to drive him to do something ill-advised if he wasn't careful.

Maximus's belly rumbled once more, interrupting his brooding.

With a groan, he sat up. *Maybe I should risk a trip downstairs.* He was debating whether or not to go when a soft knock sounded at the door.

His hand instinctively went to the dagger he'd lain on the bedside table. "Who is it?"

"It's Heather," a low female voice answered. "I've brought ye some more supper."

V

THE GREATEST

THE DOOR OPENED, revealing a half-naked man standing before her.

Heather sucked in a surprised breath. She hadn't expected to be greeted by such a sight. The stranger was barefoot and clad only in a pair of tight leather leggings that hugged his lean form. She took him in, noting the smooth, muscular, tanned expanse of his chest, and the faded tattoo that had been inked into his skin, a few inches above his right nipple: the mark of an eagle, its wings spread.

The man's black hair was damp, revealing that he'd just bathed.

For a long moment, Heather stood there, staring at him, and then heat flowered across her chest as embarrassment set in. The man didn't say anything; he just watched her, his gaze shuttered.

Releasing the breath she'd been holding, Heather brazened out the moment with a smile. She inclined her chin right, to where she balanced a tray of fresh pie and a jug of wine against her hip, before holding up the basket she grasped in her left hand.

"I thought ye'd still be hungry," she said, the words rushing out of her, "and that someone should take a look at that cut on yer arm." Her gaze flicked to his left bicep. She couldn't see the wound properly in the shadowy doorway, yet at least it wasn't bleeding.

"Thank you for the food," he said, taking the tray from her and stepping back from the doorway. "But I'm sure the wound will be fine. It's just a graze."

Heather made an impatient noise in the back of her throat. "A graze? I saw Cory's blade dig deep into yer flesh. I wouldn't be surprised if the wound needs stitching. Lucky for ye, every good Scottish lass knows how to tend wounds."

She was burbling, but his intense look was making her nervous. Keen to break the tension, Heather bustled past him into the chamber, nudging the door closed behind her. There was a chill draft in the hallway, and she didn't want to let the heat out of the room, especially considering this man's state of undress.

"Very well then," he replied, not bothering to hide the long-suffering edge to his voice. He set the tray down upon a narrow table opposite the bed and poured himself a cup of wine before taking a deep draft. "Take a look at my arm, if you wish."

The stranger set the cup down and moved back, perching upon the edge of the bed. And when his dark gaze settled upon her, the heat that still stained her chest started to creep up Heather's neck.

He had an unnerving look, as if he were reading her innermost thoughts.

It was disconcerting—and compelling.

It was bold to knock on a stranger's door and invite oneself in. But Heather felt responsible for the injury he'd sustained, and she wanted to make sure that he was alright. She'd been unable to settle downstairs, and when she'd ensured the other customers had been served their supper, she'd left Alana—Aonghus and Morag's daughter—to see to them should they need anything else.

Visions of the man bleeding out all over the floor in his room had tortured her, making Heather gather the healing basket Morag kept in the scullery before hurrying upstairs.

However, when her gaze alighted upon the cut Cory had inflicted, she caught her breath in surprise.

As the man assured her, it wasn't as deep as she'd first thought. Setting down the basket of ointments, herbs, and bandages, she bent close, peering at the wound. It looked to have only cut the skin, and not the muscle underneath as she'd thought.

"Mother Mary ... ye were right," she murmured. "But I should clean and bandage it all the same."

The stranger shrugged, his gaze never leaving her face. "If you think it needs it."

Heat was now creeping up her neck in a warm tide. His stare made her feel flayed bare. This close, she noticed what long, dark eyelashes he had. The warm scent of his skin—spicy male mixed with the smell of lye soap—enveloped her.

It was hardly appropriate for a widowed woman to be standing so close to a partially clad man, yet the evening's events had shattered the reserve between them. Forcing herself to focus, Heather reached for a small stoppered bottle of vinegar, which would cleanse the wound. It was good to have a purpose, for her belly was fluttering at his nearness.

"This will sting a little," she warned him. Not waiting for his response, she removed the cork stopper and took hold of his arm, pulling it horizontal so that she could pour vinegar straight into the wound.

The gentle hiss between his clenched teeth was the man's only response, although Heather barely noticed. She was too aware of the warmth and hardness of the flesh of his upper arm underneath her fingertips.

His muscles were as solid as carven rock.

Blinking, she forced herself to remain focused on her task. Deliberately, she let go of his arm and reached for a clean scrap of cloth to wipe away the blood that stained the skin around the cut.

Yet with each passing moment, her awareness of him grew.

It both flustered and excited her. In the two years since Iain's departure, she'd kept her distance from men. Frankly, those who frequented *The Bogside Tavern* weren't the type to set a woman's blood aflame.

But this stranger was different.

His presence drew her in, as if he were a roaring fire on a cold winter's night. It took all her will to fight the pull.

She hadn't felt such attraction since the beginning of things with Iain—when she'd been so besotted, she'd broken with her family in order to follow the handsome smithy south to Fintry.

Reaching for a bandage, Heather cleared her throat. "Do ye have a name, stranger?"

A beat of silence stretched between them before he answered. "Maximus."

She inclined her head. "Maximus." The name wasn't a Scottish one, which wasn't surprising. "That's an odd name."

For the first time since she'd entered the chamber, the man smiled. The expression was subtle, the merest lifting of the corners of his mouth. "It's Latin ... it means 'The greatest'."

The man spoke with such unconscious arrogance, such supreme confidence, that Heather grinned. "Is that so?"

Their gazes fused, and the man's—Maximus's—smile widened just a little.

The stare drew out, and suddenly the room felt stuffy and airless. Heather realized then that she was out of her depth with this enigmatic, oddly-named stranger.

"I didn't get a chance to thank ye ... downstairs," she said finally, breaking the weighty silence between them. "I appreciate what ye did ... Cory had that coming. I'm sure I wasn't the only one who was pleased to see him get a beating. I have to say that I've never seen anyone fight like ye."

She really was babbling now, yet she couldn't help it. Heather was usually unflappable, but this man's presence unraveled her. Gently, she started to wind the bandage around his upper arm. At the same time, she was painfully aware of how quickly she was breathing. And the heat in her chest and neck was now spreading to her face. Lord preserve her, she was blushing.

"I take it that isn't the first time he's harassed you?" Maximus murmured.

Heather shook her head, grateful that she could focus on their conversation and not on this man's lithe, strong body. Her fingertips itched to trace the smooth skin of his sculpted chest, to outline that eagle tattoo.

She couldn't believe she was having such lusty thoughts. This man's nearness was addling her brains. She needed to get out of here before she did something foolish.

"Aye ... but he's never been so bold," she replied, avoiding his gaze as she continued to wrap the bandage. "Now that he's as sure as he can be that I'm a widow, there's no chance of my husband returning to whip his arse."

"So, I had the honor instead."

Heather lifted her gaze to his. "Aye ... but don't think Cory Galbraith will ever forget the slight. The men of his family are mean-tempered."

Maximus shrugged. "Why did you wed one of them?"

Heather went still. The question was bold, but just. Indeed, why had she bound herself to Iain? She'd asked herself that enough times over the years not to hesitate over the answer.

"Because I was young and foolish," she replied. "And Iain Galbraith was everything my parents warned me about."

VI

LUST UNLEASHED

MAXIMUS SMILED. HE couldn't help himself. There was something about this woman that drew him in. She had a bold, saucy air undercut with vulnerability. It enticed him.

Careful, the voice of good-sense cautioned him. *If you bed her, you'll regret it in the morning.*

Maximus ignored the warning. Heather's nearness was intoxicating. He forgot his protesting belly; the demands of another part of his body overrode his usual restraint.

"So, you're a woman who likes a bit of excitement and danger?" he asked softly. He knew his tone was suggestive, deliberately so, and he liked the way those grey-green eyes darkened, her pupils growing large. He also liked the way her cheeks stained pink, and how her breathing now came in short, sharp bursts. Those lush breasts of hers were close to brushing against his arm as she finished wrapping the bandage.

What do you think you're doing? Sanity tried to speak up again, yet he shoved its protest aside. Maximus knew he was playing a foolish game, but he was enjoying himself too much to stop.

It felt as if he were emerging from a ten year famine, and someone had just laid out a feast before him.

In this warm chamber, with the comely Heather standing so close, lust barreled into him. He'd just come from spending months in the wilderness, trapping and hunting the animals he skinned for their pelts, and the femininity and softness of the woman before him was a balm to his jaded soul.

He'd taken to brooding too much of late, and maybe a lusty night would lighten his spirits.

Heather cleared her throat. She was struggling to cover up her embarrassment.

"In the past, I longed for excitement," she admitted. "But since I'm now reduced to serving ale at *The Bogside*, I'd say I'm a little warier these days."

She tied his bandage, straightened up, and was just about to step back from him when Maximus caught her hand.

"Thank you, Heather ... it's been a long while since someone took such care over me."

It was true. One of the many negatives of living forever was that all his wounds healed with the coming of the dawn. He hadn't needed a healer to tend him, for none of the earthly sicknesses touched him either. He hadn't had a sniffle, a cough, or a fever since he'd been cursed.

The blush in her cheeks bloomed further. However, she didn't take her hand from his. She had long, elegant fingers, and Maximus wound his own through them.

Her sharp intake of breath filled the chamber, and yet she still didn't yank her hand away. Instead, her lips parted, and Maximus's attention fastened upon that plump lower lip—the lip that begged to be bitten.

Desire arrowed through his groin, a deep ache following.

Hades take him—he had needs like any other man.

Still holding Heather's hand, Maximus rose to his feet and gazed down at her. They were standing so close he could feel the warmth of her body. He inhaled the scent of rosemary from her hair.

A heartbeat later, he reached out and tangled his fingers through those light-brown waves with his free hand, enjoying the weight and softness of the long hair sliding across his skin. And all the while, Heather didn't move.

Instead, her eyes hooded.

She felt this as much as he did—this pull. The moment he'd set eyes on her in that smoky common room below, he'd felt the stirrings of attraction. This woman had a spark—an aliveness—that made it difficult for him to take his eyes off her.

She was fire; he knew it in his gut.

And so, sensing that she wouldn't recoil, Maximus lowered his lips to hers and kissed her.

Ye shouldn't be doing this.

The warning whispered through Heather's mind before disappearing like smoke caught by the wind. Common sense was trying to prevail, yet lust overrode it.

She'd never been kissed like this, and she liked it. Iain had always kissed so roughly, but this man was gentle.

Maximus's lips were warm, yet firm, as they moved over hers. He tasted faintly of bramble wine: a sweet, heady flavor that made her already racing pulse thunder in her ears. His strong fingers tangled through her hair before spanning the back of her head, drawing her against him. And when his tongue swept her lips open, she was lost.

Rational thought fled, and she groaned into his mouth, her tongue sliding against his.

The sound unleashed him.

He drew her hard against his body, letting go of her hand so that he could grasp her around the waist and pull her against him.

Heather went pliantly, molding herself against the hard length of his torso and hips. Immediately, she felt the hardness of his rod against her belly.

Dizziness swept over her, the sensation intensifying when his hand spanned the small of her back possessively, pressing her closer still.

The kiss deepened, growing hungry now. Maximus's lips were a brand upon hers, tenderness shifting into something else entirely.

And when he gently bit her lower lip, need rose up within her—a furnace that made her lose all timidity, all inhibition.

She wanted to lie with this man.

This was her last chance to stop things. She should really break off the kiss, should step back and put some distance between them. He would let her go; she sensed it. And maybe it was that instinct, the knowledge she was in safe hands with this stranger, that caused all thoughts of self-preservation to dissolve.

A lustiness she hadn't even known she possessed surfaced. She suddenly didn't care what the dawn would bring—most likely regret and self-recrimination—right now, she felt as if she'd die if she didn't have him inside her.

He stripped her clothing off, his hands moving with deft, intense purpose. And then when she was naked, he feasted upon her. His hands, his mouth, his tongue were everywhere. The sensitive peaks of her breasts ached as he suckled hard. His hands parted her thighs and stroked between them. All the while, Heather clung to his shoulders, her body trembling with want.

He then pushed her onto her back upon the bed, the healing basket and all its contents scattering across the floor. Heather barely noticed. Instead, she was intent on the fact that Maximus was unlacing his leggings and then stripping them off, revealing the most impressive erection she'd ever seen.

Admittedly, she'd witnessed none besides her husband's over the years. But the hard, throbbing length of this one made her breathing tear from her in short, needy pants. The swollen head of his shaft glistened as he climbed onto the bed and crawled over her.

A soft cry escaped Heather. He'd literally prowled to her—predatory, yet controlled. Heather parted her already spread thighs wider, and when he grasped hold of her hips, she lifted them to meet him.

He drove into her.

Heather was lost. Her cries filled the chamber as she writhed up against him, welcoming the aching sensation of being stretched, filled completely.

Sweat beaded upon her skin; she bucked against Maximus, meeting him thrust for thrust. Pleasure hit her hard, cresting and rippling out from her lower belly. Her thighs trembled from the force of it, and she arched back, a ragged cry tearing from her.

Maximus continued to take her in hard thrusts, although he picked up the pace now. Heather peaked once more, vaguely aware of his own release as she did so. He reared back against her, his fingers digging into the soft flesh of her hips. Then he gave a deep, animalistic moan.

A moment later, he collapsed upon her, the ragged sound of their breathing echoing through the chamber.

VII

BELONGING

HEART STILL GALLOPING, Heather rolled over onto her side and propped herself up on an elbow. Maximus had shifted off her and now lay on his back, his chest rising and falling sharply, one arm flung above his head.

The sight of him made heat pool in the cradle of her hips once again. She couldn't believe it. She'd just had this man, and she wanted him again.

Her mother had names for lusty women—names she'd shouted at Heather right before she'd departed Dunnottar.

Those insults had cut deep, and if she were honest, they were another reason she'd never returned to her kin.

Unexpectedly, Heather's vision blurred and a tightness coiled in her chest. Sometimes she felt so alone here in Fintry. The memory of the rift between her and her parents caused a hard knot of sadness to pulse in her breast.

Don't think of them, she counselled herself, blinking rapidly. *Not now*.

Reaching out, she traced her fingers over the concave plane of her lover's belly, up over the cage of his ribs, to the hard muscles of his chest. And there, she explored the Eagle tattoo that fascinated her.

"What's this?" she asked, her voice husky.

Maximus opened his eyes, that peat-dark gaze settling upon her. "It's a soldier's mark," he murmured.

Heather inclined her head, her fingertip running along the curve of the eagle's wing. The tattoo was a welcome distraction from her own thoughts. "There are letters under it ... SPQR."

"Senātus Populusque Rōmānus," he replied, in an accent that was entirely foreign to her. "The name of the imperial Roman republic."

"Really ... and why do ye bear it?"

His mouth curved, although those dark eyes shuttered slightly. "Surely, you've realized I'm not from this land. I'm from Rome ... and in my past life, I was a warrior."

Rome.

Heather had heard of the city, and of the Pope that lived there. Nonetheless, she found it hard to comprehend what a soldier of Rome was doing in a tiny Scottish village.

"You're wondering why I'm here?" he asked, as if reading her thoughts.

"Aye," she admitted. "I've never met anyone who's so distant from home. My kin are far enough away as it is ... but I can't imagine having to cross seas and a continent to reach them."

"My kin are all dead," he replied, his half-smile fading.

"So why are ye here?" Heather asked after a pause.

"I came to Scotland many years ago as a mercenary," he replied, his gaze shifting from hers and fixing upon the rafters above his head. "I now earn coin by trapping wild animals and selling their pelts."

"And ye have business in Fintry?" she asked, incredulous. The village didn't even have a furrier.

He shook his head. "I'm headed to Stirling, where there are plenty of buyers for my furs." His gaze shifted right once more, pinning her to the bed. "So, tell me, bonny Heather. Where are you from?"

Heather swallowed. She preferred it when they talked about him. "I'm a De Keith ... of Dunnottar."

He nodded. "Dunnottar. I visited once ... years ago now. It's an impressive fortress."

Indeed, perched upon a cliff edge looking over the North Sea, Dunnottar had no equal when it came to its awe-inspiring setting. Heather had missed it over the years.

"And why don't you go home?" he asked.

Heather gave a brittle laugh. However, there was no mirth in it. Once again, the urge to weep rose within her, and when she answered, her voice was strained. "Ye heard my exchange with Cory earlier?"

Maximus observed her, his brow furrowing. "Yes ... you were wed to his cousin, and now you're his widow. You don't belong in Fintry, Heather."

"I'm not sure I belong anywhere now," she admitted, her voice wobbling slightly. "My parents were against my marriage. Before I left Dunnottar, we argued ... ugly things were said ... on both sides."

He raised a dark eyebrow. "Things that can never be taken back?"

Heather drew in a shaky breath. "Maybe not."

"You'll never know if you don't try."

They stared at each other, and Heather swallowed hard, in an effort to ease the tightness in her throat. She didn't want to bare her soul to this stranger, and yet the urge to let someone see just how sad she was inside rose within her.

"I feel as if I was given a good life, a fortunate one, but I set fire to it," she said softly, "and now I sit amongst the ashes."

A pause followed before his mouth curved. "Then you're a phoenix?"

"A what?"

His lips stretched into a full smile. "It's a long-lived bird ... that dies in flames and then is reborn from its own ashes."

Heather huffed. "Ye think I can be reborn?"

"I know you can," he replied, his smile fading. "You're still young, Heather. You've still got time."

They fell silent then before he reached up to caress her face. The pad of his thumb traced her lower lip. It was a sensual gesture, and one that made the sensitive flesh between her thighs ache. The look he was giving Heather caused her body to melt.

A phoenix ... what a strange bird.

"Even so, you don't want to leave things too late," he continued. "Your parents won't live forever."

Heather's mouth curved. He hadn't met Iona and Donnan De Keith; her parents were as tough as the land that had bred them. Her smile faded then as she caught the shadow that moved in the depths of his eyes.

"Pride is a lonely companion," he added softly. "And it steals time like a thief. Don't let it rob you of your family."

Heather inclined her head, observing him. Maximus was a man with regrets. She wanted to ask him about his past, yet she prevented herself.

Tonight wasn't about baring their souls to each other. Tonight was about pleasure, about two strangers sharing their bodies. With the dawn, everything would change.

And so, she said nothing, her eyes fluttering closed as his thumb resumed its caress of her lower lip.

A moment later, he rolled over and flung a possessive leg over her hip, drawing her toward him. His hands cupped Heather's face, and his lips found hers. She leaned into him, tasting him, breathing him in.

Aye, tomorrow all of this would be but a memory. But tonight belonged to them.

It was still dark when Heather slipped from the bed. Maximus had fallen into a deep slumber and didn't notice when she padded across the floor and reached for her lèine and kirtle in the darkness. She would have to collect her basket and its contents later.

Her limbs felt loose and languorous, and she had been tempted just to snuggle up to the warm male body next to her on the bed. Yet now the madness of lust had faded, Heather was aware that she was still under her employers' roof.

Witless goose, Heather thought as she dressed quickly, fumbling with the laces of her bodice. *Morag will flay ye alive if she catches ye in here.*

Indeed, the reminder was a sobering one.

Just like Heather's mother, Morag would have a name for women such as her.

Heather's pulse fluttered, and the knot in her breast—which had subsided for a short while—tightened once more.

What have I done?

With that thought, Heather tip-toed from the chamber and closed the door as gently as she could behind her.

Back in her own chamber, she started to shiver. The small lump of peat in the tiny hearth had long since gone out. Beside the bed, a stubby candle had nearly burned down to a molten pond. Lighting another, she sat down on the narrow cot.

Heather wrapped her arms about her torso and squeezed her eyes shut. Her eyelids burned, not from fatigue, but from the urge to cry.

She was good at presenting a tough, confident face to the world—yet it was as if Maximus had held up a looking glass to her, revealing the sadness that pulsed within.

And the pride that prevented her from going home.

Heather rubbed her closed eyes. She should really try and get some rest. Dawn came early at *The Bogside.* Morag got her and Alana up before daybreak to help in the kitchen, and there was always linen to be cleaned and floors to be scrubbed. The chores never ended, and just thinking about the coming day made Heather's chest ache.

Maximus was right: she didn't belong here.

And yet as the months had stretched out into years, she'd remained in Fintry. She'd exchanged the odd letter with her sister over the past couple of years. Aila had written, begging her to return to Dunnottar, but she'd resisted. She'd told herself that going home wouldn't solve anything.

But after speaking to Maximus, Heather realized that she'd let her stubborn nature get the better of her. She didn't want to face her family, and yet he'd made her see that she'd eventually regret not doing so.

Not only that, but Cory's parting threat had made it clear that life in Fintry was about to get difficult for her. And when Aonghus heard what had happened, he'd be furious. Most likely, he'd blame her.

Heather opened her eyes and knuckled away a tear that had escaped and was now trickling down her cheek. Blinking, she looked around the shadowed chamber. This was her only private space, her refuge from the rest of the world. She had few belongings, as she'd had to sell what few things of value she possessed, in order to buy food when Iain didn't return from battle.

To look at this room, one would never have thought that she'd grown up in a comfortable household, and had wanted for nothing before coming here.

Perhaps that was part of the problem. She hadn't known hardship. She'd felt jubilant to finally taste freedom when she accompanied Iain south. She'd been overjoyed at escaping her parents' yoke, and hadn't taken an honest look at the man she was escaping with— a man she'd soon learned to fear.

The years since had taught her that freedom came at a price. Not long after departing from Dunnottar, it became clear that she'd chosen unwisely.

Her mother had been right, although it would be galling to face her again.

Heather drew in a shaky breath and gathered her courage. *It's time to go.*

She'd been wrestling with this decision for a while now. But it didn't matter how she procrastinated, life marched on regardless.

Fate had taken control tonight, in bringing Maximus into her life. Cory and his kin ruled here—none of them would forget this insult. Maximus would disappear with the dawn, and if she stayed, she would regret it.

That last thought galvanized her.

Rising to her feet, Heather pulled a leather satchel from under the bed and dusted it off. The time for dithering was over.

VIII

THE BROOM-STAR

MAXIMUS WRESTLED WITH his conscience as he
prepared to leave with the dawn.

*So, you're just going to leave her to Galbraith's
mercy?*

You aren't even going to say goodbye.

He clenched his jaw and slipped on the pony's bridle.
One lusty night and this was what happened? It was
easier when he visited a brothel. There, it was just an
exchange: no hard feelings and no responsibilities.
Earlier in the night, he'd been relieved to awake and find
Heather gone. But now he felt like a rogue for slipping
out of the tavern without seeing her again.

It wasn't the woman's fault; it was his over-developed
sense of responsibility. Heather De Keith had asked
nothing of him—yet he worried about her nonetheless.

Enough. Maximus started strapping on his garron's
harness. *The sooner I get on the road, the better.*

He'd just finished buckling the straps when footsteps
scuffed behind him.

The pony snorted, its nostrils flaring. Calming the
stocky beast with a stroke to the neck, Maximus slowly
reached for his knife with his free hand. Then, as his

fingers curled around the hilt, he turned, peering into the shadows.

He hadn't been in Fintry long, but he'd already managed to make enemies here. One couldn't be too careful. "Who goes there?" he demanded.

A shape detached itself from the darker shadows inside the stables, outlined in the faint glow of starlight behind the open door. "It's me ... Heather."

A pale hand raised, pushing back the cowl of the long woolen cloak and revealing her face.

Maximus's hand shifted from the hilt of his dagger, the tension in his shoulders uncoiling. "You shouldn't creep up on people."

"Sorry." She moved closer. "I didn't mean to startle ye."

Maximus noted then that she wore a large satchel slung over her front. He arched an eyebrow. "Going somewhere?"

The woman tilted up her chin, meeting his gaze. "I decided ye were right. I don't belong in Fintry. I'm going home."

"What ... today?" Maximus was torn. On the one hand, he was relieved that she'd taken his advice, but on the other, seeing her again just complicated things.

Heather's mouth curved, an expression that made warmth kindle in the pit of his belly. Last night had been unexpected. He hadn't enjoyed bedding a woman that much in many long years—so many, he couldn't remember the last time he'd let go like that.

The fact that this woman had a body to make Mithras beg for mercy probably had something to do with it. Stripping her naked had been a joy, as had feasting upon her soft, milky skin.

Even so, seeing Heather here, dressed for travel, put him on edge.

"Aye ... today," she replied. The deep shadows within the stables made it difficult to glimpse the expression in her eyes. Yet he imagined a stubborn gleam in their grey-green depths. "Ye said ye are bound for Stirling this morning. Can I travel with ye?"

Maximus tensed. Once again, he felt torn. It was partly his fault she was leaving. "I travel alone, Heather," he replied after a heavy pause.

She made an impatient sound in the back of her throat, the same sound she'd made before insisting she take a look at his injured arm. Heather De Keith wasn't a woman who liked being thwarted. "God's bones ... it's only until Stirling." The note of exasperation in her voice was evident. "After that, I'll find my own way north."

Maximus didn't answer for a few moments. She was right: they'd reach Stirling by mid-afternoon. Even so, when he'd told her he traveled alone, he hadn't lied.

Maximus Flavius Cato was a loner.

Last night, this woman had woven a spell over him, and he'd willingly succumbed. For just a few hours, he'd been able to forget who he was. He'd been able to lose himself in pleasure.

But allowing Heather to accompany him to Stirling made things messy—and Maximus preferred to keep his life simple. He didn't want another Evanna. He never again wanted to stare into his lover's eyes and see her hurt, disappointment, and vengeful rage.

The silence between them lengthened, and he could sense her rising irritation, the tension vibrating off her cloaked body.

It's only one day. Surely, even he could manage that.

"Very well," Maximus huffed, turning his back on her. "I take it no one knows you're leaving?"

"Of course not," she replied crisply. "They'd make a fuss. Not that Aonghus and Morag would miss me personally, mind."

"I can't see why they wouldn't," he muttered, taking hold of the garron's bridle and leading it from the stall.

"Excuse me?"

"Keep your voice down. Let's try and leave without alerting the whole village."

Maximus led the gelding out into the yard. Starlight bathed the space and the small wooden wagon laden with sacks of furs that awaited him. He then started to harness the garron to the cart. "Get in," he instructed.

"Aren't we riding the pony?" she whispered back.

Maximus snorted. "*I'm* riding Luchag," he replied. "You're not."

"*Mouse.*" He heard the smile in her voice. "What kind of name is that for a pony?"

"A fitting one. Now get in ... and try to hold your tongue till we get out of the village."

Once again, he could sense her bristling displeasure, yet the woman did as bid, climbing onto the cart and making a nest for herself against the sacks.

Satisfied that Luchag was ready, Maximus swung up onto the garron's broad back and urged him forward, turning toward the archway that led out into Fintry's main street.

Maximus's gaze traveled east, to where the horizon was just starting to lighten.

I should have left earlier.

The thought was uncharitable. Nonetheless, part of him wished he'd risen from his bed an hour before. That way, he would have already been on the road when Heather went looking for him.

She'd only have set off on foot alone, he reminded himself. *This way, at least she's safe from Galbraith until Stirling.*

Maximus tensed. What did he care? One night in her company and this woman had clearly bewitched him. The sooner they parted ways, the better.

Fintry slumbered as Luchag clip-clopped his way through the village. It was a still, frosty morning, and Maximus's breathing steamed in the gelid air. Fintry huddled in the Strath of Endrick Water—a large wooded valley nestled between the Campsie Fells and the Fintry Hills. In daylight, it was a pretty spot, yet Maximus was relieved to bid the village goodbye.

Rarely had a night at an inn caused him so much trouble.

The unpaved road led them out of Fintry and into an oakwood. And there, looming against the dark sky, its grey walls glowing in the silvery starlight, rose Culcreuch Castle.

The home of the young man Maximus had humiliated the night before.

Maximus's mouth thinned at the sight of the fortress. Heather really did have to get away from Fintry. Galbraith wouldn't leave things be now, not after last night's shaming.

Turning his gaze from the castle, he looked north-east. Beyond those wooded hills was Stirling, and he was impatient to reach his destination.

"Look!" Heather's voice cut through the predawn stillness. "That must be the star folk are talking about?"

Maximus turned in the saddle, his gaze rising to the heavens and the comet he knew his traveling companion had seen. "Yes," he said softly, his gaze settling upon the bright smudge against the inky void beyond. "The Broom-star."

"One of the customers called it the 'fire-tailed star' yesterday. I meant to go out and look for it last night ... but I forgot." Her voice trailed off, and he caught the note of embarrassment in it.

Maximus shifted his attention to the cloaked figure perched behind him. Heather was gripping the sides of the cart in an attempt to make the bumpy ride more comfortable. She was deliberately keeping her gaze trained up at the sky, to avoid looking his way.

"It goes by many names," he replied. "For it appears in the sky every seventy-five years or so."

Silence fell between them for a few moments before Heather replied. "How do ye know this?"

Maximus's mouth curved. "You'd be surprised what I know."

"The old man who told me about it said the star heralds change," she said after another pause. "Do you think he's right?"

Maximus glanced away. To him, the Broom-star meant much more than that. The cycle of the comet's return had guided his existence over the last thousand years. He looked to its coming with both anticipation and dread. Anticipation that he might finally break the curse upon him, and dread that still—cycle after cycle—the time wouldn't be right.

The star was why he was traveling to Stirling, reluctantly emerging from the wilderness to see if his time had finally come. The Broom-star was the first part of the riddle that he, Cassian, and Draco had struggled to solve.

Maximus could still remember the bandrúi's cold voice filtering through the hut as she said the words he'd memorized.

> *When the Broom-star crosses the sky,*
> *And the Hammer strikes the fort*
> *Upon the Shelving Slope.*
> *When the White Hawk and the Dragon wed,*
> *Only then will the curse be broke.*

All this time, and they'd only ever solved the first line of the riddle. Maybe, with the Broom-star's arrival this time, the rest would be revealed to them.

"To many, its coming represents a portent or ill omen," he replied finally. "Three centuries ago, the English saw it in the sky ... not long before the Normans conquered them."

"Maybe it bodes ill for them again." Maximus noted the fierce edge to Heather's voice. Like most folk of this wild land, she loathed the English. "Maybe we will finally drive them away."

Maximus turned from her, his gaze scanning the shadowed road ahead. "Perhaps," he murmured. "After all ... your ancestors repelled invaders, time after time, in the past."

"They did," she agreed, pride lacing her voice.

The fighting between the English and the Scots had gone on for a long while. But in all his years in this land, Maximus had never known their relationship to be as fraught as it was now.

An ambitious man named Edward sat upon the English throne, and he'd launched a number of campaigns north of Hadrian's Wall. The last had ended in bloodshed for the English, but that didn't mean they were defeated.

In Dumfries, Maximus had heard that English soldiers were raiding north of The Wall again. Word was that they were gathering for another push north.

Maximus's mouth thinned then. War. When you lived as long as he had, you knew it was one constant. No matter what changed through the centuries, man's need to conquer remained. And it would until the world ended.

IX

ALONE

*Culcreuch Castle
Fintry*

"I TAUGHT YE better than that, lad ... didn't I say 'never let a stranger beat ye on yer own lands'?"

Cory Galbraith shifted awkwardly, pain lancing up his left leg. His knee throbbed dully like toothache, as did his left hand, yet he didn't take his attention from the man who sat sprawled upon a high-backed chair before him.

Logan Galbraith, laird of these lands, wasn't a man you took your eyes off. A wolf-skin cloak covered his father's broad shoulders, making the man look even more intimidating than usual.

"Aye, Da," he muttered. "I underestimated the stranger." Cory's belly cramped at the memory. He was rarely beaten in a fight, and defeat tasted like vinegar in his mouth.

Laird Galbraith's sharp green eyes narrowed. "He made a fool of ye."

Cory clenched his jaw. He didn't need his old man to state the obvious, especially not with a hall of his warriors looking on.

Seated next to the laird upon the dais, his mother, Lena, fixed her son with a wintry look. As always, an embroidery project sat upon her lap. Her mouth pursed in displeasure, and she looked down her nose at him. Clearly, she was taking her husband's side on this one. "Let me guess," Lady Galbraith spoke up, her tone sharp. "Ye were making a nuisance of yerself over *that* woman again?"

Humiliation, hot and prickly, washed over Cory. He could imagine the smirks on the men lolling at the tables around him as they broke their fast with fresh bannock, oaten porridge, and tankards of fresh milk.

Wisely, he kept his gaze fixed upon the dais.

Diarmid and Brodric stood behind him. He knew they wouldn't be smirking, for his friends both shared his humiliation.

That stranger had wiped the floor with them.

"I thought as much," his mother continued, taking his silence as agreement. "Yer cousin's widow isn't worthy of ye, Cory. Why aren't ye setting yer sights higher?"

Cory ground his teeth. He'd tried—but all the matches his parents presented him with didn't interest him.

He'd wanted Heather for a long while. He remembered the day she'd arrived in Fintry, perched behind his grinning cousin. The man had looked unbearably smug that day, returning home from Dunnottar to take up his father's forge and bringing his bonny De Keith wife with him.

Cory had watched Iain help Heather off the horse—his gaze devouring the lass's curvaceous form, her saucy smile, and mane of walnut-colored hair—and had decided then and there that one day, Heather would be his.

"Heather should wed again," he growled finally. "And I will be her husband."

"Well, clearly the lass doesn't want ye," his father rumbled. Logan Galbraith leaned back in his chair, stretching out his long legs before him and crossing them at the ankle. "Ye can't force a woman's affection, lad."

Cory inhaled deeply. He'd had just about enough of his father's condescension. "Maybe she'll look upon me differently if I lop off that stranger's head," he snarled.

His mother's lips compressed. "What a barbaric notion."

However, next to her, the Galbraith laird let out a soft chuckle. "Ye think fear will make her succumb to ye?"

Cory held his ground, even if the throb in his hand now pulsed in time with his heartbeat. "Aye. Once she realizes that I'll kill any who thwart me, she'll see sense."

"Heather De Keith isn't the type to be cowed," his mother pointed out coldly. "Lord knows, yer cousin tried."

Indeed, he had. All of Fintry knew of Iain and Heather's fiery union. Their shouting could be heard across the village at times, and more than once, Heather had emerged from the forge with a blackened eye.

"If ye want to avenge yerself on that stranger, go ahead," his father said with a swipe of a ring-encrusted hand. "But don't do it for that widow ... do it for yer clan." Logan Galbraith's face had gone hard.

"He'll likely be long gone by now," Lena pointed out. "No man lingers in a place where he's not wanted."

The laird cast his wife an irritated look. "Then Cory will have to track him down and teach him what happens when ye cross a Galbraith."

Heat ignited in Cory's belly. This time, the warmth was not due to humiliation, but to anticipation. His father's words made him long for that dark-haired foreigner's blood.

"I *will* hunt him down," Cory growled. "If I have to follow him across Scotland to do it."

"If ye leave now, ye'll catch up with him soon enough," his father replied, his expression still fierce. "But don't think I'm giving ye a host of men to assist in yer mission."

Silence fell across the hall of Culcreuch Castle, a damp space that even the roaring hearths at each end couldn't warm.

Cory swallowed the hot words that bubbled up within him. His father knew he couldn't do this without help—not when he was injured. Nonetheless, he choked back his response. He could tell by the hard look in his father's eyes that the laird was daring Cory to challenge him.

It had been like this for a while now—the push and pull between father and son. At forty-two winters, Logan Galbraith was still strong, but with each passing year, his warrior sons grew more of a threat to his hold over this keep and the clan. He knew that one day the eldest of them, Cory, was likely to rise against him, as Logan had done against his own father.

It was the way of things in their family. Old Macum Galbraith lay buried under six feet of dirt on the hill behind the castle, and it was Logan who'd put him there.

"Take Diarmid and Brodric on yer quest." The laird broke the wintry silence. "And ye may choose three others from my guard to join ye, but no more." His mouth twisted then. "If six of ye can't take that foreigner down, I don't wish to see ye grace my door ever again."

Around him, Cory heard the sharp intake of breaths. Even his mother stiffened in her chair, her gaze sweeping to her husband.

There it was—finally—the gauntlet laid down.

Cory's attention veered right, settling for the first time upon the table where his three younger brothers sat. Rory, Aran, and Duglas stared back at him, their gazes unflinching. The eldest of the three, Rory, wore a smirk that Cory itched to sink his fist into.

Just like him, they were the image of their father: tall, broad-shouldered, and green-eyed with wild auburn hair. And just like Cory, they'd been rivals from the moment they'd come out screaming into the world.

None of them would join him on this hunt, he knew at a glance.

They'd let him fight to recover his honor alone.

Alone. That's how he'd been all his life, save for two friends who'd had his back since childhood. He didn't expect things to change now.

Cory dismissed his brothers with a cool glance, his focus shifting once more to the muscular figure sprawled upon a carven chair.

"Six is all I need," Cory finally replied, his tone gruff. Then, without another word, or glance at anyone present, he turned and limped from the hall.

X

AWKWARD QUESTIONS

"HOW IS IT ye know all about this Broom-star?"
Heather asked, breaking the morning's long silence.

Maximus allowed himself a grim smile. He'd been
waiting for the question, and he could hear the wariness
in her voice. This always happened when he spent more
than a few hours with folk. You couldn't live for as long
as he had and not appear strange to others.

"My father told me," he lied smoothly.

They rode north-east through a golden morning. The
sun had melted the light frost, likely the last one of the
year, and now warmed their faces. The oakwood had
given way to a series of undulating hills, where burns
glittered and the sounds of trickling water and birdsong
filled the air.

Heather lapsed back into silence, digesting his
answer. "So, ye were once a soldier ... but now ye trap
animals for their skins?" she finally asked.

"Yes, stoats, weasels, pine-martins ... and on
occasion, a wolf or a bear." He glanced back over his
shoulder, checking the road behind them. He felt
strangely on-edge this morning. The nervousness wasn't
for himself, but for his traveling companion.

Heather was mortal. One strike of a blade to that lovely pale throat and life would leave her. She didn't realize how vulnerable she was.

His attention shifted from the road to the woman perched on the cart. The morning sun caught the golden highlights in Heather's hair and accentuated her lovely skin; the sight was distracting, and he resisted the pull. He needed to keep his wits about him today.

"You're sitting on a sack full of ermine," he continued, "which will bring me a good price in Stirling." Ermine was the stoat's winter coat—a pristine white fur favored by lairds.

A groove appeared between Heather's brows. "So, ye spend yer days traveling the wilds ... alone?"

"I do."

A beat of silence followed before Heather's frown deepened. "Isn't it a ... lonely life?"

Maximus turned away from her. He knew where this conversation was headed. "Not really ... I prefer my own company."

"And ye have never sought a wife?"

And here they were—she'd arrived at the point sooner than he'd expected. After only a short while in Heather De Keith's company, he'd realized that the woman wasn't one to bandy words. She could be disarmingly direct.

"No," he replied, his gaze settling upon the garron's furry ears.

"Why not?"

"Because I don't wish for one." He too could be direct.

"Oh," she replied softly, and then fell silent.

Relief filtered over Maximus, and he released a heavy sigh. He didn't like to be rude, yet this woman wouldn't leave him be.

A man like him didn't take a wife—not if he didn't want to answer awkward questions as the years wore on. Such as, why he didn't seem to age, why illness never touched him, and how he could suffer a mortal wound and be healed again by morning.

The women in Maximus's life over the years had been many—yet until Evanna, none of them had lasted longer than a couple of weeks. He always found an excuse to move on. There had been one or two he'd been truly sorry to leave, ones that had wept to see him go, but it was for the best—for them both. Out of all of them, only Evanna had refused to be 'left'. A warrior woman to the core, she'd hunted him down, and the ugly scene that followed still pained Maximus to dwell on.

It had been his fault: he'd stayed with her for too long. It was a mistake he hadn't repeated since. These days he kept his encounters brief, and usually paid a woman to warm his bed rather than risk tears or anger.

He couldn't give a woman a family anyway, so there was little point in him forging a lasting relationship. In many ways, it was fortunate that the curse had rendered him infertile. The last thing he wanted was a daughter or son to track him down years later, only to wonder why their father was so youthful in appearance. More awkward questions.

Maximus Cato had been thirty-three winters old at the moment of the curse, and he hadn't aged a day since. On the outside at least, he appeared in the prime of life, yet how he felt on the inside told a different story.

He was tired, stretched thin.

Each passing year drained him.

Heather shifted upon the sack of ermine. She'd seen Robert, the laird of the De Keiths, wear a cloak of ermine during winters past. It was a plush white fur that Heather's mother had always coveted. But despite her husband's position as steward of Dunnottar, they'd never been able to afford the luxurious pelt.

Amongst the sacks, Heather spied a longbow and a collection of sharp-toothed iron traps. She didn't envy Maximus the life he'd chosen. She couldn't think of anything she'd like less than living in the wilds alone for months at a time.

Although it was thanks to men like him that the people of this land had cloaks to warm them during the bitter winter months.

The cart bumped over a particularly deep pothole, jolting Heather off her perch. Swallowing a cry, she grabbed hold of the edge of the cart and hauled herself back into position.

Then, she swung a dark look in Maximus's direction.

The highland pony he sat upon appeared strong enough to take both of them on its back, yet her traveling companion had made it clear he'd ride alone.

If she'd had any illusions about what last night meant to him, they were shattered by now.

Just as well then that Heather was a practical woman.

When she'd slipped from the sleeping tavern and crept into the stables to find him, she hadn't done so with a fluttering heart. She wasn't infatuated with the man. Instead, her belly had felt as if a troupe of brownies danced inside her because of the choice she'd made. She didn't like sneaking out of *The Bogside* like a thief. She didn't like leaving without saying goodbye.

Aonghus and Morag hadn't been particularly warm to her, yet they'd given her a job and a safe haven. And she was fond of their shy daughter, Alana.

Heather had imagined the day she'd leave the tavern, she'd walk out of there in daylight with her head held high, off to pastures new.

Instead, she'd held her breath and prayed that the floorboards didn't creak too loudly as she made her way downstairs and crept out into the stable yard through the scullery door.

They'll be furious with me.

Aye, her employers would—but as she'd sat alone in her dreary bed-chamber and contemplated the sum of her life so far, Heather had known it was time to go.

And she was grateful that Maximus had agreed to let her travel as far as Stirling with him.

Her gaze settled upon his broad shoulders, lingering there.

He sat up straight and tense, his gaze scanning the road ahead. She noted that he often cast glances behind him, as if he expected them to be followed.

She appreciated his vigilance, although she couldn't see why he was being so jumpy. Did he expect Cory to ride after them?

Heather stilled at the thought, a chill feathering down her spine. Surely, Cory wouldn't bother? But as she dwelled upon it, she realized he might. A Galbraith never forgot a slight.

It's just as well I'm traveling with Maximus, she thought. Having seen how he handled himself in a fight, she felt reassured.

She continued to observe her traveling companion. His present focus on their surroundings allowed her to do so without being caught.

Damn him, but the man was even more attractive in daylight. She liked the way his ink-black hair curled at the nape of his neck, his proud profile, and the sun-kissed color of his skin. Now that she knew he'd been a warrior in the past, she could see it. He carried himself like the guards at Dunnottar. A watchful, coiled tension emanated from his tall, lean body.

Like a wolf ready to spring.

Heather's breathing caught, a strange sensation quivering within her belly. Suddenly, she was back on that narrow bed, naked and spread wide for him as he crawled over her—his gaze black in the firelight, his face a picture of feral lust.

Swallowing, Heather dropped her gaze to where her fingers clenched around the side of the cart.

It was best she didn't let herself relive those moments. They were too raw, too intense—and they made her want for things she shouldn't. It was clear that he hadn't been pleased to see her at dawn. Maximus hadn't wanted to take things further than one torrid night. She'd sensed his discomfort when she'd appeared in the stables, but he was mistaken. She wasn't looking for anything but a traveling companion.

Even so, his chill welcome had stung.

Heather's mouth compressed, and she mentally shrugged off the lingering hurt.

Best that she focused on getting to Stirling and then finding passage north to Dunnottar.

The man who rode before her may have saved her from Cory, yet she knew instinctively that spending too much time with him was hazardous. She had a poor history when it came to her choice of men, and she didn't trust her judgement at all.

Maximus was little more than a stranger.

And so, she kept her mouth shut, holding back the torrent of questions that built up inside her.

Their last conversation had made his reluctance to converse with her clear, and although Heather hated long silences, she forced herself to bite her tongue. As such, it was a long ride to Stirling over swiftly rising hills and through thick forest.

They stopped briefly at noon, sharing some bread and cheese by a gurgling creek. Few words passed between them, just practicalities about the road and when they would reach their destination. Then, as soon as they'd eaten and slaked their thirst from a skin of ale, Maximus vaulted onto Luchag's broad back and they resumed their journey.

And as they traveled, Maximus scanned their surroundings and cast regular glances over his shoulder.

"Ye look nervous," Heather finally commented, unable to hold her tongue any longer. "Are ye looking out for Cory?"

His dark gaze shifted to her, and he nodded. "You're vulnerable out here."

"And ye aren't?"

With a snort, he turned away, making it clear he wasn't interested in continuing the conversation. Heather took the hint, and they lapsed into silence once more.

Eventually, as the afternoon shadows started to lengthen, the cart bumped over a series of ruts and crested the last hill before the trees drew back and a wide strath stretched before them.

Despite her aching posterior and cramped hands, Heather caught her breath.

Ahead, its castle perched upon a crag above a huddle of grey stone houses, with a backdrop of snow-capped mountains behind it, was Stirling.

XI

THE GATEWAY

THE CART RUMBLED across the wide stone bridge spanning the River Forth, and Heather craned her neck to gaze upon the fortress perched on the volcanic outcrop above.

She hadn't been here since the town had been liberated. She and Iain had passed through Stirling five years earlier when the English had controlled it. A year afterward, the Wallace and his men had freed Stirling from the English yoke.

Now that they'd almost reached their destination, Maximus picked up his pace. He urged his pony into a fast trot across the bridge, the small cart bouncing along behind it.

"Ye'd never know a battle took place on this bridge," Heather called out, raising her voice to be heard over the thumping of the cart wheels.

Maximus glanced back at her, his gaze sweeping over the glittering water. The tide was up, and boats bobbed against the jetty at Riverside. Heather caught a glimmer of impatience in his expression.

"They say whoever holds Stirling holds Scotland," he called back. "William Wallace and Andrew Moray knew what they were doing when they chose to face the English here."

Heather nodded. Her lungs expanded, pride swelling within her. Indeed, Stirling was the gateway between the Lowlands and the Highlands—and was known as the brooch that clasped the two areas together. "Never again will those bastards rule us," she muttered.

Maximus snorted, turning from her. "Never is a long time," he replied. "You know that the English are raiding north of the border again?"

Heather frowned. "Aye … filthy devil-spawn. Why don't they keep to their own lands? England truly must be a vile place."

To her irritation, Maximus merely shrugged. "Edward's not finished with Scotland it seems." His gaze faced forward now. Impatience bristled off his broad shoulders, and Heather wondered at his mood. Was he eager to visit the furrier before they shut up shop for the day?

His reminder about the hated Edward Longshanks soured her mood. Dunnottar too had been occupied by the English when she left it with Iain. She remembered how those English soldiers had strutted about the castle like lairds, how they'd leered at her from the battlements. Fortunately, the Wallace had crushed them not long after her departure. Now the fortress was under Scottish rule once more—and she wanted it to stay that way.

"The Wallace will rally more Scots to his side and defeat them," she announced after a pause.

"William Wallace has disappeared, and Andrew Moray is dead," Maximus replied, his tone distracted. "Some say Wallace is in France, trying to gather support for the Scottish cause."

Heather frowned. She wondered if he cared at all for the plight of her people. However, she couldn't see his expression, for he was still turned away from her, focusing on the end of the bridge that neared and the cobbled way that led up the hill into town.

"Where to now?" she asked, aware that she didn't have the slightest idea what to do now that they'd arrived in Stirling.

"There's a good guesthouse in the upper town," he replied briskly. "*The Golden Lion* is a safe place for a lady to lodge for the night."

Heather swallowed a wry laugh. *A lady.*

She was the daughter of a steward, a man who was second cousin to the De Keith laird, and although she wasn't exactly a commoner, she wasn't of the ruling class either.

She wondered if Maximus was making fun of her, especially after what had transpired between them. However, his tone wasn't snide.

"And where will ye stay?" she asked.

"I'm sure *The Golden Lion* has enough rooms to accommodate both of us." His voice held a guarded edge that warned her from asking anything else. But his reply made their relationship clear: they'd shared a bed yesterday, but they wouldn't tonight.

Heat crept up Heather's neck, embarrassment rising within her.

Not that I want that either, she reminded herself hastily. Last night had been foolish and reckless. Letting lust getting the better of her had indeed been a mistake— one she wouldn't repeat.

The Golden Lion was a sturdy building made of grey stone, with yellow shuttered windows. Nestled into a lane in the upper town, the establishment sat under the shadow of the castle.

And as Maximus had predicted, the inn-keeper had rooms available—although they were the last two.

"There's a monthly market at Riverside," the man told them as he led the way up creaking stairs to the top floor. "Town's full of traders, farmers, and merchants ... and soldiers." The inn-keeper paused and glanced over his shoulder, his expression clouding. "Word has it that we'll be raising arms against the English again soon."

"I knew they were raiding farther south of here ... but are they pushing north already?" Maximus asked.

The inn-keeper's mouth thinned. "Aye ... the bastards didn't like the beating we dealt them last time."

"Who's Steward of the Realm these days?" Heather spoke up. Scotland had no king presently, and she wondered who'd taken up the role of guardian.

"John Comyn," the man replied, turning from them and continuing up the stairs. "Let's hope he's got the spine to defend Stirling when the English arrive."

Heather digested this news, tension rising within her. The peace after the last attacks had been so brief. It was just as well she was returning to Dunnottar, for it was likely the lowlands would be overrun soon.

When they reached the landing, Heather called out to the inn-keeper once more. "Is the market still running?" She carried little coin on her, and what she had she'd need for the journey north. However, it had been a long while since she'd attended a decent-sized market. After the inn-keeper's somber news, she needed something to distract her, to brighten up the afternoon.

"Aye, lass ... although ye want to hurry, for they pack up at dusk."

"Take care, if you're going down to Riverside alone," Maximus murmured when they were alone once more. He'd pressed a silver penny into the inn-keeper's hand and put an order in for supper later. They now stood at the end of a narrow hallway, the doors to their bed-chambers facing each other. "Rowdy types frequent such places. Plus, folk might come to Stirling looking for you."

Heather snorted. "I'll be careful." On one level, she appreciated his concern for her welfare, yet she was starting to find it overbearing. "Don't worry, I can handle myself."

Maximus favored her with an incredulous look that made her irritation rise. And then, to her surprise, he unbuckled a knife from around his leg and handed it to her. "This one has a thin blade," he said, his gaze snaring hers. "But it'll do some damage nonetheless. Carry it on you till you reach Dunnottar."

Heather took the knife and fastened it to her belt. She didn't know how to respond. She wanted to be irritated, but it was a kind, protective gesture. Iain hadn't ever bothered after her safety like this man did.

"Thank ye," she said, feeling uncharacteristically shy. "So, I take it ye won't be joining me at market?"

Maximus shook his head. "I have business in town." He stepped back from Heather and favored her with a quick smile. "I'll see you back here for supper."

Leaving *The Golden Lion*, Maximus descended the tangle of cobbled streets to the lower town. Upon his back, he carried two sacks of his finest pelts. A sunny day had stretched out into a golden afternoon. Stirling really was glorious, sparkling in the spring sunshine. The warmth of the sun on his face—welcome after so many months of bone-numbing cold—made Maximus's spirits rise.

I spend too long alone in the wilderness, he thought ruefully. *I should make more trips to town*. Indeed, it felt good to be amongst folk again. Women in green and blue kirtles, woolen shawls about their shoulders, walked by, some of them favoring Maximus with an appreciative look. Children's laughter echoed off the stone walls, and there were burly men everywhere, their deep voices booming through the streets. Many of them carried weapons—heavy broad-swords strapped to their hips. These were the soldiers the inn-keeper had warned them of.

Maximus observed the men with interest, taking in the plaid of their sashes: Bruce, Eskine, Boyd, Stewart, and Comyn. They were mostly lowland clans, proud warriors determined never to bend the knee to King Edward of England.

Maximus's mouth thinned as a strange sensation stirred within him. He wasn't Scottish, yet he felt their pride—their savage resolve made the hair on the back of his arms prickle.

He wished he had something to live for, something to defend.

The aroma of roasting mutton distracted him then, wafting out from kitchens. And somewhere in the lower town, he caught the mournful wail of a highland pipe drifting across the waters of the Forth.

Maximus's mouth relaxed, and his lips curved into a faint smile. The sound of Scotland.

He had an odd relationship with this land. At first, he'd hated it. The bandrúi had cursed him to remain here for eternity, and he'd rebelled. He'd even tried to leave a year or two after the cursing, to ride south over the border, where Emperor Hadrian was just beginning to build his Great Wall.

But his horse had bucked him off before bolting into the hills—and when Maximus had tried to continue south on foot, his feet refused to obey him.

He literally couldn't leave these lands. It was as the bandrúi had said.

With the passing of the years, his hatred had softened to a simmering dislike. Then, finally there had come a day when he'd breathed in the scent of damp, peaty earth and flowering heather, looked up into the wild sky, and realized that despite that he'd never chosen to stay here, Scotland had somehow gotten into his blood.

But he'd never be Scottish—not in his heart, where it really mattered. He'd never be able to don a clan sash and feel the sense of belonging the warriors who filled the streets of Stirling did.

The knowledge saddened him.

The furrier Maximus always visited here was just off a square in the lower town. The merchant greeted him eagerly, his eyes shining when he dug his fingers into the thick, snowy ermine. Even so, the man haggled.

Sometime later, Maximus emerged from the shop, unburdened by his sacks of pelts, but with his coin purse considerably heavier.

Out in the alleyway, he could hear the cries of the vendors at the market at Riverside below. Maximus paused a moment, listening. He didn't like the idea of Heather wandering down there alone, even with a knife at her waist. She was a spirited, plucky woman—but she seemed to have a knack for getting herself into trouble. If he didn't have pressing business elsewhere, Maximus might have gone down to check on her. Instead, he turned left and retraced his steps to the upper town.

Quickening his stride, Maximus scowled.

Stop fussing over her, man.

Heather wasn't his concern.

He hadn't come to Stirling just to offload his furs, but for news. He had to pay a visit to a special place: somewhere he always visited when he came to this town.

Increasing his speed further, Maximus stalked back up the hill.

High in the upper town, just below the craggy outcrop where the castle perched, sat Holy Rude. The grey stone kirk with its steep slate roof had sat on this spot for nearly three hundred years—but Maximus had been visiting this site for a while longer than that.

Entering the church, Maximus slowed his step, taking in the imposing columns that lined the nave, the sweeping arches between them, and the soaring wooden ceiling above. His booted feet whispered on the floor, just audible over the sound of monks chanting, and he inhaled the fatty odor of tallow blended with the heavy scent of incense.

He wasn't of this faith, yet every time he entered Holy Rude, a sense of peace settled over him. The kirk was a welcoming place. A few robed figures knelt near the altar, their chants a haunting melody.

Maximus ignored them, heading instead for the shrine of Saint John the Baptist.

A painting of the saint himself, preaching in the wilderness, rose above a bank of guttering candles. Maximus placed a penny in the iron box before them and lit a candle—as he always did when he entered the kirk.

A candle for his parents and brothers. He couldn't even remember their names these days. Yet lighting a candle for them reminded him that somewhere in the mists of time, he'd been part of a family. He'd belonged somewhere.

Then, once the candle had been lit, he slid in between the bank of candles and the wall, placed both hands upon a stone block, and pushed inward.

The ancient door opened, the soft rasp of stone against stone echoing through the alcove. Maximus hesitated, casting a glance over his shoulder. The chanting continued.

Turning back to the opening, he ducked his head and slipped inside.

XII

SLAYER OF THE BULL

MAXIMUS DESCENDED THE stairs in darkness before he reached a narrow tunnel where a torch hung from a bracket upon the wall, its golden light illuminating damp stone. Taking another, unlit, torch from the sconce next to the guttering torch, Maximus lit it and made his way down the tunnel to the cave beyond.

Carved out of the volcanic rock on which this town stood, this sanctuary was all Maximus, Cassian, and Draco had of their past lives.

Water coated the pitted stone walls—for there was a spring just behind the cave—the sound of dripping filling the space.

This place was a mithraeum, a temple of the ancient god Mithras.

The altar rose before Maximus, a slab of rock flanked by two long stone benches. Above it, a relief had been carved into the rock: a scene showing the god himself, slaying a bull. Either side of the altar stood two stone statues of the god's torchbearers—Cautes and Cautopates.

Maximus hung his torch up on the wall and then lit a wand of incense. Kneeling on the chill stone before the altar, breathing in the woody scent of the incense, his gaze went to the closed iron box that sat before him.

Unsheathing his dagger, he sliced the blade across his thumb. Blood welled. Reaching out, he smeared it onto the stone altar, making the ritual sacrifice. Almost immediately, he felt the pad of his thumb itch as the bleeding stopped.

"Great God Mithras," he murmured, his voice cutting through the hazy, incense-filled air. "Slayer of the Bull, Lord of the Ages. The wheel turns, and the Broom-star is again in the sky. Draw back the mists and grant three men of the lost legion peace ... at last."

How many times had Maximus uttered this invocation over the centuries—each time with hope in his heart? He hardly dared hope now, for they were still no closer to solving the rest of the riddle. They could make no sense of the words. And yet, with each rare visit to Stirling, Maximus made sure he traveled to this secret temple—a place where he, Cassian, and Draco left each other messages.

The three men had spent little time together over the years, each running from their own demons, chasing their own destiny. But their shared curse and faith in the Bull-slayer bound them.

Maximus's gaze shifted once more to the closed iron box. His pulse quickened, a pressure building in the center of his chest. Would there be a message from one of them inside?

Rising to his feet, he reached forward and lifted the lid. His breath caught when he saw that there was a small scroll.

Hope flickered, like a guttering candle, in his breast.

Maybe, just maybe, one of them had discovered something.

He broke the wax seal, which bore the mark of the imperial eagle, and unfurled the message.

The words inside were dated, written in Latin, and to the point:

XV Martii MCCCI
Ego aliquid de valorem inventum omnibus nobis.
Statim veniet ad Dunnottar.
Cassian.

15 March 1301
I have discovered something of value to us all.
Come to Dunnottar immediately.
Cassian.

Maximus smiled, his fingers tightening around the
parchment. Impatience thrummed within him.
What has he discovered?
He lowered the message before rolling it up and
placing it back inside the box. Since the seal hadn't been
broken, he knew that he was the first to come here.
Draco hadn't yet made a trip to Stirling.

Turning, his gaze alighted upon the cloaked figure
that now stood at the entrance to the cave behind him—
the figure he'd known would be waiting for him.

The man's cowled face was shadowed, although his
gaze gleamed. "Good news?" he asked, his voice a low
rumble in the temple's silence.

"I believe so ... I've lost track of the days, Norris. How
long ago did Cassian visit?"

It was true. He knew it was spring, but could only
guess that they were now reaching the end of March. He
had no idea what the actual date was.

"No more than a week ago," the hooded man replied.
"There's been no sign of Draco."

Maximus stepped forward and removed the heavy
pouch of silver pennies he wore upon his belt. He then
dropped them into the guardian's outstretched hand.

Maximus, Cassian, and Draco had carved this temple
out of the rock themselves, using hammers and picks—
long before Christians built their kirk atop it. But soon
afterward, they realized they couldn't remain in Stirling
to keep the temple safe. And so, they'd hired guardians:
torchbearers who served the three immortal centurions,
generation after generation. And every time one of the

three visited the mithraeum, they brought coin—so that these men and their families could continue to aid them over the coming years. They paid them for their service—and their silence.

Maximus had no need of most of the silver he earned from his trade. He required very little to live on. Over the years, he'd given nearly everything to the guardians.

With a smile at Norris, Maximus retrieved his torch and retraced his steps back up the tunnel. As he did so, he realized his step was lighter than it had been in a long while.

The market was even more vibrant and exciting than Heather had expected. It seemed as if traders from every corner of Scotland had converged upon the quay to sell their wares. As she strolled the length of Riverside, inhaling the muddy tang of the tidal river, Heather spied stalls selling all kinds of dried and preserved meats she'd never seen before, barrels of exotic-scented spices, an array of breads and baked goods, and pungent cheeses.

Surveying the crowd, Heather noted a number of armed warriors wandering amongst the locals. The sight both reassured her and put her on edge: they were Scottish soldiers at least, but their presence was a reminder of the shadow the English had cast over her country.

Stopping by a stall that sold bolts of brightly-colored cloth, Heather let the beautiful fabric distract her. She traced her fingertips over a bolt of gold-colored silk. How she loved all the different types of material one could buy—silk, wool, cambric, and linen—and the rainbow of shades they came in.

I wish Aila could see these. The thought of her sister made Heather stifle a pang. She'd often thought of Aila over the past few years, and wandering through the market made her remember all the times they had visited the market in Stonehaven, near Dunnottar, together.

I'll see her again soon.

As she stroked a bolt of patterned green damask—ignoring the hopeful stare of the vendor—rough male voices drifted over the crowd.

Heather tensed, her gaze flicking right in the direction of the voices.

One of them was familiar.

Peering through the crowd, she caught a glimpse of a tall man with long auburn hair. He walked with a pronounced limp and was flanked by a group of armed warriors.

Heather's heart leaped in her breast. *Cory!*

Judging from the mean look upon his face and the way his narrowed green eyes swept the crowd, the Galbraith laird's son wasn't in Stirling to enjoy the market.

Heat flushed through Heather. *How dare he follow us here?*

Her first instinct was to storm across to Cory and give him a piece of her mind, but then self-preservation checked her. Maximus had warned her to be cautious. She probably shouldn't have come down to the market without an escort; she should have treated the threat Cory posed seriously.

In situations like this, discretion was the better part of valor.

I'll just slip away unnoticed.

Heather stepped back from the bolts of cloth.

At that moment, the crowd parted—the men and women providing a barrier between Heather and Cory moving away. And as he surveyed the market, he saw her.

Cory's stride faltered, and he halted.

For a heartbeat, the pair of them merely stared at each other, frozen.

Heather was the first to recover. Gathering her cloak tightly around her, she spun on her heel and dove into the crowd.

Behind her, an angry male shout echoed through the market. "Heather! Stop!"

Heather didn't look back, didn't chance a peek over her shoulder. She knew that, despite his injured knee, Cory was only a few yards behind her. Fortunately, she was fast. Heather had always been quick on her feet, and she fled like a hunted hare now, racing down the quayside.

Shoppers—mostly women with baskets under their arms, or couples strolling arm in arm—blocked her path. Fortunately, there were few soldiers on this edge of the crowd, for one of them might have made a grab for her. Heather swerved around the shoppers, although once or twice she was forced to dig her elbows into folk in order to get them to move out of her way.

Disgruntled shouts now dogged her steps—but still she didn't look back.

Any moment now, she expected to feel Cory's heavy hand slam down upon her shoulder and drag her to a halt.

Yet it never came.

"Heather!" She could hear the rage in his voice, and to her relief, he sounded farther behind her than she'd thought.

Maybe she could lose him after all.

The crowds on the quay were both a hindrance and a boon, for although they slowed Heather's flight, they also made it harder for Cory and his friends to follow her. As soon as she burst out onto the wide cobbled square at the bottom of the lower town, Heather felt dangerously exposed.

Heart galloping, she sprinted across the square and into the network of narrow streets beyond.

Please, dear Lord, don't let this be a dead-end.

Heather didn't know Stirling at all. How many of these streets led to stone walls where Cory could corner her?

But, fortunately, this one didn't. Left, right, left, and left again—Heather kept running, and slowly the shouts of her pursuers died away.

Finally, Heather couldn't run any farther. Her heart felt as if it were about to burst from her chest, her lungs were on fire, and sweat poured down her face. Slipping into an alleyway next to a bakery, she bent double, drawing in deep breaths of air.

And all the while, she listened for any sign of pursuit.

But—save her gasping breath—she heard no such sounds.

She waited a while, until her heart and breathing had slowed, until she was sure that Cory had abandoned the chase. And then—hand on the hilt of the knife Maximus had given her—Heather crept from the alleyway.

Dusk was settling over Stirling now, the last of the sun's rays gilding the castle. Most of the streets lay in shadow.

Glancing over her shoulder, her nerves now stretched taut as if she expected Cory to jump out at her at any moment, Heather hurried up the hill toward *The Golden Lion.*

XIII

MAXIMUS THE MERCIFUL

MAXIMUS WAS SITTING with a cup of wine near the fire, when Heather burst into *The Golden Lion's* common room. One glance and he could tell something was amiss. Her bosom was heaving, her cheeks were flushed, and strands of her light brown hair stuck to her sweaty brow.

Her gaze seized upon Maximus, and picking up her skirts, she bustled across the floor toward him. She wove in and out of the tables, ignoring the curious—and lewd—looks some of the customers were favoring her with.

"You look like you need this." Maximus pushed the tankard of ale he'd bought Heather toward her she took a seat opposite him. "A trip to the market can be thirsty work."

"Aye." She grasped her fingers around the tankard, raised it to her lips, and took a deep draft. However, when she lowered it, Maximus saw the panic in her eyes.

"What is it?"

"Cory Galbraith," she replied, her voice husky as she still struggled to regain her breath. "He's here."

Maximus tensed, his gaze sweeping around the common room. With the Riverside market and many soldiers in town, the inn was busier than usual. He suddenly felt exposed. "Where?"

"Down at the market. He has a group of men with him ... around five or six of them, I think." Heather took another gulp of ale. "They chased me through the town, until I finally lost them."

Maximus's mouth thinned. He'd anticipated Galbraith following them—but he hadn't expected him to catch up with them so soon.

"Come on." He picked up his cup of wine and rose to his feet. "We can't stay downstairs ... I wouldn't be surprised if he spends the night visiting every inn in Stirling. I'll have our supper brought up to your chamber."

Heather broke off a piece of bread, her gaze lifting from the dish of stew before her to settle upon the man seated opposite. They sat at a narrow table before the fire in her room.

Since entering the chamber, Maximus had hardly spoken a word. He now wore a shuttered, brooding expression.

"Are ye worried about Cory?" she asked finally, breaking the weighty silence between them.

Maximus snorted before swallowing a mouthful of bread and venison stew. He then reached for his cup of wine. "I am ... and about you." He took a sip of wine, his dark gaze settling upon her. "I was prepared for Galbraith seeking his reckoning. But I hadn't wanted you to be drawn into it."

Heather met his eye. Now that she'd managed to escape Cory and was safe, the panic that had gripped her ribs in a vise had eased. "I got away ... no harm done."

Maximus frowned. "For the time being."

Heather loosed an irritated breath. *There's that protectiveness again.* Although she found it endearing on one level, it was also a little smothering. She wasn't used to having a man look out for her.

They finished their supper in silence, and then Maximus rose from the table and crossed to the window.

Heather watched him go, her gaze tracking him. She'd never seen a man walk like him: he had a predatory, stalking gait that made her breathing and pulse quicken.

Last night was still fresh in her mind, and she wondered if the memory of their passionate coupling was as vivid for him.

Behave yerself, Heather, she chastised herself. *Last night isn't to be repeated.*

She didn't need to complicate her life further. Dunnottar loomed like a specter on the horizon. Soon she'd have to face her parents.

Heather started to sweat. She could almost hear her mother's crowing voice: *I told ye this would happen. I knew ye would come crawling back here eventually.*

Opening the shutters ajar, Maximus peered into the street below. Flaming torches hung either side of the entrance to the inn, illuminating the surrounding street clearly.

Forcing herself not to dwell on her mother's self-righteous face, Heather focused on him instead. "See anything interesting?"

"No," Maximus murmured. "Just a drunk taking a piss against a wall ... no sign of your friends."

Heather pulled a face. "They're not my friends."

Maximus turned from the window and rested his backside against the sill, crossing his long legs before him. As always, when his gaze settled upon her, Heather's belly tightened.

Uncomfortable, she cleared her throat and rose to her feet. She then unbuckled the knife he'd loaned her and placed it upon the table. "Ye'll be wanting this back."

He shook his head. "Keep it. You shouldn't be traveling during lawless times such as these without a weapon on your person." He then patted the dagger that hung at his side. "I am well enough armed."

Heather inclined her head, studying him a moment. "That dagger ... is it the one ye stabbed Cory through the hand with?"

He nodded.

"I've never seen a blade like it ... can ye show it to me?"

Maximus pushed himself off the window sill and crossed to Heather. He then unsheathed the dagger and handed it to her.

Heather took the blade, examining its bone handle and gleaming, leaf-shaped blade.

"It's called a pugio," Maximus said softly. "Every Roman soldier carries one."

"It's nothing like a dirk," Heather replied. She noted how old this weapon looked: the bone handle was polished with age and use.

"No ... the pugio is for stabbing your enemy repeatedly with. While a dirk's long blade can kill in one thrust, the pugio creates a bit of damage first."

Heather swallowed at the blood-thirsty description before she handed Maximus back his knife. "Well ... that should have maimed Cory for life."

His mouth quirked. "Not really." He resheathed the knife before taking her hand and tracing a fingertip between two of the thin bones that stretched from the top of her wrist to knuckle.

His touch had an instant response upon Heather. She stilled, her breathing hitching. Did he have any idea what he did to her?

"I deliberately drove the dagger vertically, in between the bones," Maximus explained. "If I hadn't, the blade would have ruined his hand."

Heather exhaled sharply. "Merciful of ye."

She glanced up to see Maximus was smiling. "Maximus the Merciful," he murmured. "I like the sound of that."

His proximity was almost too much. It was getting hard to draw breath, and Heather was starting to feel hot and flustered. In contrast, the man before her appeared as cool and collected as ever. Did he ever lose that veneer of control? She was yet to see it.

He stepped back from Heather then, letting go of her hand.

Heather drew in a steadying breath. His touch had made her legs go weak and shaky. Her fingers traced the line on the back of her hand, where he'd just touched her. She could still feel the heat of his fingertips there, and it filled her with an aching want that made her chest hurt.

Not good. Not good at all.

Gathering her wits, she shifted her attention to his left arm. "I should take another look at that wound he dealt ye ... and change the bandage."

"No need," he replied, waving away her concern.

Heather stiffened. "Even a shallow wound can sour," she reminded him. "Ye should really let—"

"Leave it, Heather," he cut her off, his voice terse now. "I can look after myself."

Heather scowled to mask the hurt that constricted her chest. She'd only offered to help him; he didn't have to be so rude, so dismissive.

A brittle silence settled in Heather's bed-chamber then. She moved over to the hearth and sank down onto a low stool before it, signaling that supper was over and that he could leave now.

"Have you made arrangements for your trip to Dunnottar yet?" Maximus asked, shattering the tension between them.

Heather shook her head. "I meant to this afternoon ... but events prevented me," she replied coolly, deliberately fixing her attention upon the lump of peat glowing in the hearth.

"It's just as well then that I'm headed that way too. I can accompany you."

Heather's chin snapped up, and she turned upon the stool. Maximus was still watching her with that veiled look she'd already come to know well, although his mouth had curved in a half-smile.

"Ye are going to Dunnottar?" she asked.

"I wasn't ... but my plans have changed. I now have business there."

Business.

Heather watched him, her gaze narrowing. Once again, his tone warned her from pushing him. The man might make a living as a trapper, but he was full of secrets—layers and layers of them.

"I don't want to put ye out," she said, her voice turning from cool to frosty. As much as she was drawn to this man and appreciated his protection, he also unsettled her. It wasn't a good idea to continue traveling with him.

"You aren't," he replied, his tone brisk. He crossed to the table, threw back the last gulp of wine, and set his cup back on the table with a thud. "But since you're a woman with a taste for trouble, I'd prefer to know you're safe ... especially with Galbraith on our tail."

Heather caught her breath. The arrogance of him. How dare he assume she even wanted him as her escort?

Oblivious to her outrage, he headed toward the door. "I suggest you get an early night ... we leave before daybreak tomorrow. I'm hoping we can slip out of town unseen."

XIV

THE ROAD NORTH

CLOD-HEAD. THIS ISN'T wise.

Maximus's mouth twisted as good sense needled him yet again. Ignoring the whisper, he tightened Luchag's girth. Ever since leaving Heather's bed-chamber the evening before, he'd regretted his insistence on accompanying her to Dunnottar.

The woman was trouble—and in more ways than one.

It was bad enough that after coming to her rescue he now had a revenge-maddened warrior and his friends after him. But even worse was the attraction he felt toward her.

Last evening, as they'd stood together in her room, he'd been sorely tested.

All through supper, he'd found himself stealing glances at her. Watching her eat was erotic. She ate in small bites, chewing slowly. It had been a struggle not to stare at her mouth and that plump lower lip that drove him to distraction.

The firelight had played across her pale skin and the light scattering of freckles that dusted her nose. It highlighted the coppery strands in her brown hair.

He wasn't sure what had possessed him to take her hand either. The feel of her soft skin against his fingertips had sent a jolt of lust straight through his groin. He'd had to leave the chamber before he forgot himself.

Even so, he couldn't just abandon her to be hunted down by Galbraith. If she stayed with him, at least she'd be safer.

Strapping on a saddle bag, Maximus counselled himself to keep his distance from Heather De Keith for the rest of the journey.

He wasn't sure what had come over him. These days, he refused to be led by his rod. But around Heather, he found it hard to concentrate.

I clearly left it too long without bedding a woman, he thought, his gaze flicking toward where a cloaked figure waited in the shadow of the stable doorway. *It's turned me into a randy goat.*

"I'm leaving the cart and my traps behind," he said, breaking the hush between them. "The inn-keeper has agreed to look after them till I pass this way next. We'll travel faster if we both ride Luchag."

Did he imagine it, or did she tense? He felt it, even though Heather was shrouded by her traveling cloak. It wasn't his choice either, for them to ride together. However, there was no time for him to purchase another pony. Each moment they lingered here in Stirling put Heather in danger.

"It's around four days to Dunnottar," he continued when she didn't reply. "Three and a half if we travel fast."

With that, Maximus untied the pony and led him from the stable. Outside, a swathe of stars stretched across a wide night sky. And there, hanging amongst them, was the bright silver Broom-star.

Maximus paused at the sight of it. For centuries that star had mocked him. It had taken him and the other two a while to figure out what the Broom-star actually was, and then, once they had, all three of them lived for its coming.

But with each cycle came disappointment.

Perhaps this is the time ... maybe Cassian has deciphered the rest of the riddle?

Excitement flickered deep in his chest.

The sensation surprised him.

What was it he was looking forward to exactly? If they broke the curse, he'd become mortal again. If a dirk blade didn't end his life, he'd age and eventually become an old man. But would anything else change? He'd still be an outsider, a loner. And what good was mortality if he had no one to share his life with? Seeing the warriors gathering in town the day before had highlighted just how empty Maximus's life had become. Those men had kin to protect and a cause that drove them.

Shifting his attention from the Broom-star, Maximus turned to check Luchag's girth. The tiny flicker of excitement within him died, leaving a cold numbness in its place.

Immortal or not, without something in his life worth dying for, what was the point?

Luchag cantered out of Stirling, taking a road that would lead them north-east, over mountainous land, toward the coast.

It was a different route to the one Heather and Iain had taken five years earlier when traveling south—a long, winding road that cut through wooded vales. Nonetheless, there were a few villages they could stay at on the way.

Heather sat perched behind Maximus, her arms looped around his waist. Having grown up with horses, she balanced easily. There was no need to grip onto the man for dear life; even so, the pony had a jolting gait that threw her up against him with every stride. That, and the slope of the saddle, made it impossible to keep her distance.

It was ridiculous to worry about her virtue now—after all, two nights earlier they'd been as intimate as it was possible for a man and woman to be—but there was an awkwardness between them this morning. His attitude toward her the night before still rankled. Heather hadn't liked the heavy-handed way he'd taken charge of the situation. However, since she hadn't had time to make plans of her own and Cory's presence in Stirling alarmed her, she'd decided to leave with him all the same.

Maximus seemed in a dour mood this morning. He'd barely looked her way as he led Luchag out of the stable. He just vaulted onto the pony's back and reached down a hand to help her up.

Few words had passed between them since.

Like the previous day, Heather noted that Maximus kept scanning his surroundings. He also looked repeatedly over his shoulder to ensure they weren't being followed. His vigilance made Heather tense.

It was a reminder of the man that now hunted them both.

Mist wreathed in from the River Forth this morning, drifting between the folds in the hills and casting a chill over the dawn. But as they headed north, the sun rose, burning off the fog and basking the earth in warmth. And as they rode, Heather saw the signs of spring all around them: bluebells carpeting wooded glades; snowdrops, crocuses, and daffodils poking up from the damp earth.

Spring. New beginnings. Warmth filtered over Heather at the thought.

Despite her nervousness at facing her kin and worries about her future, she was glad to leave Fintry behind, glad to be going home.

They spoke little that day, reaching the village of Crieff at dusk. The hamlet was tiny, just a scattering of white-washed cottages and a pretty stone kirk surrounded by green hills and thick woods. Long-haired cattle grazed the hillsides on the way in, the tinkle of their bells drifting across the valley.

"We won't stay in the village," Maximus informed Heather gruffly, breaking the long silence between them. "It's too small ... Galbraith and his men will find us easily if they've taken this road." He jerked his chin toward the wooded valley to their right, where oaks and birch were just coming into leaf. "We'll make camp down there instead."

This news didn't thrill Heather. After a day in the saddle, she longed for some comfort. Still, Maximus was right. Crieff had just one tavern—a tiny establishment. If Cory arrived at the village tonight, he'd head straight there and find them.

The thought chilled her, and so she allowed Maximus to guide Luchag off the road and into the trees without complaint. A short distance in, the press of silvery birch trunks and wide oaks became too thick to stay on horseback, and so the pair of them dismounted. Maximus led the garron into a copse of oaks while Heather brought up the rear, grateful for the chance to stretch out her back and legs.

Finally, Maximus halted at the bottom of the valley, next to where a burn trickled by. Turning to Heather, he met her eye for the first time in hours. "We'll rest here tonight."

Heather nodded. "I take it we won't be lighting a fire?"

He shook his head. "Too risky ... worry not though, we have enough bread and cheese to last us till tomorrow." Indeed, they'd stopped off at the hamlet of Braco earlier in the day, where Maximus had picked up provisions.

Taking a seat upon the mossy bank next to the burn as the gloaming deepened around them, Heather watched Maximus unsaddle and rub down Luchag.

"Why exactly do ye call him 'Mouse'?" she asked finally.

Maximus glanced up, his eyes crinkling at the corners as he smiled for the first time all day. "His coat is a nondescript shade ... much like a field-mouse."

Heather huffed. It hadn't escaped her that the pony's coat was a very similar shade to her own hair. Yet she doubted Maximus had made the comparison.

When she didn't comment further, Maximus resumed rubbing the garron down with a twist of reeds. When he'd finished, he sat down a few yards away and pulled a small object from a leather pack.

The sun had almost set now, the last rays of light streaming through the trees.

Maximus held what appeared to be a figurine up to the light, and Heather saw that it was a man with a lion's head, a serpent wrapped around his torso. Ignoring her for the moment, Maximus murmured words Heather didn't understand. They reminded her of the prayers that priests said in Latin.

"What's that?" she finally asked, curiosity getting the better of her.

"A leontocephaline," Maximus replied, glancing at her. "A friend carved it for me ... many years ago. I often say a few prayers with the setting or rising sun."

Heather arched a brow. "Don't the folk of Rome worship the same god as us Scots?"

Maximus's mouth quirked. "Most probably do these days ... but I'm different."

Heather watched him, questions bubbling up inside her. The man really was an enigma.

The pair lapsed into silence before Maximus tucked away his figurine and turned to her. "So, have you thought on how you will approach your kin in Dunnottar?"

Heather tensed at the question. "Not really," she admitted warily. "I suppose I just have to brace myself for a tongue-lashing from my mother."

"I take it she's a fiery woman?"

Heather pulled a face. "Aye ... Ma's got quite a temper on her ... as have I."

"I've noticed," he replied, a wry smile curving his lips now.

Heather tensed. "Iain thought I always had too much to say for myself," she said, her tone turning guarded. She was tired of men criticizing her. She'd taken after her mother—and although her father had never minded his wife's fiery nature, Heather had never found a man who'd accept her as she was.

His smile faded. "You think I'm disparaging you?"

"Ye wouldn't be the first."

His head inclined. "You are a clever, capable woman, Heather De Keith. It's been a long while since I've met a woman with a mind as sharp as yours."

Heather arched an eyebrow. "Aren't ye referring to my tongue? Plenty have told me that it's sharper than a dirk blade."

"Men are often threatened by a woman with something to say for herself," he replied.

Heather smiled. "And ye aren't?"

"No."

Heather snorted, making it clear she didn't believe him. Even so, she felt herself warming under his words. His tone was sincere, although she sensed he was teasing her now. She welcomed it, as the tension between them since the night before had started to get to her. She still had three more days' journey in this man's company. She didn't want to spend it in pained silence.

XV

I DON'T REMEMBER

HUDDLED IN THEIR cloaks, Maximus and Heather took refuge under the spreading arms of a large oak, where the first green leaves were bursting to life. It was a cool, misty evening, as it often was in the hills, and Maximus wished he could have lit a fire to keep them both warm.

But he was wary tonight. Galbraith knew that Heather's kin resided in Dunnottar. Many roads led out from Stirling, and Maximus had taken a less traveled one. Yet he doubted that would fool Galbraith for long.

Glancing left—at where Heather had pulled up the fur-lined hood of her cloak, her profile just visible— Maximus studied her a moment. The woman was hard to fathom. Confident, sensual, and sharp-witted, there was also a vulnerability to her that he found compelling.

"Tell me," he began, breaking the silence. "What made you rebel so strongly against your parents?"

Heather glanced in his direction, and he saw from the way her features tensed that she didn't welcome the question. It was bold, perhaps too much so. Nonetheless, he held her eye. A long, cold evening stretched before them. Maximus didn't suspect he'd get much sleep.

Instead, their earlier conversation had made him curious to know more of this woman's history—of the choices and twists of fate that had ended with her serving ale to drunks in *The Bogside Tavern*.

Heather sighed. "They were … oppressive. My father is steward of Dunnottar … and my mother has always had social pretensions. As such, she and Da were very strict with my sister and me … me particularly. As soon as I was old enough, I fought them."

"They were probably just looking out for you," he pointed out.

Her gaze swung away, her eyes shadowing. "Aye … but I didn't see it that way. I thought they were trying to cage me."

"A steward's daughter," Maximus mused. "I'm surprised you and Galbraith's paths ever crossed."

"I met him one day when I went to the forge to pick up a knife for my father. He worked with his brother." She scowled then. "I imagine Blair is still at the fortress."

No love lost there, Maximus noted.

"Iain was big, rough, and as restless as me," she continued, her gaze turning inward. "We both hated that the English held Dunnottar. We wed in the kirk at Stonehaven without my parents knowing." She faltered there before clearing her throat. "Ye can imagine the scene that followed." Her fingers plucked at the hem of her cloak, her brow furrowing. It was evident that she wished to drop the subject.

"So, you ran away?"

"Aye." Heather scrubbed a fist over her face as if the memory pained her. "But once we left Dunnottar, Iain changed. He became aggressive and controlling … and we'd barely settled at his father's forge in Fintry when he struck me for the first time." Her voice turned brittle then. "Things worsened fast after that … and when he rode off to join the Wallace's cause, I was relieved."

"And when he didn't come back?"

Heather's mouth twisted. "I started to worry … survival is hard for a woman without a man's protection."

Maximus nodded, taking her words in.

"I'm not good at admitting when I've made a mistake … but it's time." Her gaze settled upon Maximus then, and she fixed him with a penetrating look that he'd come to know well over the past few days. It was now his turn to be questioned. "What about ye, Maximus … why don't ye go home?"

He shook his head, schooling his features into a blank expression. "I can't. There's no one to go home to."

"Yer kin are all dead?"

He nodded. It was the truth, at least.

"Are ye from Rome itself? I hear it is a marvel?"

"It is … but I come from Ostia—near Rome."

Ostia had been a port when he grew up there, but a few years back Maximus had met a traveler who'd informed him that it had been sacked during a Barbarian invasion centuries earlier. And then, when the river silted up, the old port had apparently been abandoned. The Ostia he barely remembered these days no longer existed.

"Do ye miss yer homeland?" Heather asked after a pause.

"I did … in the beginning."

That too was the truth.

Heather's gaze didn't waver from his face as her brow furrowed. Clearly, she found him even more of a mystery than he did her. "Did ye part well from yer kin?" she asked finally, her voice soft in the gloaming.

Maximus looked away, severing the connection between them. Heather had been open with him, but he couldn't answer her with the same candor. "I don't remember," he replied.

Maximus urged Luchag into a brisk canter, through a meadow where the first of the spring flowers bloomed, a deep frown creasing his brow.

Heather was at risk. He needed to get her to safety, although he had a feeling they wouldn't get as far as Dunnottar unhindered.

Galbraith would likely be hot on their trail by now.

They had successfully outrun their hunters for a day— but Maximus knew their luck wouldn't last. Galbraith and his warriors would also be on horseback, and with each passing day, the warrior's hunger for vengeance would grow. The longer it took for him to catch them up, the more dangerous the man would be.

The urge to watch out for Heather swept through Maximus. He'd only known the woman less than three full days, and already he was taking responsibility for her.

A chill swiftly followed this realization. Try as he might to resist her, Heather De Keith was getting under his skin.

He'd dismissed the pull he felt whenever she was near as lust. But it was more than that. The sensation that crept over him when he locked eyes with Heather was deeper—and infinitely more hazardous.

Maximus liked her.

He liked the way she talked to him, the way she responded to him. He rarely teased women, yet he had to fight the urge to do so with her. He enjoyed watching her jaw firm, watching her chin raise as she squarely met his eye.

A man could live a thousand years and never tire of a woman like that.

The thought brought Maximus up sharply. He could feel the softness and warmth of Heather's body flush with his, her ripe breasts thrusting against his back with every stride the garron took.

The sensation had distracted him the day before, as it did this morning. But reminding himself that he was immortal, and the woman who rode with him wasn't, was like having a bucket of icy water poured over him.

He knew where this road led—he had to fight harder against his attraction to the comely Heather.

Cassian and Draco also had cautionary tales when it came to women.

Maximus knew Cassian had once loved a woman deeply, and that his heart had never mended in the centuries that followed. Meanwhile, Draco, after losing his lover during a brutal raid years earlier, seemed incapable of loving anyone now. Whenever they met over the centuries, Maximus had watched Draco grow increasingly hard and bitter.

Maximus didn't judge his friend for that—immortality was a harsh curse. All three of them struggled to live with pasts that now spanned many lifetimes. Eternity heaped a number of regrets upon a man's shoulders, and some were harder to live with than others.

Pushing aside his brooding thoughts, he urged Luchag on.

Galbraith would be drawing ever closer. Maximus didn't share his worries with Heather, but he'd developed an instinct for such things over the years. His scalp had been crawling all morning, as if someone was glaring at the back of his head. Despite that he pushed his pony hard, it was only delaying the inevitable.

They wouldn't outrun them. Sooner or later, he was going to have to turn and fight.

When they stopped at noon to eat the last of their bread and cheese, Maximus's gaze shifted south.

He'd deliberately halted at the brow of a hill—the highest for miles around—with a view over the wooded valleys below. Luchag snorted as he grazed nearby while Heather chewed at her piece of stale bread.

Maximus didn't touch his food. The prickling sensation upon his scalp now crawled down his spine.

He couldn't take his gaze off the southern horizon.

"What is it?" Heather asked after a short while. "Ye have a frown so deep today it would frighten bairns."

Maximus heaved a sigh. He didn't want to alarm her, and yet the time was coming when he'd need to share his worries. Heather was brave and fiery, and he was sure she'd wield that knife he'd given her valiantly—the women of this land weren't a cowardly lot—yet he didn't want to put her in danger.

His lips parted to answer her, but at that instant, he caught a glimpse of movement to the south. And as he watched, a knot of riders crested a hill, dust boiling up under the hooves of their horses.

Maximus whispered a curse, his gaze fixed upon the approaching company.

Heather uttered a curse of her own and leaped to her feet, casting aside the remnants of her meal. "It's Cory?"

Maximus nodded. "I sensed he was near." He swung his gaze around, spearing her. "Go now, Heather. Take Luchag, and ride into those woods."

Her lips parted. "I'm not going to let ye face them alone."

Maximus favored her with a humorless smile before he went to his garron and retrieved his sword, buckling it around his waist. The rasp of steel filtered through the warm air as he drew the weapon. "I can handle them."

"Six men against one ... this is madness."

"So is letting you fight at my side."

"Excuse me?" Her nostrils flared, her anger rising. She then reached for her knife. "I'm not abandoning ye!"

"Enough," Maximus barked, his patience fraying. "This isn't a request, but an order. Get your backside onto that saddle now, woman!"

Their gazes fused for a heartbeat, Heather's grey-green eyes narrowing. His manner had angered her, but there was no time for discussion.

Panic flared within him, his heart slamming against his ribs. She had to go. Now.

Heather's mouth thinned. She then went to Luchag and swung up onto his broad back with ease.

"Maximus, I don't—" she began. But he moved toward her, closing the gap in two strides, and slapped Luchag hard upon the rump. The garron squealed and surged forward, bolting toward the line of trees to their left.

Satisfied Heather was taken care of, Maximus then turned and watched the riders gallop toward him.

XVI

BLOODY

THEY THUNDERED TOWARD him. Maximus tensed, his shoulders rounding as he braced himself to be run down. It was just as well he'd sent Heather and Luchag careening into the woods.

This wasn't going to be a pretty sight.

Just because Maximus couldn't die, didn't mean he looked forward to an unfair fight. He was a skilled warrior, but being outnumbered like this wouldn't end well for him.

And it would hurt.

Maximus's belly clenched in anticipation. He'd learned early on that the worst part of dying was the pain. The bandrúi's curse was especially cruel, for she hadn't robbed him and his friends of the ability to fear or to feel agony. Maximus felt every stab, every slash just as much as mortal men did. But unlike them, he could not escape pain through death.

Pushing down icy dread, Maximus held his ground.

The pounding hoof beats shook the earth, yet he didn't move. His fingers flexed around the hilt of his sword. His gladius was an old friend—the legionary sword had been with him through the ages. Its wide blade had sent many men to their maker, and it would sing once more today.

However, the riders didn't run him down. A few yards back from Maximus, Cory Galbraith pulled up his courser. The chestnut mare was breathing hard, foam splattered across its neck and shoulders. Galbraith had pushed the beast to the limit.

Behind Cory, Maximus recognized two of the men—one dark and wiry, the other blond and heavyset—as the two he'd fought at *The Bogside*. Three others reined in their horses behind the laird's son.

A swift assessment of the band and Maximus saw that they were all heavily armed with claidheamh-mòrs—great Scottish broadswords. The blades were so heavy that warriors had to wield them two-handed.

And it was safer to fight on foot when doing so.

Galbraith swung down from the saddle, followed by his men. Maximus watched, unspeaking, as they all drew their weapons. He noted too that each man carried a dirk at his hip.

Maximus's mouth compressed, and he readied himself for what was to come. *This is going to get bloody.*

Cory Galbraith spat on the ground between them. "Ready to face us again, filthy cèin?"

Cèin—foreigner. All these centuries in this land and Maximus still stood out like a wolf amongst sheep here.

Maximus shrugged. "I thought I'd give your horses a rest."

Galbraith took a threatening step toward him. The man's left hand was tightly bound. He would need both hands to wield his claidheamh-mòr. This fight was going to hurt him. Maximus had noted too, how Galbraith winced when he dismounted. His knee was also bound, yet it pained him.

Cory Galbraith's narrowed gaze scanned the hillside behind Maximus. "Where is she?"

A little of the tension in Maximus's chest uncoiled as he realized that they hadn't seen Heather and Luchag gallop away into the woods.

"Who?"

"Don't act the lackwit," Galbraith snarled. "Heather. Where. Is. She?"

"How should I know?" Maximus gave another shrug, aware that it would infuriate the man before him. "We parted ways in Fintry."

"Liar. I saw her in Stirling. Ye are traveling together."

Maximus cocked his head and favored Galbraith with a hard smile. "And yet, here I am ... all alone."

"Scabby, shit-eating cèin," Galbraith growled back. "I'm gonna cut that smirk off yer face."

Maximus widened his stance before he flipped his sword and caught it by the hilt—a flourish that usually enraged an aggressor.

Cory Galbraith was no exception. With a roar, he raised his broadsword and charged.

And the moment he did, battle fury descended upon Maximus in a crimson haze.

Fighting was timeless. How often had he swung his sword since the bandrúi had cast her curse upon him? Too often to count, and yet every time he did, he was back in the misty, pine-clad mountains of northern Caledonia—many centuries before this land would be known as Scotland—under the shadow of a ruined Roman fort.

The instant blood lust took him, the fear of the pain to come subsided.

Maximus gave a hoarse bellow of his own. For a few instants, the years rolled back. He was young again, leading a cohort of soldiers into battle for the glory of Rome.

Galbraith was skilled with a blade. Although young, he was big and broad-shouldered. He swept the claidheamh-mòr in a deadly arc at his opponent's head— a strike that Maximus ducked, before he raised his own blade to block a killing blow from his right.

Galbraith's men surrounded him now, each looking for a way in.

Maximus whirled, ducked, blocked, and stabbed—in a dance that he knew as well as the thunder of his heart against his ribs. He thrust his sword under a warrior's guard—the stocky blond man he'd head-butted in the tavern—and slammed his blade up under his ribs.

The warrior crumpled, his cry echoing through the spring sunshine.

Maximus battled on, felling another warrior moments later. But even as he fought, he felt the bite of steel against his left flank.

Agony lanced down his side.

It was four against one now, and the warriors remaining fought like cornered hounds. Pain throbbed across Maximus's back and bit into his right shoulder— but still he fought on.

It didn't matter how many blades they stuck him with, the curse was stronger than any of them. They could reduce him to a bloody pulp, and he would live to see the next dawn. He always did.

These men, however, were mortal. Just one blade in the right place and they would go to their god.

A howl rent the air as Maximus slammed his sword into a warrior's belly. He drew his pugio with his left hand, spinning around to face his next attacker. As he did so, he saw that his hand was slick with blood. Someone had stabbed him in the shoulder, and he hadn't even noticed.

On and on they fought—grunts, cries, and curses filtering across the hillside—and one by one, Maximus's attackers fell while he remained on his feet.

But he was staggering now, his body wracked with agony. He didn't know how many times they'd stabbed him across the back and shoulders, yet his entire torso felt as if it were on fire. He felt sick with it.

And then, finally, only Cory Galbraith was left.

The laird's son was injured. Maximus had sliced him across the cheek with his dagger and cut him deeply upon his already injured leg. Galbraith now dragged the leg after him, pain rendering him savage.

Weakness flooded through Maximus as he staggered back, clumsily blocking the next blow. He was bleeding heavily now, and nausea pulsed through him. It was almost over—he had to kill Galbraith before he fell.

He had to know the bastard wouldn't live to hunt Heather down.

Howling curses, Galbraith lunged for him. He'd abandoned his broadsword and slammed into Maximus, knocking him onto the grass.

And then he stabbed him in the belly with his dirk— again and again.

Maximus choked out a breath, agony knifing through him.

Great Bull-slayer, why did it have to hurt so much?

Darkness clouded the edges of his vision. Damn him, but he was going to lose consciousness before he finished Galbraith off.

Rage flooded through Maximus, piercing the pain, as he struggled against his attacker. Then Galbraith stuck him in the ribs, and suddenly he couldn't hear anything against the roar of blood in his ears. His vision speckled, and just for a moment, Maximus wondered if the curse was indeed broken.

Maybe, this time, he would die?

Galbraith's mouth was working, he was screaming insults at him while he stabbed once more. But Maximus couldn't hear him.

And then, Galbraith froze.

The young warrior's green eyes widened, his mouth gaping. Maximus's vision was blurring now, yet he still saw the thin blade that protruded from his attacker's throat. The knife blade drew back, and Galbraith slumped sideways onto the ground.

Behind him stood a comely figure with thick light-brown hair. Heather's eyes were huge on her pale face— and in her right hand, she grasped a bloodied blade.

The one he'd gifted her.

Yet Heather didn't pay the knife or the dead bodies that lay scattered around them any notice. Instead, her attention was upon Maximus, horror etched upon her features.

"Dear Lord, have mercy!" she gasped. An instant later, she was at his side, her hand gripping his. "What have they done to ye?"

XVII

TIME FOR WEEPING

"I TOLD YOU to run," Maximus croaked, staring up at Heather. "Why are you here?"

"I couldn't." Her voice cracked, betraying her. "I couldn't let ye face them all alone." Heather's gaze gleamed with tears as it swept down his bloodied torso. She made a soft choking sound. "Oh, Maximus ... I'm so sorry."

"Why?" he grunted, his breath bubbling as blood surged into his throat. "This isn't your fault."

"Aye, it is."

"Enough." It was difficult to speak now. "We can't ... stay out here on the road."

She stared down at him, tears trickling down her cheeks. "What do ye want me to do?"

"Drag the bodies away ... hide them ... in the trees." Maximus's gaze fluttered shut. "And set the horses free."

That was it. He was done for now. Pain cocooned him. He couldn't summon the strength to speak again.

Heather was saying something else, but he couldn't make out the words. Her voice sounded as if it were coming from far away. He just needed to rest, to take refuge from the agony that wracked his body.

With a groan, he let darkness swallow him.

Heather stared down at Maximus and choked back the sob rising in her breast.

She'd never seen injuries like this. His chest and belly were slick with blood and riddled with gaping wounds. Dark blood pooled out around him, staining the grass.

He'd die soon, but she'd do her best to make him comfortable.

For now, she had to do as he'd bid.

Trembling, she rose to her feet and set about dragging the dead warriors into the trees. They were heavy, and by the time Heather had finished the task, sweat poured down her face and back. She then removed the saddles and bridles from their horses, which grazed nearby, and let them go. She threw the tack into the undergrowth as well.

Apart from Maximus's prostrate body and the pools of blood and gore on the hill, no one would know a violent fight had taken place here.

Approaching the fallen man, Heather knelt beside him. She wouldn't have been surprised if he'd died in the interim, his wounds were certainly bad enough. However, Maximus's eyes flickered open when she stroked his blood-streaked cheek with the back of her hand.

"It's done," she murmured. "Now, I need to get ye off the road."

"Help me up," he replied, his voice a wheeze. Heather knew that sound—'the death rattle' healers called it. The sound that meant the Grim Reaper was coming for him.

"Ye won't be able to stand," she answered, her throat constricting. This man was tough, stronger than any she'd ever met. Yet even he couldn't fight death.

"I can ... if you help me."

Heather didn't have it in her to argue with a dying man, and so she helped him sit, and then placed a shoulder under his armpit so that he could stagger to his feet. Frankly, it amazed her he could even manage it.

Now that he was on his feet, she saw that he bore a number of stab wounds to his shoulders and back.

She led him into the woods, taking him to the clearing where she'd left Luchag.

The garron greeted them with a snort, clearly relieved that it hadn't been abandoned. But Maximus didn't greet his mount.

Instead, he gave a pained groan when Heather lowered him to the ground, his eyes flickering shut once more.

Heather sat back on her heels and ran her gaze over him.

There was no doubt Maximus would die here in this glade—but she would do this brave man the honor of staying by his side.

He wouldn't die alone.

Her throat thickened, her vision blurring.

Stop it. She knuckled away the tears. *There will be time for weeping later.*

"I'll light a fire," she said. But Maximus had drifted into unconsciousness, and so didn't reply.

A small fire crackled in the woodland glade, sending out a soft glow over the man who lay dying beside it. Heather sat at his side, feeding the flames with the twigs and branches she'd collected, while around them the light gradually faded.

Where had the afternoon gone? Heather had lost track of time. Had it taken that long to clear away the bodies, set the horses free, and light a fire?

Leaning forward, Heather felt Maximus's neck for a pulse.

"Mother Mary," she whispered, "he still lives."

The man hung onto life like a drowning man clinging to a fraying rope. Most of Cory's men had died of lesser wounds, yet Maximus refused to fade.

And the sight of the struggle he was clearly waging made guilt claw at her chest.

Aye, this was all her fault.

He'd come to her rescue back in Fintry, and then had insisted on accompanying her north. She'd chafed at his overbearing manner, but she'd never dreamed it would come to this.

She should have realized.

The Galbraiths were well known for their tempers. Cory wasn't the type to let a slight pass.

Her only solace was that the mean bastard was now dead.

"I'm so sorry, Maximus," she whispered, her fingers entwining with his. "I brought this upon ye."

His eyes flickered open. "I told you that you aren't to blame, woman," he croaked. "I made my choice."

Maximus's face was ashen, his dark eyes sunken into their sockets. Why was the Lord so intent on making him suffer?

"But I'm virtually a stranger to ye," she replied, tears running freely down her cheeks. She could no longer hold them back. It was true, they hardly knew each other, and yet it felt as if someone were squeezing her heart. "Better to give up yer life ... for something ... someone ... that matters."

"You matter." His fingers tightened around hers. "I'd fight any man who dares threaten you ... but you should go now, Heather. Take Luchag, and find somewhere else to spend the night."

"I'm not leaving ye," she gasped, swallowing a sob.

"It's better that you do ... *please*."

The pleading edge to his voice nearly undid her. Why on earth did this man want to die alone?

"I'm staying with ye ... to the end," she answered, squeezing his hand. "I will never leave, so save yer breath."

His eyes closed, a spasm of pain rippling across his face. "If you stay, you'll regret it," he gasped.

Heather frowned. "Let me be the judge of that."

"You don't understand ... I'm not who you think I am." The words came out in pained grunts. "I'll be healed by morning ... and you will think me a demon for it."

Heather stared down at him, sorrow grasping her around the throat. *Poor man. His mind is going.* He was muttering nonsense now, yet she wasn't surprised.

He wouldn't last till the witching hour, let alone the dawn. But she would stay at his side nonetheless.

They lapsed into silence then, and Heather watched Maximus's breathing gradually grow slower and shallower. His skin already had the pallor of a corpse. It was no sleep he'd fallen into, but something much deeper.

Watching him, an ache rose under Heather's breast bone. She reached up with her free hand, for her other still grasped Maximus's, and rubbed her knuckles against her chest, trying to ease the pain.

How was it possible to spend only three days with someone, and yet feel as if you'd known them a lifetime? No man had ever protected her as Maximus had. No man had ever really s*een* her. Last night, when they talked as dusk settled over the land, she'd sensed she had his full attention. He'd been curious about her. Given time, they might have lain together again. Given time, they might have forged a bond.

Yet now, Heather would never know.

"Sleep, brave warrior," she whispered, hot tears flooding down her cheeks. "And know that I will never forget ye."

With that, she bent her head over his bloodied body and let the tears flow.

XVIII

THE COMING OF THE DAWN

MAXIMUS AWOKE TO the warmth of the sun on his face.

For a moment, he just lay there, enjoying the heat of it, and the fact that his body was no longer wracked with agony. The shadow of yesterday's injuries was still there—deep scars that no one could see—yet he knew without even opening his eyes that his body was whole and healthy once more.

With the rising sun, the curse had worked its magic.

Slowly, he opened his eyes, his gaze settling upon the woman who lay sleeping next to him. Heather's eyes were puffy, her cheeks reddened from tears, and yet she'd never looked lovelier to him. With her hair spread out around her, she appeared a fairy maid sleeping there.

But as Maximus watched her, a cold lump settled in the pit of his belly.

He'd done his best to avoid this moment—but he'd been too injured the day before to prevent her from remaining at his side. And yet, maybe there was still time.

She was in a deep sleep, having wept until exhaustion claimed her.

Perhaps, Maximus could simply disappear into the trees? Later, she'd wake and wonder what had happened to his body. But it would be better that way. Better that he didn't have to look into her eyes and see horror there.

Pushing himself up onto his elbows, he looked down upon his ruined hunting leathers. He'd need to find a new vest, yet the flesh that showed through the slashes in the leather was healthy, no longer raw and gaping.

Maximus rolled to his feet and glanced over at where Luchag dozed under the shade of a beech tree. He'd leave Heather the garron and continue his journey on foot. But since they were both headed for the same destination, he'd have to be careful in Dunnottar lest she accidentally saw him.

Maximus took a step away from the smoking fire pit, his gaze swiveling back to the sleeping woman.

I'm sorry, Heather.

He then took another step, his boot landing upon a twig. The snapping sound echoed through the glade, and Maximus froze.

Heather's eyes flickered open and fixed upon him.

The moments that followed were the most awkward of Maximus's long life.

At first, Heather just stared at him, her mind and senses still fogged by sleep. And then, he saw realization flood across her face.

It was a terrible thing to watch, a dawning that made his belly twist.

The gentle expression upon her face vanished, and her eyes widened. Her throat bobbed, her body tensing. Slowly, she sat up, her attention never leaving him. It was as if he were a predator standing before her—no longer a man, but a beast.

"I warned you, Heather," he said, breaking the brittle silence. "If you'd left me as I asked, you'd have spared yourself this."

She didn't answer him. Instead, a nerve flickered in her cheek as her gaze shifted down from his face to his chest and belly, where those mortal wounds had vanished.

"What are ye?" she finally rasped.

"Does it matter?"

"Aye," she choked the word out. "What kind of man receives injuries like that and *lives*?

Maximus drew in a slow, steadying breath. "A cursed one."

She continued to stare at him, her face draining of color. Slowly, as if expecting him to pounce and rip her throat out, Heather rose to her feet. Her hand strayed to the knife at her waist. Her trembling fingers fastened around the hilt.

"There's no need for that," he murmured. "You know I'd never harm you."

"Do I?" With her free hand, she hastily crossed herself. She looked at him as if Satan himself stood before her.

"One thousand, one hundred and eighty-three years ago, I was part of a Roman legion that marched into the wild north of this land," he began softly. Maximus didn't know why he was bothering to tell her his story. Heather's eyes had that glazed look that terrorized folk often got. She probably wasn't taking any of this in. And yet, he had to tell her. "We were sent to put down the 'barbarian savages' and secure the northern frontier for our emperor." Maximus's throat tightened as he spoke. Even after all this time, the tragedy of the Hispana's fate still affected him. "We were the Ninth legion ... a force of five thousand men who crossed the border and never returned. They slowly picked us off on our journey north, and by the time we reached the ruins of our northernmost outpost, there were barely five hundred of us left."

Maximus halted here. Heather was watching him as though he'd slipped into another tongue, her features taut, her body coiled. He should stop there, for nothing he said would make any difference, yet Maximus pressed on. She might as well hear everything.

"Three of us were taken alive after the battle and brought before a Pictish druidess. She cursed us to an immortal life, damned us to remain forever within the boundaries of this land ... and so, here I am before you, Heather. Maximus Flavius Cato, commander of a lost legion ... a soldier of an empire that fell long ago."

He stopped speaking then and let the twitter of birdsong in the surrounding trees dominate. Behind him, Luchag snorted, as if he found the story preposterous. Indeed, spoken so baldly, it sounded like utter fantasy.

Maximus didn't expect Heather to believe him, but all the same, it felt as if a weight had been lifted to share who he truly was with one mortal soul. It had gone as badly as he'd expected.

"Take Luchag and continue north on your own," he said finally, taking another step back. "I shall make my way to Dunnottar on foot."

Heather merely stared at him, her expression frozen. He felt a pang of pity for her. She'd be sorely regretting her choice in travel companion now.

"Go well, Heather," Maximus said, attempting a smile yet failing. "I wish you health and happiness ... but here is where our paths diverge."

Still, she said nothing. The fingers clutching the hilt of the knife tightened.

Without another word, Maximus turned and left the glade, disappearing into the trees.

Heather stood there for a long while after Maximus vanished. She stared at the spot where his tall, lean figure had disappeared, as if expecting him to reappear.

But thankfully he didn't.

Whispering a curse, Heather let go of the knife hilt and wrapped her arms around her torso. She realized then that her legs were trembling. She needed to sit for a moment.

She lowered herself down next to the smoldering ruins of last night's fire and attempted to net her racing thoughts.

Immortal.
Lost legion.
Pictish druidess.

Curse.

The words tumbled through her confused mind. None of it made any sense, and yet Maximus had stared at her with a look of complete sincerity. Who would make up such an outrageous story anyway?

No man can live a thousand years.

But no man could sustain the wounds he had the day before and live to see the next dawn. She might not believe his outlandish tale, yet she'd seen how all the wounds on his chest and stomach had miraculously healed.

Groaning another curse—a filthy one she'd learned from Iain—she scrubbed at her face.

Maybe I'm dreaming.

But she wasn't. She was wide awake, with a cool morning breeze stirring her hair and the call of birds echoing through the trees around her.

She had actually lain with that man, had given her body to him. Betrayal robbed her of breath and made her pulse flutter like a trapped moth in her throat.

To think she'd actually fantasized about him taking her again, about the relationship between them blossoming into something far deeper.

She'd have ended up shackling herself to a fiend.

Her head felt as if it were stuffed full of wool. As hard as she tried, she couldn't make sense of anything Maximus had told her. The Ninth legion? She'd never heard of such a thing.

Rising to her feet, Heather kicked dirt over the embers of the fire pit and crossed to the garron. She appreciated that Maximus had left her his pony. It was a generous act; even if she was loath to receive any help from someone—or something—so unnatural.

Nonetheless, Luchag would save her legs.

She started to saddle the pony. However, she was now on edge and kept glancing over her shoulder. Part of her expected Maximus to return.

If he was a demon, he was dangerous. Folk said that such creatures stole the souls of unwary travelers.

Heather hastily crossed herself and muttered a prayer to the Virgin. Right now, she needed protection.

She needed to put as much distance as she could between her and Maximus Flavius Cato.

XIX

I HAVE QUESTIONS

THE CRY OF a red kite circling overhead made Maximus crane his neck up at the sky. The bird of prey, with its russet underbelly and forked tail, was gliding upon the air currents, and the sight made Maximus halt to watch it.

How glorious it must be to be able to fly high above the world. Why couldn't the Pict witch have turned him into a kite all those years ago? He wouldn't have minded that so much.

Shaking his head, Maximus cast the foolish thoughts aside and continued on his way up the hillside. It was another glorious spring day, although the wind that blew in from the north had a bite to it—a reminder that winter had only recently loosened its grip and could return on a whim. The weather in this land was notoriously capricious, something that had taken him a long while to get used to.

Yesterday's events had slowed his progress north. Cassian would be waiting for him at Dunnottar—and he hoped after all the ill luck he'd had over the past few days his fortune was about to change.

Cassian had tried the hardest of all three of them to solve the riddle. He'd spent the last few centuries working for the personal guards of Scotland's most powerful clan-chiefs, all the while searching for clues that would help them break the curse.

Unlike Maximus and Draco, who'd let the years turn them despondent and bitter, Cassian had never given up.

Maximus wondered where Draco was these days. He clearly hadn't made a trip to Stirling, which meant that he was probably off on some perilous adventure, testing his curse to its limits. Draco was a man who continued to look for death, even though it steadfastly eluded him.

The heat of the sun on his back lightened Maximus's mood a little, and with each furlong that he walked north, the humiliation of that scene at dawn eased a little. Nonetheless, there was a heaviness upon him today, a disappointment.

He hadn't expected things to go any better than they had between him and Heather, but the confrontation in that glade had left a sour taste in his mouth nonetheless.

It was always the same. If he tried to spare women the pain of discovering who he was, they condemned him as a heartless rogue. But if they discovered his unnaturalness, it was as if he'd just turned into a wulver before them.

At least Heather had let him tell her his story, although he wasn't sure she'd listened to any of it.

Maximus's mouth twisted. Perhaps women's reactions to him were part of the bandrúi's curse.

His belly growled as he walked, reminding him that he hadn't eaten anything since morning the day before. Galbraith and his friends had turned up before he'd been able to take a bite of bread and cheese.

He felt famished now and, as such, Maximus was relieved to arrive at a tiny hamlet mid-morning. The village sat near a swiftly flowing river, its banks overhung with willows wearing their bright green spring coats. There was a market taking place by the river, and Maximus bought himself a loaf of bread, some cheese, and a large pork pie, to eat while he traveled.

He walked on. To the west, large, wooded mountains rose to greet him, their bulk etched against a windy sky. Those peaks led into the Highlands, the wild and beautiful land where the Ninth had met its inglorious end.

Noon came and went. Maximus had finished his pie and was considering eating the bread and cheese as well, when he spotted two figures upon the crest of the hill before him.

A sturdy highland pony nipped at grass, while next to him, a woman perched upon a boulder, her long walnut-colored hair blowing in the wind.

Maximus's step faltered.

Heather.

Had she deliberately waited for him?

He slowed his pace as he climbed the hill, for part of him dreaded facing her again. Yet another part of him was curious. She was a brave woman indeed if she wished to face the immortal demon again.

He kept his gaze upon Heather as he approached; her face was expressionless, her gaze narrowed. She was a different woman to the frightened one who'd stared at him across the smoldering fire pit that morning.

All the same, Maximus noted the tension in her shoulders and the way her fingers clutched at the skirt of her kirtle. She was still afraid of him.

That being the case, he stopped a few yards back from her.

"Good afternoon," he greeted her with a half-smile.

Heather swallowed hard. Her heart was hammering, the noise of it distracting her. Wiping her sweaty palms against her skirts, she rose to her feet.

Her gaze swept over Maximus, and like that morning, a cold sensation of shock rippled through her. There was no sign of the terrible wounds he'd sustained. The chill intensified when she noted that the leather vest he wore appeared mended.

What devilry was this?

"Yer clothing," she said. Her voice came out in a strangled croak, betraying her.

Maximus glanced down, his mouth quirking once more. "Ah, yes. I helped myself to one of Galbraith's men's vests ... he won't be needing it now."

Heather's shoulders relaxed a little at this news. The fact that there was a practical answer, one that she had the wits to understand, eased her.

She'd struggled all morning with the desire to wait for him on the road, and when she finally sat down upon the brow of the hill, her belly had cramped from nerves. Curiosity battled with the instinct to get as far as possible from him. Then, when she'd spied Maximus appear in the distance, she'd fought the urge to leap to her feet, mount Luchag, and gallop off.

If he really was a demon, he'd rip out her soul and feast on her heart.

Only stubborn will had kept her seated. That and an inquisitiveness that had always gotten her into trouble.

"Why have you waited for me?" he asked when she failed to say anything else. Like at dawn, her tongue felt as if it were stuck to the roof of her mouth.

Maximus stood before her, a proud, dark-haired man with sun-bronzed skin and peat-colored eyes. But he wasn't what he appeared.

"I have questions," she said finally. Once again, her voice sounded strangled, and she cursed it.

He cocked his head. "You do? Wasn't my tale this morning enough?"

She heard the challenge in his voice, and heat ignited in the pit of her belly, quelling the chill of fear that seeing him again had brought. He thought her a coward.

Folding her arms across her chest, Heather looked down her nose at him—easy to do, for he stood below her on the slope. "No," she bit the word out. "Ye owe me more than that."

He raised a dark eyebrow. "What exactly do you want to know?"

"I want to know how it's even possible?" Heather could hear her voice rising, yet she didn't care.

"I wish I could answer that," he replied, his gaze never leaving hers. "But I can't. The druidess who cursed us was powerful. She had the three of us tied up in her hovel ... and the moment she approached me, I knew we were in trouble." He paused, and Heather could have sworn she saw a shudder pass through him. "She had eyes and a voice as cold as a winter's dawn. She made some ritual sacrifice before painting marks upon our brows with blood."

It was Heather's turn to shiver. She'd heard about the druids and druidesses of ancient times, and the power they'd wielded over folk. Her father, who'd taught her to read, had explained that the authority of such figures had in fact been based largely on superstition and fear, and when Christianity had come to this land, they'd lost their influence and become part of the old ways.

"Surely, ye mustn't have believed her at first?" she asked, interested to know how he'd reacted.

Maximus's mouth thinned. "None of us did ... we thought her mad. We believed that once she'd had her fun with us, she'd kill us ... but she didn't." He shook his head. "Instead, the bandrúi set us free ... and sent a host of warriors after us." Maximus's expression grew darker still as he relived the incident. "They stuck us full of arrows, drove swords and daggers into our backs ... and one of them stabbed me in the guts with a pike. They then left us to the wolves—all with mortal injuries."

Maximus stopped there and dragged a hand down his face. "I remember lying there on my back on the banks of a burn, staring up at the stars ... waiting for death to come. But when I woke just after daybreak, my companions and I were healed. All those terrible injuries had disappeared."

"And ye knew then the curse was real?"

Maximus nodded, before he sighed. "You can see why I kept all of this a secret ... and if you'd done as I'd bid and fled, you wouldn't know either."

Heather clenched her jaw. "I came back to help ye ... how was I to know that ye ... ye—"

"Say it, Heather. I'm *immortal*."

Heather swallowed and fought the urge to cross herself as she had that morning. A priest would say such a man had been possessed by the devil. And yet something about Maximus's tale rang true.

Who would make up such an unholy lie?

"Ye are immortal," she said grudgingly. She stepped closer to Maximus then, holding his eye. "Many folk dream of eternal life, yet ye clearly hate it ... why?"

His eyebrow quirked. "Folk like the *idea* of living forever, of escaping death's cold touch. And maybe if everyone you love was immortal too, it would be easier. But when you walk the centuries alone, when you can never stay longer than a few years in a place lest locals notice that you don't age, it becomes a lonely existence." Maximus paused there. "I've watched kingdoms rise and fall, Heather. I've lived among your people for countless lifetimes, and yet I've been forever cursed to remain an outsider."

His words moved her, and when Heather replied, her voice was subdued. "This curse ... can it be broken?"

He smiled then, the expression illuminating his face. Telling his story had carved severe lines into it, but the smile erased them. Heather's breathing caught. Immortal or not, this man had a visceral effect upon her.

Maybe that was why she'd waited for him upon this hill, why she'd wanted an explanation from him.

"That, bonny Heather, is why I'm bound for Dunnottar," he replied.

XXI

HOPE

"I'M LISTENING." HEATHER took hold of Luchag's reins and followed Maximus on foot. He'd walked past her and rejoined the road that would take them north. Heather fell in step beside him. "Ye can't say something like that and not explain yerself."

Maximus cast her a rueful look. "Have you always been this bossy, woman?"

Heather frowned. "Aye ... but don't avoid the question. Tell me ... what does Dunnottar have to do with breaking the curse?"

"I'm not sure," Maximus replied, his tone cautious now. She could tell he was regretting his candor. "But my friend Cassian—one of the three of us who were cursed— left word for me in Stirling to travel there. He has news."

Maximus paused there, his own brow furrowing now.

"Go on," Heather prompted. She sensed his reluctance, but her interest was piqued.

"Very well," he growled. "I might as well tell you the rest. When the bandrúi cursed us, she decided to give us a chance to save ourselves with a riddle. Once we solve it, the curse shall be broken."

Heather sucked in a breath. "Can ye tell it to me?"

Maximus's frown deepened. "I'm not sure that—"

"Go on ... don't be miserable. I'm good at riddles. Perhaps I can help."

Her companion gave Heather a doubtful look. However, after a few moments, he acquiesced, his voice rumbling across the hillside.

> "When the Broom-star crosses the sky,
> And the Hammer strikes the fort
> Upon the Shelving Slope.
> When the White Hawk and the Dragon wed,
> Only then will the curse be broke."

Silence fell while Heather digested the words. She hadn't lied; there was nothing she liked better than a good riddle. Yet this was the strangest one she'd ever heard.

"The Broom-star," she murmured. "That's the star ye pointed out to me on the morning we left Fintry ... the one that comes every seventy years."

"Seventy-*five* years," he corrected her. "We've had to wait for each coming of the Broom-star for a chance to break the curse. But till now, we have only ever managed to decipher the first line. The rest of it makes no sense."

Heather tensed, excitement quickening in her veins. "Then it's just as well ye met me. For I can tell ye what one of the other lines means."

Maximus abruptly halted and swiveled around to face Heather. "What?"

The woman had better not be making fun of him; he wasn't in the mood.

However, Heather merely raised her pert chin and met his gaze in that fearless way of hers that both intrigued and exasperated him.

"I'd say yer friend has already discovered it, which is why he's bid ye to travel to Dunnottar," she said, holding his stare. "The old name for the fortress is 'Dùn Fhoithear' ... the fort upon the Shelving Slope."

Maximus stared at her a moment. "Are you sure?"

Heather nodded, before her gaze shadowed. "Aye, but as for the White Hawk and the Dragon ... those names make no sense to me at all. I have no idea who or what 'The Hammer' is either ... but it would seem that the riddle refers to a siege upon Dunnottar."

"It appears so, but it may not refer to *this* cycle of the coming of the Broom-star," Maximus pointed out, heaviness replacing the spark of hope that had flared to life within him.

He couldn't bear the disappointment, the knowledge that he must wait another seventy-five years till the Broom-star returned to the sky. Eternity had taught him to be patient, but these days his patience was starting to wear thin. He was tired of it all.

Once the curse was broken, he could finally grow old and die.

"But it *could,*" Heather replied. She was studying him with a penetrating look that made Maximus tense. This woman already read him too well. "However, it might mean that Dunnottar will be attacked soon. How long does the Broom-star remain in the sky?"

"It depends ... usually for two to three months."

Heather nodded before she turned and resumed her path up the hill, leading Luchag behind her. "Then, ye will find out soon enough."

They spoke little during the afternoon. Maximus was grateful for the silence, for he felt as if he'd spilled his guts before Heather. He had no other secrets to reveal. It was a strange sensation to travel in the company of someone who knew who he truly was.

After her initial shock, Heather had rallied. She was a practical woman, and had already started seeking solutions to his predicament. He appreciated her concern, yet if it were as easy as that, they'd have broken the curse centuries earlier.

As dusk settled over the mountains to the west and the green hills and woodlands to the east, they entered the village of Alyth. Crouched in a valley, it was a little larger than the hamlet where Maximus had bought food that morning, but barely so. White-washed cottages with thatched roofs lined a meandering river, and birch copses carpeted the slopes of the hills around it.

The only tavern in town was full, and so they found lodging at a guesthouse on the eastern edge of the village.

An elderly widow named Ainslee ran the lodging, which consisted of a cottage with a hay barn out the back. The two rooms in her cottage were occupied, and so she led Maximus and Heather to the barn.

Dumping a pile of blankets onto a hay bale, the widow turned to face them. "It might not look like much," she announced, her gaze sweeping over the newcomers. "But it's warm and dry. There's a wash room with water, soap, and drying cloths next door, and I shall bring ye supper in a wee bit."

The widow motioned then to the dusty table that sat next to the door, where an unlit lamp sat. The place was dirty and in need of a sweep, and thick cobwebs festooned the ceiling. There also weren't any beds in here—he assumed they were supposed to fashion them from the hay bales that lay scattered around.

Maximus nodded, turning back to Ainslee. "It'll do." He handed her a silver penny, which she snatched from his hand, her dark gaze gleaming.

"Very generous ... thank ye."

"Make sure we get a decent supper, please," Maximus replied, holding her eye. "Some meat would be appreciated."

The widow nodded before turning for the door. "I shall see what I can manage."

Watching her bustle away, Maximus frowned. If he hadn't been so tired and hungry, he'd have suggested they sleep outdoors.

He then turned to Heather, noting from her frown that she too shared his view of their lodgings. "Sorry about this," he murmured. "I didn't think we'd find accommodation as comfortable as *The Golden Lion* in this neck of the woods ... but I'd hoped to do better than a barn."

Heather sighed before she shrugged. "Frankly, I'm just grateful that we've stopped for the day and have a roof over our heads." She glanced down at her dusty, travel worn cloak and kirtle. "I think I'll go and make use of that soap and water before the sun goes down." She then cast a leery look around her. "Hopefully, there aren't too many spiders lurking here."

"I'll have a look around," Maximus assured her with a smile. "If I find any, I'll slay the beasties before you return."

It was cold and drafty in the lean-to, and about as dirty as the barn itself. As such, Heather didn't linger over her bathing. But as she stripped off her clothing, she realized that her moon flow had arrived. She'd been so preoccupied that she'd barely noticed the ache in her lower belly during the day.

Heather paused for a moment, observing the streaks of blood upon her thighs. Of course, she'd taken a risk lying with Maximus—that of her womb quickening. She sighed then, relief flooding through her. Life was tangled enough without that added complication to deal with.

She'd never gotten with bairn during her years with Iain.

Perhaps I'm barren. Iain had accused her of that once, during an argument. Heather frowned. Such thoughts weren't helpful.

Shivering, Heather washed as quickly as she could. She sluiced cold water over her body and did her best to work a lather from the hard block of lye soap. She washed her hair too before reaching for her clothes once more.

Fortunately, she'd packed soft linen rags for this time of the month in her satchel. She secured the rag in place by pulling on a pair of woolen hose under her skirts. By the time Heather finished dressing, her teeth were chattering.

She emerged from the lean-to into near darkness. Dusk had settled over Alyth in the meantime, bringing a damp, almost wintry chill.

Heather hurried back to the barn, to find that it had a much more homely appearance than earlier. There wasn't a hearth burning, yet the oil lantern illuminated the interior in a golden glow. Pulling the door closed behind her, Heather paused, her gaze surveying the two beds someone had fashioned from hay bales and the blankets that draped over them. It appeared too as if the floor had been swept.

Shifting her attention to where Maximus sat at the table, two bowls of what smelled like mutton stew before him, she raised a querying eyebrow.

"Did the old woman decide to tidy this place up for us after all?"

Maximus shook his head and poured out two cups of ale from an earthen jug. "No such luck. She brought the stew with ill-grace and lit the lantern ... nothing more."

A smile curved Heather's mouth. She knew few men who'd tidy up and prepare beds—most of them thought of it as women's work. It pleased her that he'd made the effort.

"Take a seat," Maximus waved to the empty stool opposite him. "Let's eat while the stew is still hot."

Heather didn't need to be asked twice. The long day, followed by a cold bath and the arrival of her moon flow, had given her a ravenous appetite. She was pleased that Ainslee had provided them with a large loaf of coarse bread and freshly churned butter to accompany the stew.

Taking a seat, she picked up her cup and raised it, catching Maximus's eye. "Here's to finding a way to break that curse of yers," she said softly.

Their gazes fused for an instant. Maximus stared back at her, his patrician features tensing. For an instant, she wondered if he thought she was making fun of him. She wasn't.

"Sometimes I think we'll never break it," he admitted. "I worry that witch was just toying with us."

"And yet the Broom-star and the fort upon the Shelving Slope are real," Heather reminded him. "Ye shall break the curse. Don't give up hope just yet."

XXII

A HARD LIFE

MAXIMUS WATCHED HER, his expression veiled. Heather could sense his distrust, but wasn't offended by it.

If he really had lived as long as he claimed, life would have jaded him. She knew now why he could be so aloof sometimes.

"I can't imagine living so many years," she admitted, reaching for the loaf of bread and tearing off a chunk. She then picked up the knife and smeared on some butter. "What's it like?"

Maximus pulled a face before he raised his cup to his lips and took a deep draft. "I don't know how to describe it," he said, his tone guarded.

Heather watched him, sorry she'd brought the subject up. He'd been in good spirits when she re-entered the barn, but she'd soured his mood.

"Forget I asked ye that then," she replied. Picking up her spoon, she took a mouthful of stew. It was delicious. "As ye said ... let's eat."

They ate in silence for a short while, both too hungry to focus on much besides their food. However, as her belly filled, Heather continued to hold her tongue.

Sometimes her mouth ran away with her. Tonight, it was better if she kept her own counsel.

"It's strange." Maximus broke the silence. His voice was low now. "It's as if the longer I live, the more I lose track of time. One year flows into the next, and the seasons just seem to meld together."

Heather heard the heaviness in his voice as he admitted this. "And what of yer homeland?" she asked softly. She was curious to know of Italy. "Ye don't remember it?"

"Just sensations really," he replied, his tone wistful now. "I remember the feel of the hot sun on my face, the taste of grape wine ... and the smell of jasmine in early summer."

"Why haven't ye gone home?"

"I can't." His tone flattened with these words. "The curse forbids it. Cassian, Draco, and I can never leave the borders of Scotland. I've tried once or twice, but discovered that I cannot put a foot over The Great Wall."

Heather considered his words for a moment. Truthfully, she was having trouble fully comprehending what he'd just said. She couldn't even begin to imagine what being trapped in a land that wasn't your own for over a thousand years was like. She was surprised that Maximus hadn't lost his wits in the interim.

Yet, maybe that was part of the curse. It kept you healthy, both in mind and in body.

Sadness filtered over her as she envisaged the long years he'd spent, living in the wilderness, waiting for the next arrival of the Broom-star.

"It must be a hard life," she murmured, voicing her thoughts aloud.

Maximus's answering grunt, as he poured himself another cup of ale, told her that she had no idea just how difficult such an existence could be. There wasn't any point trying to empathize with him. She'd lived twenty-five winters. Her life was a mere blink of an eye compared to his.

"Have ye not had a few families over the years though?" she asked finally. "That must have eased things somewhat."

Maximus shook his head. "I can't father children … it's part of the curse."

Heather went still at that. She needn't have worried about her womb quickening after all. Did she imagine it, or was there a faint tinge of sadness in his voice?

"But surely, ye must have loved women during the centuries?"

"One or two," he admitted gruffly. "Although for the past four hundred years, I've done my best to avoid emotional entanglements."

Heather frowned. "Why?"

Maximus looked back at her, his expression suddenly tired. "I lived with a woman once. Her name was Evanna, and she was a Pict warrior from the ancient fort of Dunadd. Things were good between us, and I let myself believe I could stay there and forget about who I was for a few years. But then Evanna started talking about becoming my wife … about bearing my children … and I knew I had to leave."

Heather didn't answer. *A Pict woman.* His story was another jolting reminder of just how long this man had lived. Maximus's face was now set in grim lines. She had the feeling this tale didn't have a happy ending. Patiently, she waited for him to continue.

"It sounds cowardly to admit it, but I packed my things in the early dawn and left one morning," he said softly. "It tore me up to do so, yet I thought it was for the best. I didn't want her to discover who I really was. I didn't want Evanna to be saddled with a man who couldn't age, who couldn't give her the family she deserved." He paused there. "And I didn't want to see the horror in her eyes when she found out the truth."

Heather grew still at this. The same horror he would have seen in her eyes that morning.

"I should have realized that Evanna wouldn't let things be," he continued. "She was too proud, too fierce to simply let a man leave her without explanation." He winced then, as if the memory still pained him. "She caught up with me a day later. I was sharing the fireside of a group of hunters, and Evanna came riding in like an avenging fury, her flame-red hair flying behind her. She confronted me, and when I gave her some feeble excuse, she drew her blade and stabbed me in the belly with it."

Heather drew in a shocked breath.

Seeing her reaction, Maximus's mouth twisted. "The women of Scotland have always been fierce … but Evanna was any man's equal in battle. The hunters scattered, and Evanna left me to bleed out by their fire pit." He glanced away then, severing the connection between them. "But of course, I was reborn with the dawn."

"So, ye never told her who ye really were?"

"No … it would only have enraged her. You're the only mortal I've told the full story."

Heather's gaze widened at this admission. When she spoke again, her voice was awed. "And ye have never lived with a woman again?"

Maximus shook his head. "I broke my lover's heart … and my own … that day. I'll not put myself, or anyone else, through that again."

Silence settled in the barn while Heather considered his words. After a few moments, she pushed her bowl away and fixed Maximus with a level look. Feeling her watching him, he raised his gaze, meeting her eye.

"I'll not lie," she said, her attention unwavering. "Discovering that ye cannot die came as a terrible shock to me … one that I'm not yet over." She paused there, seeking the right words before she continued. "But all the same, I'm glad I know. We all need others to see us for who we really are, Maximus. I can't break the curse, but I can be yer friend."

Friend? A small voice mocked her. *Is that what ye two are?*

Aye, as they'd lain together, their relationship was a little more complex. Nonetheless, after everything that had occurred in the past few days, it felt an age since that night at *The Bogside Tavern*.

Maximus watched her. His expression was shuttered, yet his dark eyes gleamed. And when he spoke, there was a husky edge to his voice. "Thank you, Heather."

Once supper was over, Heather rose from her stool and moved over to one of the beds Maximus had made up. "I take it ye chased off the rats and spiders?"

"I did my best, My Lady."

Heather's mouth curved at the teasing edge to his voice. After the intensity of their conversation, she welcomed a lightening of the mood.

She sat down upon her bed, tucking her legs under her, and began to comb out her still damp hair with her fingertips.

Meanwhile, Maximus stood up and stretched. "I suppose I'd better use the washing facilities," he said, stifling a yawn.

"Take the lantern with ye," Heather replied. "Or ye'll trip over in the dark. There is no candle in there."

Maximus nodded and picked up the lantern. "Very well ... I'll be back soon."

He left the barn, the door creaking shut behind him, and darkness swallowed the interior. Heather didn't mind the darkness, although as soon as he departed, she heard the tell-tale sounds of scratching and scrabbling in the haystack behind her. Maximus hadn't managed to turf out *all* the rodents it seemed.

Suppressing a shiver, Heather drew a blanket around her shoulders. She hated rats.

The time slid by, and Heather finished combing out her hair. She then remained seated, awaiting Maximus's return. The situation still seemed surreal. She'd almost forgotten about the violent fight she'd witnessed on that hillside.

Cory and his men had been strong warriors; even so, Maximus had still managed to hold his own for a while. He'd told her to run, but a few yards into the woods, she'd pulled Luchag up and turned him around. And when she'd emerged from the trees, the viciousness of the fight had cowed her. Horrified, she'd watched it unfold, but when Cory drove his dirk into Maximus's chest, she'd had to do something.

Now Cory Galbraith and his men lay rotting in the undergrowth on the edge of those woods. She hadn't dragged them that far from the road, and in a few days, their corpses would start to stink.

How long before someone found them? How long before the Galbraith laird heard that his son had fallen? They'd blame Maximus. Would Logan Galbraith seek vengeance?

Her belly cramped as she imagined him tracking them down. They wouldn't be hard to find, for everyone in Fintry knew she hailed from Dunnottar.

Pushing aside her churning thoughts, Heather let out a long exhale of relief when the door creaked open and light flooded into the barn once more.

Maximus placed the lantern back onto the table and turned to her. "I see Ainslee doesn't want to waste warm water on us."

Heather huffed. "Aye ... but at least she provided soap."

Maximus pulled a face, making it clear what he thought of the hard soap and coarse cloths that the widow had given them.

"Can ye leave the lantern lit tonight?" Heather asked. "I heard rats scrabbling while ye were out."

His mouth curved, yet he nodded. "If you wish."

Crossing to his hay bale bed, which lay against the far wall, he unlaced the front of his leather vest and stripped it off.

Heather's breathing stopped. She hadn't realized he was going to undress. She'd have looked away if he'd given her warning. The sight of his nude torso—all lean, sinewy muscle and tanned skin—made her mouth go dry.

"Isn't it a bit cold to sleep naked?" she said, cursing the gasping sound of her voice.

Maximus's chin snapped up, the smile returning. This time, she caught the playful edge to it—an expression that made the pit of her belly warm. "Worry not, fair lady, I'll keep my breeches on," he said, his gaze meeting hers. "Although since you've already seen me naked, you shouldn't find the sight too … shocking."

Heat blossomed across Heather's chest. She could feel it creeping up her neck. Any moment now, her cheeks would be aflame. She couldn't believe how easily he managed to embarrass her. She wasn't a shy, blushing maid—and he was right. She'd seen him without a stitch of clothing on.

She'd seen him aroused, had stared into his eyes as he'd moved inside her. She'd run her fingertips over every hard-muscled plane, every hollow, of his body.

And yet the blush wouldn't recede. She watched Maximus's smile widen as her cheeks caught fire. He knew where her thoughts had just gone.

Momentarily rendered speechless, Heather cleared her throat, turned away from him, and lay down upon the makeshift bed of hay bales. She could feel the heat of his stare upon her back, his unspoken challenge.

Despite all that transpired over the past day, the connection between them was still there.

XXIII

THE GATEHOUSE LOOMS

THE SIGHT OF Dunnottar made Heather catch her breath. Seated behind Maximus, her arms instinctively tightened their grip around his waist. As if sensing her tension, he drew Luchag to a halt upon the clifftop.

The stronghold reared up opposite them.

Heather had known that their destination was near, yet she'd been unprepared for the impact of actually seeing it. A host of memories flooded back, thoughts that she'd deliberately buried ever since leaving this place five years earlier. She was glad Maximus had halted the garron. She needed a few moments to collect her wits before they made their approach.

"It's still an impressive sight," Maximus murmured, his own gaze sweeping over the high, dove-colored walls with a swathe of blue sea behind them.

"When were ye here last?" Heather asked, deliberately focusing on him so that she could avoid her own thoughts for the moment.

"I don't recall ... fifty years ago maybe," he replied. "It was smaller then ... the keep hadn't been built." He paused. "But when it comes to location ... and sheer brooding impregnability, Dunnottar can't be beaten."

He was right about that, Heather reflected. The castle perched high upon a green headland, with sheer cliffs plummeting to the rocks below. A narrow strip of land joined the outcrop to the mainland. The castle stood like a sentinel, watching out over the North Sea.

The skin on Heather's forearms prickled. How she loved this place—but returning here brought mixed feelings with it.

"You're nervous," Maximus noted when Heather didn't speak. "I can feel it vibrating off you."

Heather forced a laugh. "I didn't realize I was that transparent." Her belly cramped then, and she struggled with the urge to scrabble down from the saddle and sprint away.

Coward.

Aye, when it came to facing her kin, she was. And yet, she didn't run, but remained perched upon the saddle behind Maximus. She wouldn't let him know just how much she was dreading this. The day she'd been putting off for too long now had come.

"You are easy to read, Heather," he replied, without the slightest teasing edge to his voice. "I've never met a woman who wears her emotions for the world to see as you do."

Heather tensed. That was ill news indeed. "I imagine that's why my life has turned out the way it has," she murmured. "I must learn to don a mask like most folk do."

"That would be a shame." His hand—warm, strong, and steadying—covered hers and gently squeezed. "The world has too few folk like you in it."

Heather swallowed. Now he was making the flaw sound like a strength. She wasn't sure she agreed with him. "Aye, well, since we're about to ride into the wolf's den, I need to be wary of being too open," she replied. "Dunnottar isn't for the meek."

"Who rules here now then?" he asked. Although the conversation had moved on, Maximus hadn't removed his hand from over hers. Heather welcomed his touch. If she was being honest with herself, she actually *craved* it.

But at the same time, it was distracting. The past two days, during which they'd completed their journey north, had grown increasingly uncomfortable.

The pull between them hadn't disappeared with the shock of Heather's discovery. If anything, it had grown. Maximus only had to look her way and Heather's pulse quickened. Traitorously, her gaze always sought him out and lingered upon him when he wasn't looking in her direction. She couldn't help herself.

Over the last couple of days, she'd realized why he'd been so protective of her. Of course, as an immortal she must seem incredibly fragile to him.

The realization had made her belly flutter.

It was no good. Immortal or not, she still wanted him.

Fortunately for them both though, Maximus had continued to keep his distance physically from her. The heat that flared every time their gazes locked hadn't encouraged him to take things further.

Their arrival at Dunnottar was a relief. She wasn't sure how much longer she could travel with this man before throwing herself at him—and such behavior would be unwise. Falling for an immortal man was likely to be the worst decision—in a long line of disastrous choices—she was ever going to make.

"When I left here, Robert De Keith ruled," she began, attempting to focus. "However, my sister sent word to me that he was captured by the English last year. His brother, David, is now laird."

"Your voice sharpened as you said David's name," Maximus observed. "I take it you aren't fond of the man?"

Heather's lips pursed. Nearly six years earlier, David De Keith had wed Gavina Irvine in order to weave peace between the two warring clans. However, just weeks after their wedding, he was rumored to have strayed from the marriage bed. He cornered Heather once, in a stairwell, and tried to kiss her. She'd kneed him in the cods and fled.

Fortunately, she'd departed from Dunnottar soon after.

Heather drew in a steadying breath before she answered. "No ... he's lecherous and vain. Let's hope that Robert manages to escape the English and return home before David brings Dunnottar to ruin."

Maximus laughed. "Your honesty is refreshing, Heather." He sobered then. "I will miss it."

Silence fell between them, for he'd just reminded them both that their forced companionship was now coming to an end. Now they'd arrived at their destination, everything would change.

"So, what now?" she asked, injecting a bright note she didn't feel into her voice. "Do ye have plans for after ye find yer friend?"

"It all depends on Cassian's news. If it's as you say, and Dunnottar is 'the fort upon the Shelving Slope', then I'll likely stay here while the Broom-star is still in the sky." He paused then. "And you, Heather? Once you make peace with your kin, what will you do?"

Heather swallowed. Truthfully, she had no idea. She was so focused on confronting her family she hadn't given any thought to what lay beyond that meeting.

"Like ye, it depends," she replied, deliberately cagey. "If they spurn me, I suppose I will go to Stonehaven and search for work there."

"And if they welcome ye?"

Heather gnawed at her bottom lip. "A widowed daughter will be a burden to them," she admitted. "I will have to find some way to make myself useful." If she was honest, she didn't see a bright future ahead of her at Dunnottar. A heavy sensation settled over her when she imagined the years to come.

As if sensing her tension, Maximus gave her hand a gentle squeeze. "You'll find your path, Heather."

Leaving the clifftop, they picked their way down the steep hill beyond. Reaching the bottom, they then took the narrow path that climbed to the gatehouse. Luchag made easy work of the slope, although Maximus let the garron have his head, while he and Heather leaned forward to aid him.

And all the way, Maximus was aware of stares tracking their progress. He glanced up, spying the outlines of men and spears upon the walls. He tensed under their scrutiny, aware they'd see he was armed. Yet, since there were just the two of them approaching, the guards wouldn't view them as too much of a threat.

The mood was tense throughout Scotland these days. Years of battles against the English had led to a period of uneasy peace—one the English seemed intent on shattering. As such, all the northern strongholds would be wary of strangers approaching their gates.

Maximus and Heather didn't speak on the way up to the walls. Maximus wasn't one for filling silences with prattle, and during the days they'd traveled together, he noticed that neither was Heather.

All the same, he meant what he'd just told her. He would miss Heather De Keith.

He hadn't wanted her to discover his secret, but in the days that had passed since, she'd surprised him.

Heather was a survivor.

She'd been full of questions—some of which were easier to answer than others—but her fear and horror had quickly transformed into unceasing curiosity. Sometimes that curiosity got too much, and Maximus had been forced to steer the conversation in a safer direction, but he'd enjoyed her company nonetheless.

More than enjoyed it, in fact.

She was warm and clever, with a sharp wit and dry sense of humor. He'd been content to just sit and listen to the lilting cadence of her voice. They'd shared meals together and camped out under the stars while he listened to her grumble about the tree roots that kept sticking into her back.

Maximus hadn't even minded that.

Heather's company reminded him just how lonely his life was. He'd chosen this solitary existence, and yet just a few days in this vivacious woman's company, and he longed for more.

This was what was missing in his life: a woman to love and cherish. Someone to build a future with.

But such a desire was foolish and dangerous.

Just because Cassian had summoned him here didn't mean they were on the cusp of solving the riddle. In a millennium, they'd managed to decipher two lines. There was every chance the Broom-star would fade from the sky in a month or two, and he and his friends would still be immortal.

After seeing what Cassian had endured, he didn't want to make the same mistake of falling for a mortal woman, only to see her wither and die while he remained young.

Maximus clenched his jaw and shoved his spiraling thoughts back into the recesses of his mind where they belonged. He'd only known Heather a few days, and he was already weakening. He'd told her about Evanna, and she'd seemed to understand.

But the problem lay with him.

Maximus wanted more.

Haven't all these years taught you anything?

Clearly not, for even now, the warm softness of Heather's body pressed against his back, the feel of her arms looped around his waist, both distracted and comforted him. He didn't want this journey to end.

But end it had to.

Drawing Luchag up before the gates, Maximus craned his neck up at a broad-shouldered figure who loomed above him on the battlements. "Good day!" he called out.

"State yer business at Dunnottar," the warrior shouted back, his harsh voice ringing over the high stone walls.

It wasn't a friendly welcome, although Maximus hadn't expected one.

"I'm here to see Cassian Gaius," he called back, flashing the warrior a toothy smile. "Tell him that Maximus Cato has arrived."

XXIV

WELCOME HOME, LASS

"HEATHER!"

AILA DE Keith's squeal of joy echoed through the hallway, causing two servants carrying piles of clean linen to stop and gawk. Heather had just climbed the turret stairs to the chambers where her mother and father lived, when her younger sister emerged from one of the doorways.

For a moment, the two women just stared at each other—and then a wide smile creased Aila's face. Picking up her skirts, she rushed down the hall, covering the space between them in just a few strides. She then flung herself into Heather's arms.

Tears flowed down Aila's cheeks when she pulled back from the embrace. "Ye didn't tell me ye were coming!"

Blinking back tears of her own, for seeing her sister again had made Heather's resolve to stay in control of her emotions crumble, she favored Aila with a watery smile. "Sorry about that ... I left Fintry in a rush. There was no time."

Worry clouded Aila's face at this news.

Folk always said the two sisters looked alike. However, Aila's features were more delicate than Heather's and she had smoke-grey eyes. These days, Aila was a lady's maid to David De Keith's wife and dressed almost as finely as a lady herself. Clad in a grey-blue kirtle, her thick, light-brown hair pulled back from her face, she carried herself beautifully.

"Has something happened?" Aila asked, her brow furrowing.

Heather shook her head. She hadn't been planning on telling her kin about the circumstances of her departure, and seeing concern shadow Aila's eyes, she resolved not to.

Aila would be worried for her, yet her parents would only condemn her.

"Come!" Aila looped her arm through Heather's and steered her toward the door of the steward's solar. "Ma and Da will be delighted to see ye."

"Will they?" Heather tensed. How could Aila say that—knowing how things had gone the last time she'd exchanged words with their parents?

Aila paused, her expression turning serious. "We've *all* missed ye, Heather."

Heather stared back at her sister, her throat constricting. Aila was such a kind soul. She and Aila might have shared some similarities in looks, but their characters were vastly different. Heather was willful, fiery, and difficult; whereas Aila had a sweet, even temper, and she always tried to see the best in people and situations.

The two servants were still gawking at them from the end of the hallway, and Aila sent them scurrying away with a wave of her hand. "Aye, ye can tell everyone that Heather De Keith has returned," she called after them.

The weight in Heather's belly increased. The last thing she wanted was her presence here to be shouted from the ramparts. However, she kept her mouth clamped shut and followed her sister into the solar.

Iona De Keith lowered the pillowcase she'd been embroidering to her lap. Her grey-green gaze—identical to her eldest daughter's—narrowed. "Yer return is as abrupt as yer departure I see, Heather."

A few feet away, Donnan De Keith rose from his desk and the ledger he'd been writing in, and crossed the solar toward her. As she remembered, he favored his right leg as he walked. It was a pronounced limp that came from a hunting injury many years earlier. Was it her imagination, or did the limp seem worse these days?

The look of joy on his face made a lump rise in Heather's throat. The sting from her mother's acerbic welcome faded. At least one of her parents was pleased to see her.

"Welcome home, lass," he rumbled, pulling her into a fierce embrace. "Lord, how I've missed ye."

Heather's vision blurred once more, and this time the tears spilled over. She'd thought he'd rail at her. Instead, his warmth made her want to weep. "I've missed ye too, Da," she whispered, pressing her cheek to his chest.

Her father was just how she remembered him: strong and solid, his brown hair just lightly touched with silver. However, when she drew back from his embrace, she saw that there were lines of care around his grey eyes that had been absent when she'd left Dunnottar five years earlier.

Across the room, Iona sniffed. "Don't think ye shall get such a greeting from me, Heather. I'll not forget the way ye spoke to me last."

Heather loosed a sigh before turning to face her mother. Now that her father had welcomed her, she felt galvanized. One of them she could deal with, but when they turned against her in a united front—as they had the day she'd left this place—it was so much harder.

Now she was standing before her parents, Heather fully understood the wisdom of Maximus's advice to come back here and face them. He was right: life was too short, for mortals like her at least, to bear grudges.

Iona didn't look welcoming. Her chin was held high, her nostrils flared as if she was readying herself to do battle. She'd also started to twist the gold ring she wore upon her left hand—a sure sign she was agitated.

"I apologize for the way things went that day, Ma," Heather said softly. And she meant those words too. If she could go back in time, she'd have given Iain Galbraith a wide berth indeed. "I was wrong to run away as I did ... but rest assured, I have paid the price over the years."

Iona stiffened, her full mouth compressing. She'd been expecting her daughter to bite back—for the old Heather would have—and didn't know how to deal with her contrition.

"We knew ye should never have shackled yerself to that man," her father replied. Glancing back at him, Heather saw that Donnan Galbraith's expression had darkened. "He was a troublemaker ... and wasn't going to treat any woman well."

And how right ye were, Da, Heather thought as tears prickled the back of her eyelids once more. *What a fool I was.*

"So, things were bad?" Aila asked softly, drawing near to Heather and placing a sympathetic hand on her arm.

Heather nodded, not trusting herself to speak. This wasn't how she'd expected the reunion to go. If they didn't stop being so kind to her, she'd break down and start sobbing.

"Then why didn't ye just come home?" Aila pressed, her grey eyes shadowing.

Heather swallowed. "Ye know what I'm like ... stubborn. I wanted to make things work. I was determined to."

"Yer pig-headed nature always got ye into trouble as a bairn," Iona announced, her clipped voice ringing across the solar. She was twisting the ring vigorously now. "And it has as a woman. I do hope ye have returned to us humbled ... for I, for one, won't tolerate yer headstrong ways again."

Heather drew in a deep breath. That was better. The sharp edge of her mother's tongue made the urge to weep recede. Suddenly, she was back in control.

Drawing herself up, she readied herself for a verbal assault. Any moment now, her mother would attack as she had the last time they'd faced off.

Filthy harlot!

Ye have become a blacksmith's whore.

I knew ye'd come crawling back to Dunnottar with yer tail between yer legs!

Yet the harsh words never came.

"Heather takes after ye, my love," Donnan replied, his mouth quirking. "Ye were a handful when ye were younger too."

Iona drew in an outraged breath while Aila turned away to hide a smirk. Heather had to bite her cheek to prevent her own smile.

Her mother abruptly stopped twisting the wedding band, her mouth gaping. "Donnan!"

"What, mo ghràdh?" he asked innocently.

"How dare ye!"

Heather watched her father's smile widen. "It's the truth. But it's also why I fell in love with ye."

Iona De Keith stared at her husband, and then to Heather's surprise, her mother's cheeks grew pink.

This exchange between her parents was something she'd never seen before. She knew they were happy enough together, yet Donnan De Keith could be a dour man at times, preoccupied with his role as steward of this keep. Her mother was always the sort to notice the things that were lacking in her life rather than appreciating what she had.

She'd never seen her father tease her mother so boldly. It was as if the shock of her return had unfettered something within him.

And seeing Iona De Keith's blush, he'd succeeded in rendering his wife speechless—for a short while at least.

Taking advantage of the moment, Heather turned to her sister to see Aila's eyes twinkling with delight. She too was enjoying seeing their father get the best of their mother. "Do ye think Lady Elizabeth might have some work for me in the keep?" Heather asked. "I'm not afraid of hard graft ... and will work in the kitchens if I have to."

This comment brought a choked sound from their mother. "The kitchens? Next ye shall be offering to empty privies and muck out stalls. To think a daughter of mine could sink so low."

Irritation spiked within Heather. She bit back the urge to tell her mother she'd spent the past year and a half serving ale to drunks in a rowdy tavern. None of her kin knew the truth. Instead, Heather had told her sister in her last letter that she had rented out the forge and was living off a small but sufficient income.

"Lady Elizabeth isn't in charge here for the moment," Aila replied, her expression sobering. "David's wife, Lady Gavina, is." Her sister reached out then, clasping a hand through Heather's. "Ma is right ... we can't have a steward's daughter scrubbing floors. I'm sure Lady Gavina will find ye a suitable position."

XXV

IN MY BONES

CASSIAN MET MAXIMUS in the bailey of the lower ward.

Maximus had just emerged from stabling Luchag, and was wondering where his friend had gotten to—and if he was going to bother to greet him at all—when a tall, broad-shouldered figure appeared in the arched doorway leading into the keep.

Dressed in pine-green braies, a mail shirt that reached mid-thigh, and high boots, Cassian looked every inch a soldier. For a moment, the man halted, his gaze sweeping the cobbled expanse that lay between the high curtain walls and the keep itself. Then his attention seized upon Maximus, and a smile spread across his face.

An instant later, he ran down the steps, agile for such a big man, and strode across the bailey. He wore a plaid cloak of De Keith colors—light and dark cross-hatchings of turquoise green—which rippled out behind him.

"Cassian Gaius," Maximus greeted him with a grin. "You haven't aged a day."

Cassian huffed a laugh. "And neither have you, *Great One*."

Indeed, their paths hadn't crossed in twenty years—when they'd accidentally run into each other in Perth. And just as then, Cassian's lightly tanned face was unlined, his short brown hair untouched by grey.

They clasped arms and hugged, although when Cassian drew back from him, his smile had already faded. "Have you seen Draco?"

Maximus shook his head. "Not since the last cycle."

Cassian's hazel eyes shadowed. "Let's hope he makes a trip to Stirling soon … he'll have seen the Broom-star in the night sky."

Maximus didn't reply. Draco would have seen the comet, yet with the passing of the years, the man was becoming a law unto himself. The toll of his immortal life had turned him increasingly reckless and wild. "He may not join us this time," Maximus pointed out. "You know he doesn't always." They stood alone in the bailey and so it was safe to talk.

Cassian frowned. "Surely, he wants the curse broken as much as we do?"

Maximus shrugged. "With Draco, who knows?" Seeing the concern on his friend's face, he slapped him upon the shoulder. "Captain of the Dunnottar Guard, eh, Cass? I've never had gates open so quickly before me. The moment I mentioned yer name, they fell over themselves to let me in."

Cassian's mouth curved, revealing the hint of another smile. Although he had beamed moments earlier when spotting Maximus, his friend had an intense, serious nature. Earning a smile from him could be a challenge, which was why Maximus knew that Cassian was pleased to see him.

"I told them my old friend Maximus Cato was on his way," Cassian replied. He threw an arm around his shoulders and steered him toward the gatehouse. "And our reunion requires a drink."

"Wine, I hope," Maximus quipped.

Cassian cast him a rueful look. "All these years here and you still don't like ale?"

Maximus pulled a face in reply. "No."

The two men entered the gatehouse, crossed a narrow entranceway, and made their way into a square hall lined with long tables. This was the guard's mess, where the men who defended the castle took their meals. However, since it was mid-afternoon, Maximus and Cassian were the only ones here.

"Take a seat near the hearth," Cassian instructed, waving toward the western edge of the hall, where a long table sat before a roaring fire. "I'll go and get us something to eat and drink."

His friend disappeared through a doorway into what was likely the kitchen while Maximus took a seat at the table.

He was massaging a tense muscle in his shoulder and studying the heavy beams that crisscrossed the ceiling above him, when Cassian returned bearing a tray. He placed some bread and salted pork before Maximus and then poured them both large cups of wine.

"It's sloe," Cassian advised him. "A bit tart, but good."

The two men raised their cups in a silent toast before taking a sip. Cassian was right, the wine was drinkable. His friend didn't hail from Rome like Maximus did. Instead Cassian, like most of the Ninth, was from Hispania—the land now called Spain. Like Maximus, Cassian had grown up drinking wine made from grapes. He knew good *vinum* from bad.

The two men didn't speak a toast. Instead, Maximus made a silent vow.

To breaking the curse.

Helping himself to some bread and pork, Maximus ate hungrily. In the days since the fight with Galbraith and his men, he'd had the appetite of a wolf. It was like that whenever he sustained and then healed from mortal injuries. His body needed fuel.

"I've deciphered a line of the curse," Cassian said, waiting until Maximus was halfway through his meal before speaking up. He'd shifted into Latin, the tongue they always used when discussing the curse. He leaned forward, his eyes gleaming as he continued. "Dunnottar is 'the fort upon the Shelving Slope'."

"I know," Maximus replied, swallowing a mouthful of food. "I'm surprised none of us discovered it before now ... we've certainly been around long enough."

Cassian stiffened, his excitement dimming. He clearly hadn't expected Maximus to steal his moment.
"Scotland's a big country. Just because an answer lies in plain sight doesn't mean you'll see it." He paused then, gaze narrowing. "How did you find out?"

"Heather told me ... it's the old name for this place."

Cassian tensed. "Heather?"

Maximus reached for his cup of wine and took a large gulp, stalling a moment. *Dull-wit.* He hadn't meant to let that slip. He hadn't wanted to mention Heather at all, and yet her name had just tripped off his tongue.

"The woman I traveled here with," he replied casually. "She's a De Keith and was heading home alone ... so I accompanied her."

"And you just happened to discuss this castle's old name together?"

Maximus let out a long sigh. This was it—the moment when he decided whether to lie to his friend or just tell him the truth.

Lying was easier. Cassian wouldn't be impressed by the truth. And yet, he felt weary of secrets. He'd kept so many over the years, and he'd always been honest with the man before him.

He wouldn't lie to him now either.

"She knows who I ... who *we* ... are," he said finally, glancing away. "I told her."

Silence followed this revelation, and when Cassian finally did reply, his voice was hard. "Hades! Why would you do something so daft?"

Maximus leaned back and dragged a hand through his hair. "I didn't intend to," he replied after a pause. "But things got ... out of control."

"Right." Cassian's voice was clipped. "You'd better tell me the whole story ... from the beginning." He then leaned forward and refilled Maximus's cup. "Out with it."

Maximus bristled. As Captain of Dunnottar Guard, Cassian was used to ordering men about—but the pair of them were equals. He'd not be barked at. Of course, before the curse, Maximus had been both Cassian and Draco's commander, although those days were dead and forgotten, lost in the mists of time.

Picking up his cup, Maximus took a long draft. He then glanced over at Cassian, who was watching him with a deep scowl marring his forehead. "Very well," he murmured.

And so, he started from the beginning, from that fateful night he'd taken a room at *The Bogside Tavern*. He left nothing out—even telling Cassian, albeit briefly, that he and Heather had spent the night together before leaving Fintry with the dawn. Cassian's expression didn't change as he listened, although his mouth thinned when Maximus recounted how Heather had refused to leave his side as he lay bleeding out over the ground after the attack.

Another silence, a brittle one this time, fell after Maximus had completed his tale. "As you can see, it wasn't something I planned," he added. "The situation just spiraled out of control." A heavy sensation had settled over him after completing his story. He'd made a mess of things really.

"I thought you were more careful with women these days?" Cassian spoke up eventually. "Defending the honor of a tavern wench and then bedding her sounds like a recipe for disaster."

Maximus caught the scorn to his friend's voice and tensed. "It wasn't like that," he growled. "And don't use that tone when you speak of Heather."

Cassian favored him with a smile that didn't reach his eyes. "She's the steward's daughter." His voice still held a hard edge. "If she was to tell anyone about us, news would spread like pestilence throughout this keep."

Maximus inclined his head. "Heather won't betray us."

Cassian's gaze narrowed. "And how do you know that?"

"I just do."

Cassian muttered a curse under his breath and downed the rest of his wine in one draft. "Let's hope you're right," he said, rising to his feet. "The last thing you and I need in the coming weeks is for the people of Dunnottar to turn against us. This is our chance to break the curse, Max. I can feel it in my bones."

XXVI

COMPANIONSHIP

"YER SISTER TOLD me once that ye left Dunnottar under a shadow?" The woman with white-blonde hair, seated by the window of her solar, greeted Heather without preamble.

Heather tensed, her fingers curling into her palms. She resisted a sharp look over her shoulder at where Aila hovered in the doorway. It wasn't really her sister's fault; she wouldn't be surprised if the whole castle knew the sordid tale. This was another reason why she'd stayed away for so long. Heather hated to be the subject of gossip.

"That's true, My Lady," she replied after an awkward pause. "I lost my heart to a man and ran away with him to a village near Stirling."

Lady Gavina, who was around Heather's own age, inclined her head. Then with a wave of her hand, she gestured for her to come closer. "Don't worry, I'll not judge ye. Yer past doesn't bother me, Heather ... I was only asking out of curiosity. Please, take a seat."

Reassured, Heather did as bid, sitting down in one of the high-backed chairs that sat next to the glowing hearth. Outdoors, the shadows were lengthening as the warm spring day retreated. The evenings were still cool, as Heather had noted over the latter part of the journey here when she and Maximus had slept rough.

"I was wondering if ye would employ my sister here, My Lady?" Aila spoke up, relief and hope both lacing her voice.

Lady Gavina De Keith smiled. "I don't need two lady's maids, Aila ... but I'm sure a place can be found for Heather somewhere in the castle. Ye can leave us now, please."

Realizing that she'd indeed been dismissed, Aila retreated from the women's solar—a long, thin chamber with a large window looking south down the rocky coastline.

A loom sat beside Lady Gavina, with a half-finished tapestry upon it. It bore a scene of a castle perched upon a high-cliff: Dunnottar.

"The tapestry is lovely," Heather ventured. "Ye have talent, My Lady."

Lady Gavina's mouth curved once more, and this time the smile seemed a trifle forced. Her cornflower-blue eyes were shadowed, her beautiful face strained. "Thank ye," she murmured, putting down the shuttle. "Although it's taken me nearly two years to get this far ... I fear I shall be a crone before I finish it."

Heather smiled back. "All the same, it will be worth the wait."

The lady's gaze settled upon her then, and Heather had the unnerving sense she was being scrutinized. Eventually, when Gavina spoke, her voice was as cool as her countenance. "And what of yer husband?"

Heather swallowed. "He joined the cause ... but never returned home, leaving me a widow."

Lady Gavina's slender eyebrows arched. "Ye weren't happily wed to him, I take it?"

"No," Heather admitted, her fingernails now digging into her palms. After the reunion with her parents, she was feeling a little fragile. Her mother hadn't flayed her alive as she'd expected, yet the encounter had drained her. "He turned out to be a bad man, My Lady ... only, I realized it too late."

Lady Gavina watched her steadily, her gaze shuttered now. "I always envied women who got to choose their own husbands," she said after a long pause. "But it seems even those who wed for love get it wrong sometimes."

The lady's blunt words made Heather stifle a wince. Yet after a few moments, she realized that Gavina had just revealed something about herself. Heather remembered the laird well. David De Keith had made her skin crawl—and Lady Gavina had been wed to him for at least six years now.

Lady Gavina was the only daughter of the Irvine laird. For years, the neighboring clans had feuded, but the union between David and Gavina had done much to mend relations.

Perhaps David resented the match, for he'd started straying from the marriage bed even before Heather left Dunnottar, flaunting his infidelities without a care for how his young wife would feel. Heather couldn't imagine how things had deteriorated since then.

Now she understood the melancholy in Lady Gavina's pretty blue eyes. Her breathing slowed, empathy darting through her breast. "Aye," she murmured, plucking at a non-existent loose thread on the lilac kirtle Aila had loaned her for this meeting. The clothes she'd arrived in were too shabby to go before the Lady of Dunnottar in. "Few are the women who find happiness in men, My Lady. After Iain left me a widow, I decided I'd never again place my fate in a lover's hands."

Lady Gavina watched her, and then a real smile stretched her face. The expression revealed her for the beauty she was. "I like ye, Heather," she said, still smiling. "Ye are lively, witty company, and I'd welcome ye as my companion. I have Aila to tend to my needs as maid, but there is a mountain of sewing, embroidery, and weaving that I require help with. Although Lady Elizabeth is gentle company, she is often occupied with her son. I must admit that my days have grown a little lonely and dreary of late ... I could do with the friendship of someone with yer spirit." Their gazes met and held. "Are ye willing?"

Heather stared back at her for a moment, surprised by the lady's words. Such an offer was generous. But guilt knotted her belly then, for the idea of becoming Lady Gavina's companion didn't excite her. She was the type of woman who grew restless when faced with a day of weaving, spinning, and sewing. She liked her days to be more industrious, to have more purpose; her time working at *The Bogside* had changed her more than she'd realized.

Nonetheless, Heather knew she'd be ungrateful and foolish to refuse Lady Gavina. Her family would be furious with her if she did so, and the truce with her mother would be shattered.

So, instead, she dipped her head in thanks. "That's very kind of ye, My Lady," she murmured. "I'd be honored to accept."

Dusk was settling over Dunnottar when Heather finally left Lady Gavina's solar. She should go upstairs to her parents, for her mother would want to hear how the meeting with Lady Gavina had gone. However, she felt restless.

She and Maximus had parted ways earlier outside the stables in the lower ward bailey. She wanted to know if he'd found his friend Cassian and if so, how the reunion had gone.

And so, instead of taking the turret stairs back up to her parents' rooms, she left the keep.

Outdoors, a brisk, salt-laced wind blew in from the sea. Heather wished she'd brought a woolen shawl out with her, for the dusk air was cold upon her bare arms.

There were a few men about—soldiers mostly, milling outside the barracks. One or two noticed her and stared, yet Heather ignored them. She was looking for Maximus.

Maybe he was in the stables, checking on his pony. He was fond of that hardy garron, and Heather had also developed an affection for the beast during the journey.

Even if Maximus was elsewhere, she'd check on Luchag in the meantime.

Descending the steps, she set off across the bailey, aware that even more male stares now raked over her.

She'd forgotten what it could be like here, in a male-dominated environment. Still, experience had taught her to ignore such looks, and so she did so now. It was best not to encourage them.

She was half-way to the stables when a rough male voice hailed her. "Heather!"

Halting, she drew in a deep, steadying breath. It had been a few years since she'd last heard that voice—so similar to Iain's—but with a more gravelly edge. Of course, Blair was still at Dunnottar. She'd been bracing herself for the moment when she'd run into him again.

Heather turned, her gaze settling upon a big man with curly auburn hair. Dressed in soot-covered braies and lèine, and a sturdy leather vest, the smith hadn't changed much since Heather had last seen him. However, these days he was sporting a bushy beard that only added to his formidable appearance.

"Blair," she greeted him warily. "I thought I might see ye here."

The smithy scowled. "Finally decided to show yer face, then?"

The animosity in his voice made Heather's hackles rise. Blair had resented her years earlier, had blamed her for Iain's decision to leave Dunnottar and return to Fintry. Clearly, he hadn't softened his attitude toward her.

"Aye ... and I can see ye are as charmless as I remember."

The man's face screwed up at that. "Ye were my brother's doom," he growled, dropping all pretense of civility now. "He'd still be alive, if he'd stayed here."

Heather folded her arms across her chest, raising her chin to hold his stare. "Iain made his own decisions," she said coldly. "I had very little to do with them. It was *his* choice to join the cause."

In response, Blair spat on the ground between them.

Heather gave the man the kind of withering look she'd reserved for drunks at *The Bogside*. Then, without bothering to acknowledge the man again, she turned and continued on her way to the stables.

Nonetheless, when she stepped inside, she noted that her pulse was racing and her limbs felt shaky. How unfortunate it was that Blair Galbraith still lived here.

Taking a calming, deep breath, and then another, she walked down the narrow central aisle until she found Luchag. The garron looked content as he snatched at hay from a manger, and upon spying her, he snorted a greeting.

"Hello, lad." Heather ducked into the stall and stepped close to the pony, stroking his furry neck. Now that they'd arrived in Dunnottar, this garron was the only link she had left with Maximus.

It was funny, but the realization made her feel sad.

Ye can't hold onto things, she chided herself, digging her fingers into Luchag's plush brown coat. *That journey was always going to end. Ye were always going to go yer separate ways.*

Even so, knowing something and accepting it were two different things.

Another male voice intruded then, drawing Heather out of her reverie. "Now ... that's a lucky beast."

XXVII

THE GUARDIAN RETURNS

HEATHER GLANCED UP to see Maximus standing a few feet away. Her gaze took him in, noting that his dusty hunting leathers had been replaced with dark-green braies, a long-sleeved lèine of the same hue, and a fitted leather vest. Under one arm, he carried a smooth-domed iron helmet.

"I don't believe it." Heather quirked an eyebrow. "Ye have joined the Dunnottar Guard?"

His mouth curved into a slow smile that made her pulse flutter. He then stepped forward, ducked under the wooden barrier, and entered the stall. "I may be here for a few months," he replied, his voice deliberately low. They were alone in the stables at present, but that could change at any moment. "I might as well make myself useful while I'm here."

Heather swallowed. His proximity was distracting. She remembered then the things she'd said to Lady Gavina—about how rare it was for a woman to find happiness in a man's arms. She'd been vehement at the time, yet now the words seemed tinged with bitterness.

She was still firm on one thing though: she'd never again place her future in a man's hands.

Iain had taught her how foolish that was.

Maximus wasn't the sort of man she should yearn for. He was cursed, unnatural. Wanting to spend time with him would only lead to trouble, for them both. And yet, as she lifted her chin to hold his dark gaze, Heather noted that her pulse had quickened. The desire she'd felt ever since that first evening at *The Bogside* had grown even stronger, rawer. Her mouth went dry, even as her fingertips itched to reach out and touch his face.

As if sensing her turmoil, Maximus inclined his head. "Is all well with you, Heather?"

She nodded, not trusting herself to speak.

"The reunion with your parents and sister?"

"It went better than expected," she managed, cursing the breathy edge to her voice. "I think my mother may even soften toward me with time ... and I've found employment ... as Lady Gavina's companion."

His smile widened at this news. "So, you needn't have worried about coming back here after all?"

Heather swallowed. "I suppose not," she replied weakly. They were standing so close she could feel the heat of his body. He was observing her intently now.

"And yet your voice sounds a little flat," he observed. "Aren't you happy how things have turned out?"

She huffed a laugh, in an attempt to mask her growing discomfort. It suddenly felt hot and stuffy in this stall, and they were standing far too close to each other.

"I should be," she admitted. "Lady Gavina has been more than kind ... but ..." She broke off there, searching for the right words. "I know it sounds selfish but ... it's just that I wish for more from life."

"It's not selfish at all. What do you wish for then?" His gaze didn't waver from hers.

"Aye, well ... that's a fine question." Heather cleared her throat. "My days at *The Bogside* were exhausting, yet at least I had a real purpose there. I suppose I'd like a home of my own ... even if it's just a humble one ... and a family to care for. I wish to be a wife and a mother."

Satan take her, why couldn't she still her blathering tongue? Maximus didn't need to hear all this.

"Heather," he said softly, stepping closer still. Their bodies were almost brushing now. "You'll have all those things one day ... when the time's right." When she didn't answer, he reached up and cupped her cheek. The warmth of his palm upon her skin made her stifle a gasp. "You'll make a fortunate man very happy," he continued. "And you'll have a brood of bairns, who'll exasperate you."

Heather's breathing quickened at his words. He wore an intense expression, although his dark eyes were shadowed.

And all the while, the ache to touch him grew.

He bowed his head, leaning down toward her, and unconsciously Heather swayed toward him.

They shouldn't be doing this, but she didn't care. All she wanted was to feel his lips on hers.

With a soft groan in the back of his throat, Maximus covered her mouth with his.

The kiss was hungry, demanding. Heather melted into him while his hands tangled in her hair, tilting her head back so he could deepen the kiss. Her lips parted under his, welcoming his questing tongue.

Pressure built in Heather's chest, and heat flowered in her belly. His kiss overwhelmed her, caused her thoughts to scatter and her knees to weaken.

He'd kissed her at *The Bogside* passionately. But this kiss was different. This embrace vibrated with more than just lust. Instead, it felt as if he was opening himself up to her, felt as if he was giving her a part of himself. She could feel the tension shivering off his body, his want.

And in return, Heather kissed him back wildly, her pulse pounding in her ears.

The thunder of horses' hooves and the boom of men's voices shattered the moment, rippling into the stables from the bailey outside.

Maximus froze and pulled back from Heather. Breathing hard, his gaze fixed upon the stable doors. When he spoke, his voice held a rasp to it. "What in Hades is that?"

Emerging from the stables, Maximus's gaze swept over the now busy lower ward bailey. When he'd spied Heather earlier, speaking with a belligerent looking man—her late husband's brother most likely—there had been only a scattering of soldiers about, and a handful of servants finishing up the last of their chores before the light faded.

Now flaming torches hung from the walls, casting a lambent light over the faces of the men who urged their horses into the wide cobbled space.

Maximus glanced over his shoulder, relieved that Heather had left the stables through the side door, which would take her to the stairs leading to the upper ward.

The voices that echoed off the stone walls were rowdy, aggressive—it was no place for a woman.

Maximus's heart still thundered in the aftermath of their kiss.

Mithras save him, the woman would be his undoing. Whenever she was near, he found himself doing and saying things he knew he'd regret later. Cassian was right to be angry he'd told her about the curse. In his place, he'd have been furious too. But when Heather's gaze met his, he found it difficult to hold back. She knew who he was and yet, once the initial shock of discovery had passed, she accepted him.

It was a powerful thing—to be seen and wanted after so many centuries alone.

Heather was so sultry, her grey-green eyes a blend of knowing and innocence that caused something deep inside his chest to tighten. Just a couple of hours apart, and when he saw her again, a hunger had risen inside him he'd had trouble controlling.

Even now, his groin ached in the memory of how sweet her mouth had tasted. She'd been impossible to resist: her curves in that clinging lilac kirtle, her breasts straining against the laces, and the creamy skin of her cleavage tempting him.

But when she'd told him how she longed to be a wife and mother, a heaviness settled over him. He wished he could give her what she wanted. And yet he couldn't. The bandrúi had made sure of that.

A roar went up in the midst of the crowd of soldiers, drawing Maximus's attention once more.

A stable lad appeared from the tack room, his eyes panicked. Obviously, this host of men hadn't been expected. The lad went to rush by, in a hurry to ready stalls for the horses, but Maximus caught him by the arm.

"Who are these men?" he asked.

The lad's thin face tensed as he met Maximus's eye. However, seeing that he was being questioned by one of the Guard, he didn't struggle in his grip. "It's the Wallace—William Wallace," the youth gasped. "He and his men have returned to Dunnottar."

This announcement made Maximus let go of the lad, and without another word, the boy scurried off. Frowning, Maximus turned back to view the company— this time with fresh eyes.

The Wallace had been active a few years earlier, and instrumental in repelling the English forces, but of late, he'd gone to ground. No word had been heard from him. Many folk thought he'd left Scotland. But it appeared he was back.

Maximus's gaze swept the faces of the men who were now dismounting from their horses, their rough voices deafening as they ribbed each other and called for ale. In the midst of the group sat a big man upon the largest destrier that Maximus had ever seen.

In contrast to the activity around him, the newcomer was strangely still. Instead, he took in his surroundings with calm, yet keen, interest.

It was the gaze of a leader.

Maximus had sometimes wondered if he'd ever meet this warrior in his travels, and William Wallace was indeed how he'd imagined him. A mail shirt covered his broad chest, a thick fur mantle emphasizing the breadth of his shoulders. He had long dark hair and a thick beard to match, his strong-featured face set in a severe expression.

"Wallace!" A shout rang out across the crowd, and Maximus's attention shifted to the steps of the keep, where a tall man with brown hair and a neatly trimmed beard, an ermine cloak upon his shoulders, had stepped outdoors. Shadowing him, Maximus spied Cassian.

Although Maximus had never set eyes upon the laird of Dunnottar, he realized that this must be David De Keith, the current ruler of this fortress.

"Greetings, De Keith!" The newcomer bellowed, as the rumble of voices around him died away. "I hope yer kitchen is well-stocked … my men are hungry!"

"And thirsty!" One of the warriors shouted, much to the delight of his companions. Laughter rang out across the bailey.

"Of course … there will be plenty of food and drink for the Guardian of the Realm and his warriors," De Keith called back. However, the lack of force to his voice betrayed him.

Clearly, the laird wasn't happy to have these men as his visitors.

William Wallace frowned, a formidable expression indeed. "I gave up that title, De Keith." The bitter edge to his voice made the men around him grow still. "And I'd prefer not to be reminded of it."

"Well, we welcome ye here all the same," De Keith replied, a note of brittle joviality in his voice now. "To what do we owe the honor?"

Wallace's dark gaze narrowed further. "I'm a wanted man, De Keith … and need a place to lie low for a while," he rumbled. "Plus, Longshanks is pushing north again. Soon he'll be knocking on yer door … we don't want Dunnottar to fall under English rule again, do we?"

A heavy beat of silence passed before the laird shook his head, his mouth compressing. "The occupation was my brother's doing … he couldn't repel them."

"And yet Robert is a much better military commander than ye," Wallace countered.

The silence in the lower ward bailey turned chill. Even from this distance, Maximus could see that David De Keith was scowling. William Wallace's reply had been a blatant challenge.

"I take it ye have seen the fire-tailed star in the night sky?" De Keith asked, unexpectedly steering the exchange in a new direction.

Wallace inclined his head. "Aye ... what of it?"

"It's an omen ... one which bodes ill for us all."

The freedom fighter snorted at this while around him some of his men exchanged wary looks. The people of this land were superstitious; such talk made them uncomfortable.

"It bodes ill for the English, De Keith ... as it did all those years ago when William the Conqueror crossed the Narrow Sea."

The moments drew out, and then De Keith favored the newcomer with a strained smile. "The Lord willing, ye are right." He waved his arm to the gathering of warriors before him, an expansive gesture. "Come inside ... and leave yer horses for my men to see to."

Wallace gave a curt nod. And with that, he swung down from his warhorse.

Conversation resumed once more, and Maximus's gaze shifted from the band's leader to the other faces in the crowd. Judging from the array of plaid, the Wallace had managed to recruit men from all over the Highlands to his cause—men whose clans had fought each other over the centuries were now temporarily united against a common enemy.

Maximus wondered how long the truce would last.

And as he viewed the milling crowd of horses and riders, the same sensation he'd felt in Stirling—which made the hair on the back of his arms prickle—revisited him. These men were stout-hearted Scots, proud to represent their clans and defend their homeland with their lives.

How I envy them.

The prickling sensation intensified. The feeling was so strong it made him catch his breath. No wonder even the promise of breaking the curse left him numb these days.

What was the point, if he was going to continue living this way? He was nothing but a shadow, a man who passed through the lives of others without ever belonging.

He'd spent centuries avoiding the very thing that made life worth living.

I don't believe it ... I actually want to settle down. The thought struck him with such clarity that he sucked in a sharp breath. *I want a woman ... a clan.*

Still reeling from this realization, Maximus forced himself to continue surveying the crowd of warriors. And as he did so, he spied a face he hadn't seen in many years.

The man stood out amongst the Scots—with their long hair and beards, and their fair, ruddy complexions. Dressed in leather armor, a wolfskin cloak hanging from his shoulders, the warrior was clean-shaven and had aquiline features, curly black hair shorn close to his scalp, and dark-copper skin. He was seated astride his horse, watching the surrounding activity under hooded lids.

And then, feeling Maximus's gaze upon him, the newcomer's attention shifted across the crowd of men and horses.

Their gazes locked for an instant. The man's expression was as hawkish and brutal as Maximus remembered. The years hadn't softened this centurion at all; instead, they had turned him to steel.

As such, it came as a surprise when, at that moment, Draco Vulcan smiled.

XXVIII

THE WELCOME BANQUET

THE NOISE IN Dunnottar hall was deafening. Men's rough voices echoed off the stone walls and lifted high into the rafters. The thud of tankards of ale and mead being slammed down onto tables, and the clatter of food being served, accompanied the raucous conversation. Musicians—two youths playing a harp and a flute—stood next to the huge hearth at one end of the long rectangular chamber, yet the clamor almost drowned out the music.

This was the chamber where the De Keith and his retainers took their meals. The steward and his family sat at a long table near one of the hall's wide windows. Extra tables had been dragged in to accommodate the new arrivals, which meant that the servants had to squeeze through the gaps between to serve them.

Five long years had passed since Heather had last graced this hall with her presence. Strangely, it felt like much longer; she was a different person these days.

Taking in her surroundings, Heather caught snatches of conversation around her. The table behind them were discussing the fire-tailed star. Apparently, De Keith had proclaimed it an ill omen. The edges of her mouth curved when she thought of what the 'Broom-star' meant to Maximus and his friends. To them it was a sign of hope.

Heather's pulse quickened then, as she recalled the passionate kiss she and Maximus had shared in the stables. It was a stolen moment, yet she found herself longing for another.

Forcing herself to focus, her attention shifted to the long table before the hearth where the laird, his family, and his most loyal warriors sat eating. Servants were circling the laird's table with ewers of wine.

Heather had been amazed to discover that the huge, dark-haired man who'd stridden into the hall earlier was none other than William Wallace.

Her breathing had caught when she'd found out who he was.

The Wallace was actually here—once again a resident at Dunnottar. He was her hero: a man who represented Scottish freedom.

"I don't know how the kitchen manages to accommodate all these men," Iona De Keith muttered, raising her voice to be heard over the din. "The Wallace could have sent word of his arrival ahead."

"That's not his way," Donnan De Keith replied. "I suppose it's safer if no one knows the man's whereabouts ... especially with the English up to no good again."

Heather, who'd just started on her dish of boiled mutton and mashed turnip and butter, glanced up to find her father watching her. "Who is this man ye traveled north with, Heather?"

Heather stifled a sigh, aware then that her sister also observed her closely now. Likewise, her mother stared at her, a frown marring her brow.

"It's dangerous on the road for a woman alone," Heather answered evenly. "Maximus was traveling to Dunnottar ... so we journeyed together."

"Maximus," Iona sniffed. "What kind of name is that? Is he a cèin?"

"Aye ... he's from near Rome, but has lived here a long while."

If only they knew just how long.

"And what's his business at Dunnottar?" her father asked.

"His friend Cassian invited him to join the Guard."

"The Spaniard?" Heather's mother gave another disapproving sniff. "Soon we'll be overrun with outsiders."

"Cassian Gaius is the best captain we've had in years, my love," Donnan De Keith replied, a note of chastisement in his voice. "Better a man of Rome and a Spaniard at our side than to have this fortress overrun with English again."

Iona shuddered at this, hastily crossing herself. "Don't say such things, Donnan."

Heather's father didn't answer his wife. Instead, he caught his eldest daughter's eye before favoring her with a gentle smile. "At least he brought ye home safely, lass."

Heather smiled back, although the expression was forced. It was fortunate her father didn't know what had actually befallen them on the road to Dunnottar.

Reaching for a loaf of bread, she ripped a piece off, her gaze settling upon where her sister sat at her side. Aila had been silent ever since they'd entered the hall. She realized then that her sister's attention had shifted during Heather's exchange with her parents. Her gaze was now fixed upon the laird's table a few yards away. She appeared to be staring at a big, ruggedly handsome man with short brown hair, who sat halfway down the table.

"Who's he?" Heather asked, her curiosity spiking.

Aila started, as if she'd been caught doing something she shouldn't, and tore her gaze from the man. She focused on her supper then, her cheeks flushing. "No one," she murmured.

Across the table, their parents were now conversing together, their daughters ignored for the moment. As such, Heather bent her head toward her sister's, her elbow nudging her in the ribs. "I doubt 'no one' makes a lass blush like that ... come on ... who is he?"

Aila made a strangled sound in the back of her throat. Her sister wore a hunted look, as if she wished to leap up from the table and flee. "Cassian Gaius, Captain of the Guard," she whispered.

Heather glanced over at the table, at where the man was speaking to one of the Wallace's men. *Maximus's friend*. Like Maximus, he wore his hair in that brutally short style, and he held himself with that same ramrod straight posture. A soldier's bearing—a *centurion's* bearing.

"He's handsome," she acknowledged, shifting her attention once more to where her sister now squirmed beside her.

"Enough," Aila hissed. "I wasn't staring at him ... I was just ... deep in thought."

Heather cocked an eyebrow. Aila must think her a goose if she was ever going to believe that. Nonetheless, she could see her sister wasn't in the mood to be teased. She was staring down at her plate with a fixed, pained look upon her face, her shoulders rounded. There wasn't any point in pursuing the subject.

Instead, Heather's attention returned to the laird's table, and to William Wallace. The rumors had said he was a giant, and indeed she'd seen how he towered over De Keith as he made his way to the table. David De Keith wasn't a small man, but he'd looked so next to the seven-foot warrior.

Curiosity spiraled up within Heather. *Why is he here?* She longed to be one of the servants circuiting the table, so she could catch snippets of conversation. Had he gone to France to rally support for the Scottish cause as many folk believed?

Heather's gaze slid along the table, taking in the faces of those seated there. Lady Gavina was the only woman present this eve. She was seated to the left of her husband, with Cassian flanking her other side.

The Wallace sat to David De Keith's right, and the pair of them appeared to be deep in discussion. William Wallace was frowning, while the De Keith laird wore a pinched expression.

Heather guessed that the conversation wasn't going well.

A striking man sat next to William Wallace. Jet black hair curled close against his scalp, and he bore haughty, hawkish good looks. Unlike most of the men in this hall, he didn't wear any clan colors.

Heather wondered who he was.

Nosiness will be yer undoing one of these days, she chastised herself, taking a mouthful of mutton.

She noted that Maximus was nowhere in sight. Since he'd just joined the Guard, she imagined he was taking his first watch upon the walls. Nonetheless, she found her gaze looking for him.

Careful. She washed the mutton down with a sip of ale. *Don't ye get besotted with him.*

The thought made her tense. It was probably too late for such warnings. It was time to admit that Maximus had gotten under her skin. That kiss had left her breathless and aching. She felt oddly tearful as she'd hurried away afterward.

Falling for him wasn't wise at all.

As she finished her supper, Heather became aware of a strange sensation, a prickling between her shoulder blades. It felt like someone was staring at her. At first, she resisted the impulse to glance over her shoulder, telling herself that it was probably just fatigue. It had been a tiring journey, and she was looking forward to sleeping on a soft mattress tonight.

However, the sensation intensified with each passing moment, and eventually, Heather glanced over her shoulder.

And when she did so, she froze.

A man seated at the far side of the hall was watching her. He sat in the midst of a long table, where the Wallace's men ate and drank. Around him, the other warriors roared with laughter over some joke one of them had made. Yet this man ignored them.

He merely stared at Heather. His face was taut, his eyes unblinking.

Heather stared back, a chill washing over her. She'd been enjoying her supper, but now her belly and throat closed. A moment later, she broke into a cold sweat.

No ... it can't be.

But it was. She knew that face well enough not to mistake it.

There, watching her with a glare that pinned her to her seat and robbed her lungs of breath, was Iain Galbraith.

XXIX

A GHOST FROM THE PAST

HEATHER TURNED BACK to face her parents, her pulse thundering in her ears. Her body coiled, and she dug her fingers into the wooden tabletop.

"Heather ... what's wrong, lass? Ye have gone the color of milk." Across the table, her father watched her, his brow furrowed.

Next to him, her mother also frowned. "Donnan's right ... are ye unwell?"

Heather shook her head. Shock had rendered her momentarily speechless. Her supper churned in her belly.

Run, her instincts screamed. *Get away from him!*

But she couldn't, not now. Everyone was still seated in the hall. She'd only draw unwelcome attention to herself.

One thing she knew though was that she wasn't going to keep this secret to herself. Her kin were her only allies in this hall—and none of them had liked her husband.

"Iain is here," she rasped, finally finding her voice.

Beside her, Aila gasped. "Iain Galbraith?"

Heather nodded, bile stinging the back of her throat. "He's seated at the rear of the hall ... and I can still feel his stare drilling a hole into my back."

Her parents and sister shifted their attention from Heather then, their gazes all swiveling to the back of the hall. And when she saw how her mother's face paled, how her father's mouth thinned, and how Aila's delicate features grew strained, she knew they'd all recognized him.

"I thought ye said he was dead?" There was no mistaking the accusatory edge to her mother's tone. Although the meeting between them could have gone worse earlier, there was still friction between mother and daughter. Iona didn't trust her—and to have Iain Galbraith return from the dead when she'd told everyone she was a widow didn't help matters.

She knew how it looked. Her mother thought her a liar.

"I believed he was ... when he never returned to Fintry," Heather replied, swallowing the hard lump in her throat. "No word reached me, or his kin there. Even his brother here in Dunnottar believes he's dead."

A little of the tension in her mother's face eased at this, although the glower on her father's darkened. "What kind of man deserts his wife?"

A cruel one.

The words were unspoken, yet they hung in the air between the four of them. Heather remembered well the nervousness she'd felt as she waited for Iain's return. They hadn't been getting on well, and his mercurial temper frightened her. Frankly, she'd been relieved when he joined the cause. But when some of the other men returned to Fintry, and he didn't, she'd begun to worry.

What little coin he'd left her with was almost gone. She'd done her best to grow as many vegetables in the plot behind their cottage as she could over the summer, yet they wouldn't sustain her over the winter. Still, she'd waited for him, month after month. But eventually, hunger and cold had driven her to *The Bogside Tavern* in search of work.

"So ... all this time he's been with the Wallace?" Aila asked finally, breaking the heavy silence that had descended upon the table after her father's question.

Heather drew in a ragged breath. "It would seem so." Her gaze swept over the faces of her kin, desperate. "Please ... I don't want to go back to him."

She cursed herself for her ungratefulness earlier, for her wish for more out of life than merely remaining here as Lady Gavina's companion. Such a life was infinitely better than returning to Fintry as Iain Galbraith's wife.

Heather's throat constricted. God was punishing her for her ingratitude.

"He may not want ye back, lass," her father pointed out, his grey eyes shadowing. "After all ... he probably never expected to see ye here."

A little of Heather's panic ebbed at her father's answer. He was a steadying influence, a practical man who always looked for solutions instead of getting flustered.

"Da's right," Aila soothed. "He may avoid ye while he's here."

Heather's belly clenched. "If that's the case, then why's he staring daggers at my back?"

Aila's mouth compressed. "Maybe, he's just surprised."

Her sister was trying to find some certainty to grasp onto, yet her words made Heather's pulse accelerate further. "I can't go back to him," she vowed, her gaze dropping to where her fingers still grasped the table edge. "I can't."

"Ye are afraid of him," her mother observed quietly. Her tone had lost its sharp edge. Instead, Heather could hear the worry in her mother's voice. And when she looked up, and their gazes fused, she decided to tell the truth.

"Aye," she murmured. "He's got a bad temper ... and he's not shy of using his fists. I seem to have a knack for enraging him."

Iona De Keith's grey-green eyes narrowed, her jaw tightening. "Don't worry," she replied, drawing herself up. "Ye won't have to go back to him." She cast her husband a sharp look. "Will she, Donnan?"

The steward shook his head. His gaze shadowed, although it never wavered from his eldest daughter. "Of course not," he replied.

As soon as the meal was over, Heather and her family quickly rose from their seats and hurried from the hall. Usually, after a banquet like this one, Heather's parents would linger, for there would be sweet apple wine poured, more music, and some dancing.

This evening, Donnan De Keith limped from the hall without a backward glance.

Head down, Heather followed him.

The party of four left the long rectangular-shaped chamber and entered a wide gallery that led down to where the turret stairs awaited them. As the stairwell neared, Heather started to hope that her father was right. Perhaps Iain had stared at her merely out of shock; maybe, he would avoid her for the rest of his stay here.

"Where are ye going, Heather?"

Just a few yards from the stairs, a rough male voice echoed out over the corridor, and Heather's hope shattered.

Heart pounding, she skidded to a halt. The urge to flee boiled up within her, yet she wasn't a coward. She'd faced this man down many times in the past, and she'd do so again.

At least this time she had her family with her.

Iain wouldn't want them to see him at his worst.

Turning, her gaze alighted upon the tall man who strode toward her.

He was as handsome as ever, with wild auburn hair, piercing green eyes, and a lantern jaw; although his time away had roughened his looks a little, and there was a thin, pink scar across one cheek that hadn't been there when they'd parted ways.

"Iain," she greeted him, cursing the rasp in her voice. "Ye are alive."

He favored her with a wide, harsh smile. "Aye ... as ye can plainly see, woman."

"Why didn't ye ever send word to Fintry, or to yer brother here? These past two years, we all thought ye had fallen."

Iain's smile faded. He stopped a few feet back from her, and Heather noted that he was leaner than she remembered. His work at the forge had bulked him up, yet his new life as a soldier honed his muscles differently.

"I've been in France with the Wallace," he said, irritation edging his voice. "Busy with important matters."

"More important than letting yer wife know ye still breathe?" Donnan De Keith's voice was a growl in the silence of the corridor. Although she didn't shift attention from Iain, Heather knew her father stood at her shoulder. Never had she been so grateful to have his support. Still, fear coiled in the pit of her belly when she saw how Iain's face darkened in response.

"The cause supersedes everything, De Keith," he replied, his lip curling. "Or maybe ye aren't as loyal to Scotland as I am?"

"I'm just as loyal as ye," her father replied, no trace of rancor in his voice. However, there was a hardness to it that Heather hadn't heard before. "I just know how a wife should be treated."

The curl in Iain's lip intensified, twisting his mouth into an unpleasant sneer. Casting the steward a dismissive look, his gaze settled upon Heather once more. "I can see why ye were so keen to leave these people." He thrust out a hand toward her. "Come on ... let's go, *wife*."

Heather shrank back, shaking off the hand that grasped for her forearm. "No, Iain. I'm staying here with my kin. Our marriage is over."

Iain Galbraith went still, disbelief rippling over his face. "Ye don't get to say when it's over," he replied, his voice roughening. "We made vows before God."

"Aye ... and ye broke them when ye couldn't be bothered to tell me ye were alive ... when ye left me at yer forge with no means to support myself."

He snorted. "I knew ye'd survive. One of my kin would have taken ye in."

Heather swallowed, trying to force down the hot anger that now bubbled up within her. "Yer uncle turned me away when I asked him for help, although yer cousin Cory said I could live at Culcreuch Castle ... provided I warmed his bed." Iain's gaze narrowed at that, but Heather pressed on. She'd had enough of minding her tongue. She'd had enough of this man. "I ended up serving ale at *The Bogside* ... it was the only place I could find work in the village."

Her mother's stifled gasp behind her warned Heather that, of course, Iona had no idea of how she'd earned a living since Iain's departure. She'd get a tongue lashing from her mother later for this revelation.

"I'd forgotten how much ye have to say for yerself." Iain took a threatening step toward her. "I'll enjoy shutting that insolent mouth of yers."

"Leave her be, Galbraith." Donnan De Keith growled. Glancing at her father, she noted that his hands were balled into fists at his sides. Her father was a big man, and a fierce fighter in his day, yet he wouldn't be a match for Iain—a soldier in his prime. "Heather is staying with us."

"Step back, old man," Iain replied with a sneer. "I'm taking my wife back to my quarters." He made a grab for Heather then, but she cringed back from his touch.

Behind Heather, her mother let out an enraged hiss, while her sister gasped. None of them could believe this man was going to drag her away by force—but Heather believed it. The violence in Iain Galbraith simmered near the surface, and he held his temper on a short leash.

A sickening realization welled up within Heather then. By asking for her father's protection, she'd inadvertently put him in danger.

"Enough!" Iain snarled. He reached for Heather once more, his fingers clasping over her forearm and digging in.

"No!" Heather's terrified cry rang out over the corridor. The fear he'd used to control her in the past barreled into her, but this time she wouldn't be held prisoner by it. She balled her free hand into a fist and struck him hard in the mouth.

XXX

NOT DONE

EVERYTHING TURNED TO chaos, the moment Heather punched him.

Iain reeled back, blood streaming from his split lip, his green eyes wide with shock. She'd never have dared hit him in the past, but something had snapped within her. No longer would she cower before him. Maximus had taught her how important it was to stand up to bullies.

"Whore!" He lunged for her, but this time, her father barred his way.

And an instant later, the two men were swinging punches at each other, their curses ringing off the surrounding walls.

Heavens, no!

Heather stumbled back, her gaze fixed upon where her father now slammed Iain against the wall, using his superior bulk to his advantage. But Iain was younger, fitter, and more vicious. He head-butted the steward, sending him reeling back, before he drew a dirk from his waist and went after him.

"No!" Heather screamed, rushing forward. "Stop!"

If she didn't do something, he'd slay her father.

She'd almost reached Iain when a strong hand clasped about her shoulder and hauled her backward. And then, a tall, lean figure clad in pine-green and black hurtled past her.

Heather stumbled against her sister, gasping in shock. *Maximus*. Where had he appeared from?

Her father had hold of Iain's wrist now as he struggled to keep the dirk from his throat. Donnan's face was red from the strain, although his gaze was murderous. Fury had rendered him fearless.

Maximus moved fast, with the grace Heather had already seen in those fights with Cory. His fist collided into the side of Iain's face.

Iain hadn't seen the attack coming, and his head snapped sideways from the force. His grip on the knife released, just a fraction. But that was all her father needed. He shoved the blade away from his exposed neck and wrenched it from Iain's grip before throwing it to one side. The dirk clattered onto the stone floor, but Donnan De Keith ignored it.

Instead, he punched Iain in the throat and sent him reeling.

Heather noted that Maximus stepped back, letting her father retaliate without interference.

Iain slumped to the ground on all fours, choking and retching as he clutched at his injured throat.

"I suggest you leave things be now," Maximus told Iain, his hand straying to the sword at his waist to prove his point. "Or the laird will hear of this."

With a choked curse, Iain heaved himself to his feet. Blood trickled down his chin from his split lip, and his eyes had a glazed look. Still grasping at his throat, his gaze settled upon Maximus. It raked up and down the length of him, taking the measure of the man who'd dared to interfere in his business.

His attention then shifted to Heather. She stared back, although the fury in those green eyes made her belly cramp. She'd always fear this man.

"We're not done, Heather," he croaked. Then, with one last malevolent look at Maximus and Donnan De

Keith—a stare that promised retribution, Iain Galbraith stumbled away.

A hollow silence followed his departure.

Breathing hard, Donnan rubbed at his forehead. Iain had head-butted him hard, and his eyes watered in the aftermath. However, the steward's gaze shifted to Maximus, and he favored him with a nod. "I thank ye, for stepping in when ye did ... and for letting me finish it."

Maximus inclined his head and smiled.

The steward's gaze narrowed as he scrutinized his savior. "Ye must be new to the Guard ... I don't think I've seen ye before?"

"You haven't," Maximus replied. "I just started today."

"This is the man who escorted me north, Da," Heather interrupted, casting Maximus a grateful, if shaken, smile. "Maximus Cato, may I introduce ye to my father ... Donnan De Keith, steward of Dunnottar."

Heather was aware then that both her sister and mother were now staring at Maximus as if they'd just received new pairs of eyes and were trying them out for the first time. He was rakishly attractive in the Guard uniform and held himself with that unconscious male arrogance that drew a woman's eye.

"Maximus," she continued, gesturing to the two women behind her. "This is my mother, Iona, and my sister, Aila."

Still smiling, he favored both of them with a nod.

"Thank ye for yer assistance," Iona De Keith murmured, her voice unnaturally meek. The fight had cowed her.

"You're welcome," Maximus replied, holding Iona's eye for a moment. He then shifted his attention to Heather. "Who was that man?"

Heather drew in a shaky breath. "My husband."

Maximus's gaze grew wide.

"I know," she continued, her voice barely above a whisper. Her knees weakened then as the full weight of the situation settled upon her. "I thought he was dead ... but it seems he isn't." She drew a trembling hand over her face. "I'm so sorry, Da ... I had no idea he'd react like that."

"It's alright, lass." Stepping close, her father placed a hand upon Heather's shoulder. "I shall speak with Captain Gaius ... and ensure that man doesn't come near ye again."

Relief flooded through Heather. "Thank ye, Da," she whispered.

"Come on." Her mother murmured, backing away toward the turret stairs. "We should go up to our rooms, lest that odious man returns."

"He won't," Maximus assured her. Yet his attention never strayed from Heather. "Can I talk to you alone for a moment?"

All three of her family members tensed at this request, but Heather reassured them with a wan smile. "All will be well ... ye can trust him." She waved them toward the stairs. "Go up ... I will join ye shortly."

They moved away, although Donnan was frowning. Maximus had come to his aid, but he was still worried about his daughter being compromised. Yet, since Maximus had saved his life, he couldn't really protest too vigorously.

Maximus and Heather remained in silence in the hallway, waiting until the sound of her family's retreating footsteps on the turret stairs faded. Then Maximus stepped close, his gaze snaring hers. "Did you really have no idea he was alive?"

Heather caught the note of disbelief, the slight edge of accusation, in his voice. Like her parents, he suspected she'd lied to him. Since their arrival at Dunnottar, Maximus had started to lower his shields. Their emotional kiss earlier proved it.

But this changed everything. Her throat tightened when she saw how his gaze shuttered. Swallowing, Heather raised her chin. "I told ye the truth. Do ye think I would have been serving ale at *The Bogside* ... or that I would have lain with ye ... if I'd believed my husband lived?"

"I don't know what to think." He raked a hand through his hair, and Heather realized he was agitated. This discovery had upset him. "But I do know yer kin have just earned themselves an enemy."

"As have ye," she replied softly. "I saw the look he gave ye."

Maximus arched an eyebrow. "I'm not worried about the likes of Iain Galbraith," he replied with that arrogance she found equally compelling and frustrating.

"All the same ... be wary of him. Just like Cory, he never forgets a slight."

The mention of Iain's cousin made Maximus frown. It was a reminder of their journey to Dunnottar, of a forced proximity that had bonded them. But this revelation had caused that bond to fray. Heather could feel it, and she wondered if he could too. It was hard to believe just a few hours earlier she'd been in his arms. He'd kissed her as if she was his world.

But that was before Iain crashed back into her life.

Maximus didn't need to spell the situation out. Her husband's presence here drove a wedge between them.

Disappointment constricted her chest. "It was fortunate ye were here," she said after a pause, hoping he didn't sense how upset she was. "What *were* ye doing in this corner of the keep anyway?"

His mouth curved, although his gaze remained cool. "I was looking for you ... although I should have known I'd find you in the midst of trouble."

Heather swallowed. He wasn't wrong there. Strife seemed to dog her footsteps these days. "Have ye seen the Wallace?" she asked, desperate to shift the focus from herself once more.

"I have," he replied.

"Why do ye think he's here?"

"Dunnottar has always held a strategic position on the edge of the Highlands." Maximus sighed then and rubbed the knuckles of his right hand, which he'd used to punch Iain. "William Wallace will be waiting to see what the English do next." He paused, meeting her eye once more. "And my friend Draco now serves as his right-hand."

"Draco?" Heather went still. "The other immortal ... ye are all here now?"

"We are."

Heather's breathing quickened. Excitement fluttered up under her ribcage, momentarily making her forget her own problems. "Then there might be a chance ... that the curse will be broken?"

The hint of a smile upon Maximus's lips faded, and his gaze remained shadowed. "Every coming of the Broom-star there is a chance," he reminded her. "But until we unravel that riddle, a chance is all we have."

Maximus stepped closer to her and lifted a hand, his fingers gently tracing the line of her jaw. His touch robbed her of breath, and she willed him to lean in close, to kiss her again, to ravage her mouth with his. But he didn't. "You're in danger here, Heather," he murmured. "From now on, until the Wallace and his men leave this castle, you need to keep a watch over your shoulder."

Heather drew in an unsteady breath. It was hard to concentrate when his touch left a shiver of pleasure in its wake. His closeness was intoxicating, yet she felt the reserve in him now.

Her husband's presence had made him wary of her. Even if she had no intention of reuniting with Iain, she wasn't a widow. And soon all within the castle would know it.

Her throat ached when she thought about what this would do to her parents. "I will," she whispered.

XXXI

DISTRACTION

"THIS IS IT ... we are so close to breaking the curse I can almost taste it," Cassian announced in Latin. He then held his cup of wine aloft. "Let's toast to the fort upon the Shelving Slope."

"I'll drink to that," Draco replied. He flashed Cassian a grin and picked up his cup before glancing over at Maximus. "Are you going to join us, Max?"

Maximus glanced up from where he'd been gazing down sightlessly at his untouched wine. He picked up the cup and forced a smile. "To breaking the curse."

The three of them lifted their cups to their lips and took a sip. They sat in the guard's mess hall. Since supper had just ended, there weren't many guards in here: just a few men drinking and playing dice and knucklebones at the long tables.

"That's quite a scowl you're wearing," Cassian noted, setting his cup down before him. "I thought you'd be happy about this development ... it's only taken us a thousand years to get this far."

Maximus snorted. "You know I'm pleased we've finally managed to solve two lines of the riddle," he replied. "It's just I've got other things on my mind tonight."

"Did something happen during your shift?" Cassian asked.

Maximus shook his head. "No ... but afterward I paid Heather a visit." He lifted his cup to his lips and took another gulp of wine. "She has some ... troubles." Maximus tensed as he finished speaking. He didn't like leaving Heather unprotected, for Iain was likely to try to corner her again if given the opportunity.

Damn those Galbraiths. Everywhere he turned, there was one of them ready to complicate his life. Maximus had thought Heather would be safe here within Dunnottar's sheltering walls. But she wouldn't be—not while that man resided here.

"Heather?" Draco spoke up for the first time, his voice an amused drawl. "What's this ... has the cool-headed Maximus lost his head over a woman?"

Maximus cast his friend a jaundiced look, yet didn't dignify the comment with a response. Draco was deliberately baiting him.

"What troubles?" Cassian asked. His tone was light, although his brow was now furrowed. As captain here, he liked to be kept informed.

"Her husband has risen from the dead it seems," Maximus replied, meeting Draco's eye. "He arrived here with you."

Draco inclined his head. "Does he have a name?"

"Iain Galbraith."

The slight narrowing of Draco's gaze told Maximus all he needed to know.

"Galbraith ... there's a smith here by the same name," Cassian spoke up.

"They're brothers," Maximus replied, wondering how much about Heather he should reveal. "Heather and Iain met here a few years back ... before he returned to his home near Stirling and took her with him. He then joined the cause, and when he never returned, everyone believed him dead."

"Galbraith's a hot-head," Draco said finally, "but loyal to the cause. The man accompanied the Wallace to France. He might have had good reasons for not getting in touch with his wife."

"France, eh?" Cassian murmured, pouring himself more wine. "And I take it you joined him and availed yourself of fine food, drink, and women?"

Draco pulled a face, letting Cassian know he didn't think much of his joke. The curse was the same for all three of them: none could cross beyond Scotland's borders, either by land or sea. "I made my excuses and gathered men in the Highlands before waiting for him at Inverness." Draco swirled the wine in his cup. "And how about you, Cassian?" he asked, expertly steering the conversation away from himself. "Been at Dunnottar long?"

"I arrived shortly after Wallace liberated it from the English," Cassian replied.

Draco's eyebrows shot up. "You rose through the ranks quickly."

Cassian snorted. "As did you, I imagine."

Listening to the banter between his friends, Maximus felt a stab of envy.

There it was again. Cassian and Draco had the focus he lacked. Neither of them hailed from this land, yet they'd taken Scotland into their souls in a way he never had. Cassian had proudly served a number of clan-chiefs over the years, as he did De Keith now. Draco was a Moor, a soldier of Hispania who'd been drafted into the Ninth legion. Yet these days, he followed William Wallace and had taken on the Scottish cause.

Of course, Maximus had once believed in a cause. He'd once lived for the glory of Rome. As pilus prior of the first cohort of the Ninth, he'd led his men proudly into Caledonia. But their destruction had turned his pride to ashes. He'd always secretly carried some of the blame for the death of the eight hundred men under his command.

Maybe it was time to let it go.

He'd missed Cassian and Draco. The years passed slowly between the rare times they met up. Yet there was never any need to 'pretend' when he spent time with these two.

"Maximus's friend Heather knows about us," Cassian said then. "It seems she saw him heal from a mortal wound on the way north."

Draco's shoulders tensed at this news. His lean frame stiffened. "Can she keep a secret?" he asked, a hard edge creeping into his voice. "The last thing we need is the folk of Dunnottar coming after us with pitch-forks. I suffered a lynching fifty years ago ... it hurt, and I don't relish the idea of being stoned again either."

Maximus frowned. "Heather can be trusted," he replied, his own tone sharpening.

Silence fell between the three of them then, a little of the easy camaraderie at the table slipping. Draco was scowling, and Cassian had a veiled, watchful expression that warned Maximus he wasn't convinced.

Eventually, Maximus decided he needed to smooth things between them. "Do you think this is it?" he asked, his gaze shifting from Cassian's face to Draco's. "This will be the last time we gather under the Broom-star?"

"Is that hope I hear in your voice?" Draco asked, raising an eyebrow. "I thought you'd given up years ago."

"That's rich coming from you," Maximus countered. "Before you arrived, we were about to take bets whether we'd see you this cycle."

Draco snorted, but refused to rise to the bait. Instead, he flashed Cassian a conspirator's grin. "I think our friend has found something to live for ... he's in love."

Maximus pulled a face. "Arse."

Draco smirked, although Cassian was now watching Maximus with a penetrating look that made him tense. He stroked his chin, his attention never straying from Maximus. "Draco has a point. You do seem ... different these days. Last time we met, you barely raised a smile."

Maximus shrugged, schooling his face into an aloof expression both of them knew well. It was a warning to leave this topic alone. They had a point though—he did feel different these days. The change had been recent; he knew the exact moment the shield of ice around his heart had started to thaw.

The day he'd met Heather De Keith.

She's still married, a small voice within warned him. *Keep away from her.*

The Great Bull-Slayer strike him down, he wanted that woman. That was why he'd gone looking for her this evening. He literally couldn't keep his distance from Heather. He knew he wasn't good for her, that he couldn't give her the things she desired, but he'd sought her out nonetheless.

But Iain Galbraith's presence at Dunnottar dumped a bucket of icy water over his ardor. For a few moments, he'd worried that she'd lied to him all along, but when he'd stared into her eyes, he realized she was telling the truth.

Not that it mattered. He had no wish to draw attention to himself here, or to bring trouble down upon him or his friends. Too much was at stake, and he couldn't afford to get sidetracked.

Cassian and Draco's comments made him wary. He'd be a fool to get involved, especially since Heather's situation was complicated. As lovely as she was, he needed to keep his distance from her now.

Cassian cleared his throat then, breaking the tension. "Enough distractions ... we need to get to work if we're ever going to solve the rest of the curse." He pushed aside his cup of wine and rose to his feet. "Follow me ... I have something to show you both."

Maximus followed his friends down the narrow, twisting steps beyond the curtain walls—the steps leading to Dunnottar's dungeons. He wasn't sure why Cassian was leading him and Draco there, but it appeared he had a plan.

The wind buffeted them, the scream of gulls and the boom of surf against the rocks loud now they were outside the castle's sheltering walls. Maximus breathed in the scent of salt and seaweed, and enjoyed the warmth of the setting sun on his face. After months of bleak weather, the sun finally had some force to it—although it was nothing like the searing summer heat of his homeland.

He made his way down the cliff face, trying to ignore the precipitous drop to his right. Of course, he'd survive a fall to the jagged rocks below. Even so, heights had always made his belly lurch.

Dunnottar's dungeons had been dug into the cliff. A wide stone archway greeted the trio when they stepped into an entrance way. Beyond it, yet more steps led up into a dark tunnel.

Four men stood guard in the entrance. They snapped to attention upon spying Cassian.

"Evening, Captain!" One of them greeted him.

"Good eve, Bard," Cassian replied. "Are the prisoners behaving themselves?"

"Like lambs, Captain," another guard replied earnestly.

"Good to hear."

Maximus and Draco exchanged wry smiles at this. They'd already noticed the camaraderie that Cassian had with his men. He walked the thin line between friendship and respect easily. After once leading a huge cohort of soldiers, Maximus knew that inspiring such loyalty was much harder than it looked. The Wallace had managed, yet many leaders failed.

Taking a torch from the guard nearest, Cassian led the way into the damp, dark tunnel beyond. Low stone arches stretched overhead, barely high enough for a tall man to walk under without stooping. Maximus breathed in damp, musty air before the stench of unwashed bodies and unemptied chamber pots made him screw his nose up. He took smaller, shallower breaths then, in an attempt to keep the unsavory odors at bay.

They passed a handful of cells carved out of the stone. Around half of them were occupied. Prisoners in ragged clothing, beards covering their faces, watched them pass. Their gazes glinted from the shadowed recesses of their cells.

"What are these men's crimes?" Draco asked, deliberately keeping his voice low.

"Two of them are cattle rustlers, due to be hanged on the walls within a day or two," Cassian informed him. "The other three are men who personally crossed David De Keith."

Draco raised a questioning eyebrow before shifting to Latin. "The man makes enemies? He seems pretty ineffectual to me."

Cassian huffed a laugh. "Don't be fooled. He's got a vindictive streak the folk here have grown wary of," he replied in the same tongue. "De Keith is an adder sleeping in the grass ... underestimate the man at your peril."

They'd reached the back of the dungeon now, where Cassian led the way down a narrow conduit. Both Maximus and Draco had fallen silent as they digested these words. They followed Cassian toward the end of the narrow passage, passing a chamber on the way. It was more like a large alcove, but the moment Maximus's gaze swept over the interior—taking in the twin stone benches lining the space, the carven wooden effigy of a bull upon a stone altar, and the faint scent of incense— something within him unknotted.

It was a simply furnished space. Two flaming torches replaced the usual statues of torchbearers—yet the purpose of this place was unmistakable.

"You've built a mithraeum here," Maximus murmured.

XXXII

SEARCHING FOR THE KEY

CASSIAN SMILED IN response. "This used to be a store area ... but I decided to repurpose it. Feel free to use the shrine whenever you want."

Maximus intended to. He was on edge this eve—still coming to terms with the fact that Heather wasn't actually a widow, and that her bully of a husband wanted her back.

Of course, Maximus had his leontocephaline for when he wanted to say a prayer. Draco had carved the lion-headed figurine out of marble for him many centuries earlier, and it had been his constant companion over the years. But perhaps the sanctuary of the mithraeum, and more prayer to the Bull-slayer, would help focus his thoughts.

"Follow me," Cassian continued on a few steps farther, to a where a wooden door blocked their way. Opening it, he led them into what appeared to be a tiny study. A table lined with low wooden benches dominated the space. A stack of leather-bound books sat upon it. Leaves of parchment lay scattered across the table, and a pot of ink sat next to a cup holding a collection of quills.

"What have you been doing in here?" Draco asked, his obsidian gaze sweeping the cramped chamber.

"Searching for answers," Cassian replied, closing the door behind them. He lit the sconces upon the wall with his torch before lodging it into a bracket. Warm light now flooded the cramped space.

"And these books?" Maximus moved to the table and picked up the volume at the top of the stack. "*A History of the Kings of Alba*," he read aloud. "Where did you get this?"

Cassian's mouth quirked. "I *borrowed* them from the laird's library."

Maximus glanced up. "Without asking first, I take it?"

"Fortunately, he's not much of a reader ... Lady Elizabeth or Lady Gavina are more likely to notice there are books missing."

Draco frowned. "And if they do?"

"I doubt they'd suspect me ... how many soldiers do you know who can read?"

He had a point. Out of the three of them, only Maximus had been able to read and write in Latin centuries earlier. But over the years, they'd all learned the various dialects and tongues of this land.

How else could they ever break the curse?

Maximus traced his fingertips over the cover of the book, a shiver rippling down his spine. These histories were incredibly valuable to them.

"Only two lines left to decipher," he said softly, voicing his thoughts aloud. "Surely, one of these volumes holds the key?"

"I've just started on this pile," Cassian admitted with a rueful smile. "But it'll be much faster with you two helping me."

Draco nodded. He drew close to the table, his gaze still searching the chamber. "I don't suppose you've got some ale? I guess we'll be spending a bit of time in here."

"There's a barrel in the corner, and some cups ... pour each of us a drink. Even Maximus. He can suffer ale instead of wine for a change."

Maximus snorted at this, yet didn't protest. Like Draco, he was eager to get started, eager to help Cassian trawl through the stories in these books. Somewhere, there had to be a mention of 'the Hammer' and its significance to this fortress. Or maybe they would find out what the 'White Hawk' and the 'Dragon' actually referred to.

"You've done well, Cass," he said, taking a seat at the table. "I know it feels like we've still got so far to go ... but we'll get there."

Cassian smiled in response. Then, as Draco got up to pour them all some ale, he lowered himself onto a bench opposite Maximus and reached for the next book on the top of the stack. "That damn riddle won't beat us this time," he vowed, determination lighting in his hazel eyes.

"I can't believe ye actually hit him." Aila's hushed voice was full of awe. She was sat up in bed, the covers tucked up under her chin, watching her sister with wide eyes. "Didn't it hurt yer hand?"

"Like the devil," Heather replied, drawing a brush through her hair. She then glanced down at where her knuckles were reddened. She'd barely noticed at the time, for fury had pulsed through her like a stoked ember. However, when she'd gone upstairs, her hand had started to ache. Heather flexed her fingers. It still did.

The ache reminded her of the mess she'd made of things. Maximus would keep his distance from her now, while Iain was likely to approach her again at some stage. Queasiness churned in her belly. She felt cornered, hunted, when all she wanted was a peaceful life.

Meanwhile, her sister continued to stare at her with that probing, slightly-hurt look she remembered well from when they'd been bairns. The look Aila gave her when her elder sister kept secrets.

"Why didn't ye tell me ye were working as a serving wench?" she asked softly.

Heather put down the hairbrush on the mantelpiece. She stood by the glowing hearth, enjoying the heat that seeped through the thin fabric of her night-rail. Although they were well into spring now, she'd forgotten how cold this castle could be all year round.

"Ye know why," she replied softly. "Ma would have had a fit."

"Ye could have sworn me to secrecy."

Heather cocked an eyebrow. "Ye mean she didn't rip my letters from ye and read them herself?"

Aila drew herself up, irritation flashing across her features. "Of course not! I'm no longer a lass … she knows better than to do that!"

Heather smiled at her sister's fire. Aila De Keith was no longer the blushing sixteen-year-old that Heather had left behind. She was twenty-one and maid to the Lady of Dunnottar. Heather was pleased to see that although Aila had inherited her father's quiet nature, she also had his spine.

It would serve her well in future. Life rode roughshod over the meek.

With a sigh, she went to the bed, lifted the covers, and climbed in next to Aila. It felt strange to be sharing a bed with her again, after all this time. Heather had gotten used to sleeping alone. However, there wasn't a chamber available for her.

Heather didn't mind really. She'd missed Aila during her time in Fintry. Sharing a room again meant that they'd have a proper chance to talk without their mother eavesdropping.

"Ma was quiet this evening," Heather said, lying back and staring at the wooden rafters above them.

"She's in shock … she thought Iain was going to cut Da's throat," Aila replied, her tone sharpening. "We both did."

Heather swallowed. "I had no idea Iain would do that ... he's grown even harder since he went away."

"I don't think our parents blame ye, if that's what's worrying ye," Aila said softly. She too lay down, although she rolled over on her side and propped herself up onto an elbow so she could study her sister's face. Once again, Heather felt uncomfortable under her assessing stare. "I certainly don't."

Heather shifted her attention from the rafters to her sister's face. "It's good to be back," she murmured, her throat thickening. "I just didn't want to cause problems."

"We're all happy to have ye here," Aila replied, placing a hand over Heather's, which rested upon the coverlet. Her sister's mouth curved then. "Even if ye are like a tempest."

Heather snorted. Their father had always called her that as a bairn—a tempest that raced through the castle, all long brown hair and skinny limbs. "I don't mean to be."

Aila's smile widened. "And of course, we're all dying to know more about that man ye traveled here with."

Heather heaved a deep breath. She'd been awaiting this moment, dreading it actually. She'd known Aila would interrogate her about Maximus sooner or later. Thinking about him made her chest ache. Yearning rose up within her. She couldn't let Iain ruin things between them. She just couldn't.

"There's not much to tell," she lied. "I needed an escort to Dunnottar, and Maximus provided it."

"The way he looks at ye though," Aila replied, her expression turning dreamy. "No man has *ever* looked at me like that."

Heat spread across Heather's chest at her sister's observation. "How exactly does he look at me?" she asked, feigning a lack of interest even as her pulse quickened.

A grin flowered across Aila's face, and an uncharacteristically wicked gleam lit her eyes. "Like he wants to devour ye."

XXXIII

LONGING

"OUCH!" HEATHER DROPPED the needle and raised her hand, frowning as blood beaded on her finger. *Lucifer take this embroidery.* She didn't have the patience for it.

Seated at the window seat in her parents solar, she was currently alone with her sewing—and her errant thoughts. Aila was attending Lady Gavina, her father was out overseeing things with the laird, and her mother was taking a walk in the upper ward with Lady Elizabeth.

It was a rare moment of solitude.

The window was open, letting in a warm morning breeze. Fluffy white clouds chased each other over a wide pastel-blue sky, and the air smelled of the sea and sunshine. It was a glorious day, yet a shadow lay across Heather.

Five long days had passed since she'd last seen Maximus.

Granted, she hadn't gone looking for him, even if the urge to do so grew stronger with each passing day.

The incident with Iain had left her shaken, and so she stayed within the walls of the keep, not even venturing out into the upper or lower wards for a stroll as she'd have liked. Instead, she either spent time with her parents in their solar, helping her mother with needlework while her father worked, or she visited Lady Gavina.

Heather's mouth compressed then.

Each visit to Lady Gavina made her increasingly nervous. She wondered if the lady had heard she wasn't actually a widow, and had an estranged husband inside the keep. But Lady Gavina hadn't said a word. Instead, the two women continued to spend companionable afternoons in each other's company.

With a sigh, Heather picked up her needle and resumed work on the pillowcase she was embroidering. Despite the sunlight that bathed her face and the peace here, high in the tower, her mood was low. A dull, permanent ache had lodged itself under her breastbone, and her usually robust appetite had faded.

I miss him.

Why didn't Maximus seek her out? Was he deliberately avoiding her?

Part of her understood why he might do so, yet another part grieved.

Melancholy wasn't an emotion that Heather understood well. Lady Gavina's gaze was often shadowed by a sadness she never voiced, yet Heather told herself *she* was too practical, too focused on her daily life to succumb to such feelings. As such, she'd tried to ignore the creeping sense of loss at first. Instead, she kept herself busy and worked on rebuilding her still fragile rapport with her parents.

Heather stared down at the rose she was embroidering, her vision blurring as tears welled.

The longing was growing unbearable. It was no good. She would have to seek Maximus out. It wasn't wise. Indeed, it was foolish and rash; yet the more she tried to squash the desire, the stronger it became.

She knew he'd be busy with Cassian and Draco, but surely he had time for her too?

Heather was mulling over this, and trying to think about the best way to approach Maximus without drawing too much attention to herself, when the door to the solar burst open.

Her mother rushed in. Her face was flushed, her eyes bright with excitement. "We've been invited to join the laird at his table for supper tonight!" she announced.

Heather straightened up, surprised. As a rule, Heather and her kin sat apart from the De Keith in the hall. It was rare to break bread with the laird at his own table.

Heather swallowed down the nervous sensation that fluttered in her belly. Truth be told, she didn't want to sup with the laird at all. She'd been successful in avoiding David De Keith since her arrival, and she'd hoped to keep it that way. The memory of how he'd cornered her that day on the stairwell years earlier had never faded.

"This is wonderful news," Iona stopped in the middle of the solar and clasped her hands together. However, the excitement dimmed in her eyes when her gaze settled upon Heather.

Her mouth flattened into a hard line as she took in her daughter's simple green kirtle. "This is the third day in a row ye have worn that," she chided. "Don't ye have any other kirtles?"

Heather shook her head. "I'm hoping to buy cloth for some at Stonehaven market next week."

Iona De Keith started to twist the wedding band on her left hand, her gaze narrowing. "Next week is no good. What will ye wear tonight?"

"This kirtle will do me fine," Heather replied with a shrug. "I'll do something with my hair and wear a shawl, if ye like?"

"No," her mother snapped. Irritation flared in her eyes. "That won't do at all. Really, Heather, yer father and I have a position to uphold. Now ye've returned, we need to see about getting ye accepted at Dunnottar once more. One of mine or Aila's gowns will have to suffice."

Iona fussed all afternoon, taking care to choose the right kirtle to wear, and insisting that her daughters made a similar effort. Heather was forced to borrow another of Aila's kirtles. However, her sister was slightly shorter than her and had a smaller bust. As such, the gown revealed a little too much of the lèine she wore underneath, at the hem, and certainly more cleavage than she'd have liked.

Heather really didn't want to see the laird with her breasts on display like this—she remembered David's lecherous glances well. Unfortunately though, there were no other suitable formal kirtles, and so Heather was forced to don this ill-fitting one.

The hall was busy when the steward and his family entered: men and women were taking their seats at the long tables that lined the room. Outdoors, it was a mild evening, and the huge shuttered windows on the long side of the hall had been opened wide, giving splendid views in each direction over the rocky coastline and the sea. The days drew out this time of year, and so dusk was still some way off—as such, the sun sparkled off the North Sea.

Heather's step slowed as she admired the view. Nothing compared to the panorama from these windows. She felt like an eagle perched high in its mountain eyrie, surveying the world from above.

Unfortunately, she couldn't stop to gaze upon the view, for her mother pushed her forward, propelling her toward the far end of the long chamber.

The seating at the laird's table had been rearranged this evening, so that the steward and his family flanked David's left, and his wife and retainers sat to his right. Heather took a seat between her mother and sister, opposite Lady Elizabeth, the former mistress of Dunnottar.

William Wallace had also joined them this eve. Heather's pulse quickened at the sight of the freedom fighter. The keep had been abuzz ever since his arrival. Lady Gavina had confided in Heather that he'd chosen the stronghold as a place to lie low for the time being.

Shifting her attention from the Wallace, Heather favored Lady Elizabeth with a smile. She noted the strained expression on the woman's face. She was still young, yet her face had a sternness to it that Heather didn't recall from years earlier. Dressed in a charcoal-grey kirtle, her golden hair pulled back into a severe style, she appeared a widow in mourning. But as far as Heather understood, Robert—the rightful laird of this castle—was an English prisoner, not dead.

To the laird's right, Lady Gavina sat as silent and poised as always. Dressed in a high-necked blue gown, the Lady of Dunnottar was a vision of loveliness. Still, her husband didn't spare his bonny wife a glance. Instead, he launched into a discussion with Heather's father—quizzing him over the accounts.

Such conversation wasn't of the slightest interest to Heather, and so she let her gaze travel across the table again. Captain Gaius sat next to Lady Elizabeth, and on sensing Heather's attention upon him, his gaze flicked up from where he was cutting himself some venison.

Their gazes held for a moment before Cassian's mouth curved into a polite smile. "You must be Heather?"

Like Maximus, Cassian spoke Gaelic with a light, lilting accent. Maximus had told her Cassian was a Spaniard. His looks weren't as swarthy as Maximus's, and he had a taller, broader build that was more similar to her countrymen.

"Aye," she replied with an answering smile. Hope flowered in her breast then. Maybe this man would help her. He'd know where Maximus was this evening. "And ye are Captain Gaius ... my father speaks highly of ye."

His smile widened. "That's pleasing to hear." His gaze flicked to where Aila sat next to Heather, unusually silent. "I can tell you two are sisters ... the similarity between you is remarkable."

Heather grinned. "Aye ... although folk have always said that Aila's the prettier of the two of us." She nudged her sister with her elbow as she spoke, noting how Aila's cheeks grew pink. It was cruel to tease her when she plainly turned tongue-tied in this man's presence. However, Heather couldn't help herself.

Cassian's smile softened, his attention resting on Aila for a moment longer. Heather noted that he didn't contradict her.

Farther down the table, William Wallace was talking to his captain. From what Maximus had told her, this was Draco Vulcan, the last of the cursed trio. Listening to his leader, the soldier wore an intense, almost fierce expression. Something about him made Heather uneasy—the man exuded a leashed aggression, his lean body coiled like a hawk about to dive for prey.

She wasn't sure she'd trust him.

Shifting her attention back to Cassian, Heather noted that he was observing her with a shuttered expression—almost as if he was taking her measure.

Nervousness rippled down Heather's spine. *Has Maximus told him that I know their secret?* She hoped he hadn't, yet the captain's look contradicted that hope. What if Cassian and Draco perceived her as a threat?

Clearing her throat, she forced another smile. "How is Maximus faring? I haven't seen him since our first evening here." She wanted to ask a more direct question than that but knew she had to ease into it.

Cassian inclined his head. "He's fitted into the Guard well."

"Didn't ye say he worked as a trapper before, Heather?" Aila asked, seeming to have found her tongue for the first time since sitting down at the table. Heather wished she hadn't.

"Aye … but he was a soldier before that," Heather assured her. She knew what her sister was getting at; it was indeed odd that a complete stranger would turn up at Dunnottar and be accepted so easily into the Guard.

"Maximus is an able fighter," Cassian agreed, his expression giving nothing away. "He's an asset to the Guard."

Ask him where Maximus is this eve. Now's yer chance!

Soon Cassian's attention would be drawn elsewhere and the opportunity would be lost. She had to ask him before that happened. Heather's lips parted as the words rose within her—but another man's voice echoed down the table, interrupting their conversation.

"Heather ... what a delight it is to have ye back at Dunnottar."

Tensing, Heather turned to find David De Keith watching her. She'd thought he'd been occupied with her father, yet he focused on her now, his brown eyes gleaming. His lean, bearded face was composed in a charming expression.

Heather dipped her chin respectfully. "Good eve, Laird De Keith."

"What a fair sight ye are," he continued, his voice booming down the table. He held his silver goblet up for a passing servant to refill, "although can I say, ye are even bonnier than I recall."

Heather's skin prickled. She didn't want the laird's compliments, not when she knew what he was really like. His words had caused the conversation around them to die away. Heather could feel Lady Gavina and Lady Elizabeth's gazes upon her, and when she glanced down the table, she saw that Cassian, the Wallace, and Draco were now all observing the exchange between her and the laird too.

Heather plastered a pleasant smile to her face, yet didn't answer. The sooner De Keith resumed his conversation with her father, the better.

But he wasn't finished with her yet.

"I'm sorry to hear ye have lost yer husband," he said smoothly.

Heather's belly clenched. Obviously, news of Iain Galbraith coming back from the dead hadn't reached him. She dropped her gaze to the table, resisting the urge to glance across at the two ladies opposite. Surely, they both knew that she wasn't a widow. Would one of them say something?

"Hopefully, we can find a role for ye in the castle now ye have returned," De Keith continued, his voice lowering in a sensual way that made Heather's throat close.

Heart pounding, she stared down at the platter of food before her that she no longer had any appetite for. She wished the odious man would stop talking.

"Heather has been a companion to me since her return." A cool female voice interjected then. "I value her company and wish her to remain at my side."

Lady Gavina's interruption soured the laird's mood. Heather glanced up to see that his charming smile had dissolved, replaced by a scowl. He then shifted his attention to his wife, for the first time since the meal had begun. "Ye already have a lady's maid," he muttered.

"But I also require a companion," she replied calmly, holding his eye. "Since my husband spends very little time with me."

David De Keith stared at his wife, open dislike in his eyes, before his expression shuttered. "As ye wish," he said with an airy wave of his hand. "I care not."

He looked as if he was about to say something else, when something beyond their table drew his eye.

A guard had entered the hall and was striding toward the laird's table, a scroll clutched in his right hand. Twisting in her seat, Heather watched the man approach.

"What's this?" De Keith greeted the guard. "Can't ye see I'm in the midst of supper, man?"

The guard's rugged face tensed. "A rider has just brought this from Drum Castle. He said the matter was urgent."

The laird's mouth pursed, and he cast his wife a sharp look. "What does yer brother want?"

Lady Gavina frowned. "I wouldn't know, David. I haven't heard from him since our father died."

Heather stilled at this news. She hadn't realized the Irvine laird had passed away. Lady Gavina hadn't said. That wouldn't help relations between the two clans; it was rumored that Shaw Irvine, Gavina's elder brother, had never wanted to make peace with the De Keiths.

Dismissing his wife's comment, De Keith snatched the scroll, broke the wax seal, and scanned the missive's contents.

XXXIV

UNWELCOME

"WHAT IS IT, De Keith?" William Wallace called from
the opposite end of the table. "Ye look like ye just shat
yerself."

A rumble of laughter followed this comment.
However, David De Keith didn't look amused. His gaze
narrowed, and when he lowered the scroll, Heather
noted his hands were shaking.

Face ashen, he turned his gaze upon his wife once
more, ignoring Wallace completely. "I'll have yer brother
strung up by his balls for this insult," he rasped.

Lady Gavina's eyes widened. "What's Shaw done?"

The laird's fingers tightened around the parchment.
He then raised it once more and began to read aloud. "I
duly inform ye that the valley upon the border we share
has always been Irvine land," he read, biting out each
word. "Of late, De Keith cottars have presumed to build
hovels upon it. I hereby order that ye remove them."

A mutter of anger went up at nearby tables, for other
De Keiths had overheard their laird.

"Wait," the laird barked. "That's not the end of it."
Clearing his throat, he continued to read, "Furthermore,
I insist that ye also give up the meadows south of that

valley, for they too belong to us. My father allowed ye to encroach, but I will not. Yield these lands, or I will come to Dunnottar to enforce my rightful claim. I urge ye not to bother cowering behind the walls, for if ye do, I shall use my new siege weapon—The Battle Hammer—to flush ye out. It is a great, iron-tipped battering ram. I will strike it against the gates of Dunnottar until they shatter, and then ye shall have no choice but to face me."

De Keith's voice choked off there while muttering rose up around him.

"How dare he make such threats?" Lady Elizabeth gasped. "Has he forgotten the truce between our families?"

De Keith snarled a curse, his gaze boring into his wife now. "Clearly. The bastard never intended to honor it. I married an Irvine for *nothing*."

Gavina had gone pale, her blue eyes huge and pleading. "I don't understand why Shaw would behave this way," she whispered. "I know he was against our marriage ... but—"

"He was waiting for this," De Keith exploded, cutting his wife off. "As soon as yer father died, he couldn't wait to restart the feud."

"Will ye yield those lands to him?" Wallace asked, his powerful voice intruding once more.

This time, the laird turned to the freedom fighter, staring him down. "Never," he snarled.

Supper concluded swiftly. De Keith tossed Irvine's missive upon the fire and started drinking heavily. Sensing their laird wished to be left alone, the surrounding retainers and guests started to rise from their seats and file from the hall. Outdoors, the sun was now setting in a blaze of red and gold; the fiery sunset reflected off the rippling surface of the sea.

Heather glanced Cassian's way when he got to his feet. She saw him lean down and whisper something quickly to Draco. Then, he edged his way along the table and made for the door.

Heather's pulse sped up. With the arrival of the missive, her opportunity to question Cassian about Maximus's whereabouts had been lost. But she had to speak to him before he left.

Hurrying ahead of her parents and sister, Heather caught up with Cassian as he neared the doors. "Captain," she gasped. "Can I speak to ye a moment?"

Cassian turned to her, irritation flaring in his hazel eyes. He favored her with a curt nod, his big body tense with purpose. He had the look of a man who wished to be elsewhere. Heather really didn't want to bother him, but this couldn't wait.

She was aware that in a few moments her family would be within earshot. She needed to speak quickly or the opportunity would be lost. "I wish to speak to Maximus. Where can I find him this evening?"

Cassian stared down at her, his brow furrowing. The moment drew out, and Heather's breathing stilled, her pulse now racing. Was he going to refuse to tell her?

"Please," she continued, hoping that the desperation didn't show in her voice. "I won't disturb him for long."

Cassian's mouth compressed before he finally answered. "He's taking the watch atop the upper ward's north tower. When ye find him, can ye pass on the message that I must speak with him ... urgently. I'll be in the dungeon."

Heather stepped out into the upper ward bailey and immediately wished she'd returned to her chamber to fetch a shawl. A crisp breeze blew in from the sea, its chill feathering across her bare arms and cleavage.

This low-cut kirtle didn't cover enough flesh. However, she risked being waylaid by her family if she went back for a shawl. She'd hurried from the hall before any of them could stop her.

She was aware of male gazes tracking her as she walked along the wall toward where the north tower rose against the sky. There were men on guard on the upper ward walls, and one or two turned to watch her progress. She felt exposed, and as such, hurried her pace.

Yanking open the tower door, she took the stairs that led past the guard room and up to the roof.

Two figures stood watch up here, outlined against the setting sun.

And as Cassian had said, one of the guards was Maximus.

Hearing footfalls on the stairs, both men had turned, their hands reaching for the hilts of the swords at their hips. However, upon spying Heather, they both stilled.

Maximus recovered first. "Heather … what are you doing up here?"

It wasn't the warmest welcome she'd ever received. Despite that it had been days since they'd seen each other last, he didn't even favor her with a smile. Instead, his dark brows knitted together and his jaw tensed.

A cold sensation settled in the pit of Heather's belly. *He's not pleased to see me.*

Heather shoved the worry aside. She'd done nothing to anger him; there was no reason why he wouldn't want a visit from her. It wasn't her fault that her husband had returned from the dead.

Aye, but it's hardly appropriate, her conscience needled her.

Heather ignored it. Despite that she was happy to be reunited with her family, and relieved that Lady Gavina had taken her under her wing, the gnawing sense of emptiness couldn't be borne.

Their journey north had been fraught with danger and discomfort, yet she'd never felt so alive. Being in Maximus's company made the world seem brighter. Seeing him now, standing just a few feet from her, made the ache under her breastbone increase in intensity.

Lord, how I've missed ye.

"I'm here to see ye," she replied, flashing him a smile and feigning a confidence she suddenly lacked. "Can we speak?"

Maximus's jaw tensed, and then his gaze shifted to the guard across from him. The man was smirking, a knowing glint in his eye.

"I won't be long," Maximus muttered with a nod to the guard. He then stalked across to Heather, took her by the arm, and led her back to the stairwell. The grip on her arm was firm, and Heather stiffened at the way he marched her off the tower top. She didn't appreciate being manhandled.

"Take all the time ye need, lad," the guard called out behind them, laughter in his voice. "I would."

Heather bristled. Why were men so crude?

Unspeaking, Maximus led her down to the chamber beneath the roof. He ushered her into the guard room—a small space furnished only with a table and a couple of chairs. Shutting the door behind them, he then turned to Heather.

"This is a poor idea, Heather ... folk talk."

Heather drew herself up, her shoulders squaring. "Let them ... I'm permitted to walk around this castle and to see whomever I please."

"Didn't I tell you to be careful?"

Heather lifted her chin, irritation surging. "And I have been," she countered. "I've hardly left my parents' rooms in the last week ... the walls are starting to close in on me."

"Galbraith will still be looking for you," he pointed out, folding his arms across his chest. "He'll be waiting for you to take a stroll alone ... you do realize that?"

"Of course, I do," Heather snapped. "But I wanted to see ye ... although right now, I'm wondering why I bothered."

"You shouldn't have sought me out ... it'll only compromise you."

Heather stilled, heat igniting in the pit of her belly and radiating up into her chest. It wasn't from annoyance, but embarrassment.

"How did you even know I was up here?" he demanded, clearly determined to make her feel even more unwelcome.

"Captain Gaius told me," she replied, taking a step back from him. How she wished she had a shawl. Now that they were alone, she was painfully aware of all the skin she had on show. "And don't scowl like that ... he wasn't happy about giving me the details."

Silence fell between them, tension rising to fill it. Heather's throat constricted. His unfriendliness stung. She felt like weeping—not that she would in front of him.

"I've missed ye," she said finally, her voice barely above a whisper. "The days have been long without yer company ... and I thought that ... maybe ... ye felt the same way. But I see I was wrong."

Those words cost her. Heather wasn't the type to bottle things up. She wasn't like her bashful sister, or the stoic Lady Gavina. She'd suffer for being so open, but she would tell him anyway.

Yet Maximus appeared carven from stone. He merely stood there watching her with a narrowed gaze, his shoulders braced as if to ward her off.

Heather's vision blurred when he didn't answer. Damn him, the man was going to make her cry after all. She couldn't let him see it.

It hit her then that she'd made her greatest mistake yet—she'd lost her heart to Maximus Cato. And he didn't feel the same way.

"I'll go now," she continued, hating the rasp to her voice. "Oh, and Captain Gaius wants to speak with ye ... it sounded urgent." With that, she stepped around him and reached for the door handle. The faster she got away from here the better. What terrible instincts she had— what a foolish goose she was.

But before she could open the door, Maximus stepped forward to block her way, his hand fastening over her outstretched arm. "Wait."

XXXV

I'LL WAIT FOR YE

THE FEEL OF her naked skin under his fingers made Maximus's heart jolt against his ribs.

Hades take him, what was this woman doing? She'd stepped out onto the tower roof like a siren, beckoning him to his ruin.

And that kirtle she wore—could the neckline dive any lower?

Every man on the northern walls would have seen her make her way here, would have ogled the creamy swell of her cleavage. She was every red-blooded man's dream come to life, and she was standing right before him.

He wasn't made of stone.

Whatever Cassian wants, it can wait.

Gripping her arm, Maximus pushed her backward two strides so that her spine hit the wall. Then he released her arm, his palm burning from the contact, and placed his hands either side of her shoulders, boxing her in.

Heather stared up at him, those luminous grey-green eyes glittering with unshed tears.

He hadn't meant to, but he'd hurt her.

Yet he couldn't believe she'd taken such a risk by coming to find him. Over the past week, he'd spotted Galbraith from time to time. The man watched him with a malevolent eye, his gaze simmering with resentment. Heather was still in danger from her estranged husband, but this evening she'd thrown caution aside in order to see him.

"I've missed you, Heather," he rasped. He couldn't the bear the hurt in her eyes. "All I can think of is you ... but I've stayed away to protect you."

Her throat bobbed before she spoke, her own voice husky now. "I don't need protecting."

"Yes, you do. Wherever you go, trouble follows, woman." His gaze dipped to where her breasts now rose and fell sharply, just inches away from his touch. "And then you come out to find me dressed like *this*?"

"My family was invited to take supper with the laird this eve," she replied, indignation lacing her voice. "This was the only decent kirtle of Aila's that fitted me."

"It *doesn't* fit you," he growled back. "You're virtually spilling out of it. My friend up on the roof started drooling at the sight of you."

Her lips parted at his words, and Maximus found himself distracted by her mouth. That plump lower lip would be his undoing.

"I don't want to stay away from ye," Heather said finally, her voice barely above a whisper. Her cheeks were flushed now; standing this close together was affecting her as much as it did him. "These past days have made me realize that I'm in love with ye, Maximus. I want us to be together."

Maximus's breathing hitched. *Mithras, Lord of Light, save me*. This woman was so bold. He adored it, loved how she spoke what was on her mind, in her heart—even if she wanted the impossible.

"But you know what I am," he said finally, his voice roughening once more as he fought a sudden tightness in his chest. "You can't bind yourself to an immortal."

"I can." She lifted a hand to his chest, her fingers splaying over his heart.

"But I can't give you a family ... you know that."

"That doesn't matter. I only need ye ... nothing else."

Maximus's belly clenched. "You say that now ... but with the passing of the years, you'd grow to hate me for denying you bairns."

"I'd *never* do that," she countered, her eyes gleaming. "And if ye break the curse ... none of this will matter."

"But we might not this time." He could feel the heat of her hand, even through the thick leather of his vest. It was making it difficult for him to think. "I will have to wait another seventy-odd years for the Broom-star to reappear ... and in the meantime, you will grow old and eventually die ... and I will have to watch."

For the first time, Maximus truly understood how Cassian had felt when he'd lost his beloved wife centuries earlier. The agony must have been unbearable. Maximus didn't want to weather such pain. He saw the toll it had taken on his friend.

"Aye ... I will age and one day die," Heather replied, her gaze never leaving his. "But my love for ye won't. Even after I leave this world, my love for ye will echo across eternity ... and one day, when ye break the curse, our souls will meet again. I'll wait for ye, Maximus. To the end of time itself ... I will always wait for ye."

He stared at her, his throat aching. "Heather," he whispered her name in a plea. "I don't think I could bear it."

"Ye would," she countered, her voice firm now. "Think about it ... few lovers leave this world at the same moment." Her mouth quirked then, even if her gaze was serious. "I'd just have to wait a little longer than most for my love to join me."

"But what about Iain Galbraith?" He was grasping to hold on to control now, trying to anchor himself in the reality that was slipping away. "You're still a wedded woman."

Her gaze didn't waver. "Aye ... but he'll leave Dunnottar eventually."

"But you'll still be his wife, Heather."

Her gaze widened. "Ye want to wed me?"

"Of course I do," he ground out the words, his heart beating so fast now he felt sick. With that he stepped close, cupped her face with his hands, and kissed her.

And the moment he did so, he was lost.

He was immortal, but that didn't mean he had a will of iron. There was only so much he could take. The softness of her lips under his stripped away the last of his self-control.

How things had changed since that night at *The Bogside*. He'd been in command of his feelings then; the night had been an escape, had been nothing but pleasure. He'd enjoyed her but had been content to leave things be afterward.

But now, just a fortnight later, he wasn't the same man.

Somehow Heather had gotten under his skin. He had a beating heart after all. The feelings she roused in him were raw, wild, and dangerous. They made him reckless.

All he wanted was to be with this woman, to lose himself in her.

Heather groaned, and he parted her lips with his tongue and tasted her, hungry for her. Within moments, he was lost, the last remnants of his self-restraint sloughing away.

He was supposed to be standing guard on the roof above—but suddenly he didn't care about that.

He didn't care about anything except this, except Heather.

She kissed him back with a hunger equal to his own, her fingers clutching at him. She unlaced his vest, and Maximus shrugged it off, his mouth never leaving hers. At *The Bogside*, he'd spent the night taking his pleasure slowly, exploring her. But not now.

Breathing hard, he broke the kiss and reached forward, unlacing her kirtle. Then, he pushed the garment off her shoulders, sliding both it and the lèine she wore underneath down so that her ripe breasts were exposed to him.

She had the most beautiful breasts he'd ever seen— large and rose-tipped, the skin the color of milk. And with a groan of surrender, he lowered his head and feasted upon them. He drew each swollen nipple deep into his mouth, suckling hard.

Heather's soft cry echoed through the chamber, her hands sliding over his shoulders and up to his head. Her fingers dug into his scalp, urging him on.

She was wild, lusty, and unforgettable.

And Maximus would go mad if he had to wait much longer.

With a growl, he released her breasts and stepped back, pulling her with him. He lifted her up onto the table, shoving her skirts up around her hips. Heather wantonly spread her legs for him, her breathing coming in excited gasps. The sight of her nakedness exposed to him made the aching in his groin almost unbearable.

Staring down at her, he unlaced his braies and released his swollen shaft. It twitched in its eagerness for this woman, and her gaze widened at the sight of his rod. Reaching out, she wrapped her fingers around his girth, a pleading whimper escaping her.

It was no good. He couldn't wait.

Grabbing hold of Heather's hips, he yanked her hard against him as he pushed inside her, working his way in to the hilt. The tight heat of her—the way she stretched to accommodate his shaft, her hips undulating to welcome him—made a deep groan well up within him.

She felt unbelievable. They fitted together perfectly.

Maximus took her hard on that table—there was no gentleness in it at all. Each thrust bordered on violence, and yet she moved against him with a ferocity equal to his own. The table rocked and thudded against the stone floor, yet neither of them paid it any mind. Heather's head fell back to expose the long, pale column of her throat. Those magnificent breasts rose each time he drove into her. She wrapped her legs about his hips, drawing him even deeper with each plunge.

He felt her body begin to shake and tremble, felt the rush of wet heat deep inside her, but he didn't stop. Instead, her response sent him over the edge.

And for the first time since the cursing, he forgot who he was. All the long, weary years of his life faded, and the future ceased to matter. All he cared about, all he wanted in life, was right here with him.

His climax rose swiftly then, driving him into oblivion. His vision darkened, and for a moment, he thought he might black out as the storm hit him. He reared back, his fingers digging into the soft flesh of her hips, pleasure beating through him like a battle drum. His raw cry joined hers, reverberating off the walls.

"I think the whole castle heard us, carissima."

Heather stirred from where she'd sprawled back on the table, breathing hard as she sought to recover from the tempest that had just swept over them both.

Frankly, she couldn't care less if everyone as far as Stonehaven had heard them.

"Carissima," she panted. "What's that?"

"It means 'dearest' in Latin."

Heather gazed up at him, warmth suffusing her. He was still buried inside her, and she never wanted him to leave. A feeling of completeness made tears sting the back of her eyes. She'd been on the verge of weeping earlier, but she wasn't sure she'd be able to hold back now.

"Come here," he said, his voice rough as he reached for her. Heather let him pull her up, and then she sank into his embrace, feeling his arms go around her. Leaning against his bare chest, which was now damp with sweat, and listening to the thunder of his heart, she was loath to ever let go.

Her lips traced the line of his collar bone, resting in the hollow at the base of his throat. "Immortality and Iain Galbraith be damned ... ye are mine Maximus," she whispered. "And I am yers forever ... remember that."

XXXVI

THE BATTLE HAMMER

BLAIR GALBRAITH STRAIGHTENED up from beating
the blade, sweat pouring off him.

Enough. He'd worked hard on the new claidheamh-
mòr the Wallace had commissioned him to craft, but it
was almost dark outside. Since the arrival of the freedom
fighter, Blair had been busier than ever. And as his
apprentice had recently left to set up his own forge in
Stonehaven, Galbraith was running the forge alone.
Supper had come and gone, and his belly now growled.

Shutting down his forge, Blair stepped outside into
the wide expanse of cobbles. His workshop sat next to a
row of storehouses on the eastern edge of the lower
ward. Across the bailey, he spied the chaplain emerging
from the entrance to his lodgings, a cramped collection
of chambers that sat below the keep's chapel.

The crenelated roof of the chapel, illuminated by
torchlight, was still blackened in places, remnants of the
Wallace's liberation of Dunnottar nearly five years
earlier. The English garrison had been overwhelmed,
and those left had sought sanctuary in the chapel. But
the Wallace had shown no mercy, burning the lot of
them alive.

Blair remembered that day well. He'd never forget the blood-curdling screams of dying men that shook the heavens.

Reaching the bottom of the steps, Father Finlay cast a nervous look in Blair's direction before raising the hood of his robes and hurrying off.

Blair watched the chaplain disappear into the gloaming, a hard smile stretching his face. Father Finlay was wary of him these days after an altercation between them. The chaplain hadn't liked the interest Blair had been showing in one of the lasses who served him. Apparently, the girl had complained to the chaplain that Blair had cornered her and taken liberties.

Blair's smile faded. *Bitch.* A punch to the nose had sent the good Father running. The chaplain then complained to the laird, and David had given Blair a half-hearted scolding. Fortunately, David De Keith had a similar view of women as Blair did.

Rubbing a tense muscle in his shoulder, the weaponsmith turned left, heading toward the postern door that would lead him to the upper ward. He planned to meet his brother in the guard hall there. Iain had promised he'd keep back some supper for him.

Blair scowled. His brother's unexpected return had shocked him. He still couldn't believe Iain had been alive all this while and never bothered to let him know.

The blacksmith had almost reached the postern door when movement on the walls above caught his eye.

He halted, his gaze traveling to where a woman with long brown hair, clad in a becoming emerald-green kirtle, made her way back to the keep. And then, a few moments later, a tall, dark-haired man clad in black and green walked into view. As Blair watched, the guard halted, his gaze tracking the woman's path.

Blair stilled, his mouth flattening into a thin line.

Iain needs to know about this.

Tearing his gaze from the couple above, he strode to the postern door, flung it open, and hurried upstairs.

Iain was seated at a table by the door when Blair entered the guard's mess. Two empty jugs of ale sat before him, and he was halfway through a third. There was no sign of the supper he'd promised his brother.

Crossing the hall, Blair pulled up a stool opposite Iain and sat down. "I need to tell ye something," he announced, "about Heather."

Iain had been lifting a tankard of ale to his lips but halted mid-way at his wife's name. "What of her?"

Blair held his gaze, savoring the moment. He realized then that as much as he wanted revenge upon Heather, he also longed to injure his brother. In his time away from Dunnottar, Iain had never gotten in touch—not even once. He'd let Blair think he was dead.

Remembering this, Blair leaned toward Iain. "She has betrayed ye, brother."

Iain's face hardened, his fingers tightening around the tankard.

"I've just seen her emerge from the northern guard tower on the upper ward," Blair pressed on. "She was flushed, her hair and clothing in disarray ... and a man followed her outside and watched her walk back into the keep."

Something feral moved in Iain's green eyes. "Who?"

"One of the Dunnottar Guard ... the one ye often see with Captain Gaius."

Iain slammed down his tankard, the dull thud echoing over the hall. His reaction told Blair that Iain knew the man.

"Is he the one who intervened last week?" Blair asked.

Iain nodded, a vein pulsing in his forehead. "*Interfered.*"

"Well ... it appears he's humping yer wife."

Iain's face reddened, fury smoldering in his eyes.

Blair bit back a smile. Heather was done for. This was his chance to get even against the woman who'd robbed him of his brother.

Leaning forward, Blair met his brother's eye. "She's humiliated ye, Iain," he murmured. "The question is ... what are ye going to do about it?"

"You took your time to track me down," Cassian greeted Maximus with a scowl. "Didn't Heather pass on my message?"

Maximus cast his friend an apologetic smile. "She did ... but I was delayed." Without further explanation, he crossed the few feet between them and lowered himself onto a stool before the table.

Seated next to Cassian, Draco poured a cup of wine and handed it to Maximus. His dark eyes held a gleam.

"What's happened?" Maximus asked, taking the cup. His gaze flicked between his friends' faces; something was most definitely afoot. "Are we celebrating something?"

"We've solved another line of the riddle," Draco drawled. "If you're interested?"

Maximus stilled. The storm he'd just experienced with Heather still warmed his veins. He'd been able to think about little else. However, Draco's words brought him up short. In an instant, his heart started to pound. "What?" His attention then shifted to the closed history volume between them. "Was it in there?"

Cassian's mouth quirked. "No ... we discovered it during supper. The 'Hammer' that will strike this stronghold is none other than a great battering ram."

Maximus's gaze narrowed. "Owned by whom?"

"Shaw Irvine ... De Keith's trouble-making neighbor," Draco replied. He was grinning now. "He's named his new siege weapon 'The Battle Hammer', and threatens to bash his way into Dunnottar with it unless De Keith cedes land to him."

"And will he?"

Draco shook his head.

"David De Keith insists that his clan are the rightful owners of the land that Irvine demands," Cassian answered, his voice tight with urgency. "He won't be negotiating with him."

Excitement quickened within Maximus. "Finally, after all these years ... the riddle is revealing itself to us," he breathed, holding his cup aloft.

A slow smile spread across Cassian's face in response, as he and Draco both raised their own cups of wine. "It is time."

"Where have ye been?" Iona De Keith lowered her sewing and cast a long look over her daughter.

"Just out for a walk on the ramparts, Ma," Heather replied with a breezy smile. "It was such a fine evening that I wanted to watch the sun set."

"Ye shouldn't wander alone lass," her father's voice rumbled across the solar. He sat in the corner, near the fire, his lame leg up on a settle and a cup of wine in hand. "Not while Iain still resides here."

"Don't worry, I was careful." Heather glanced away. "Where's Aila?"

"She's with Lady Gavina," her mother replied, still surveying Heather.

It was hard not to wilt under her mother's stare. She had eyes like boning knives sometimes.

"Ye are flushed," her mother observed, "and yer hair is tangled."

"It's windy up on the ramparts," Heather answered, guilt tightening her lower belly. She didn't like lying to her parents. Yet she could hardly tell them what had just transpired with Maximus.

She was still reeling in the aftermath herself.

She'd sought him out on instinct, and hadn't been prepared for the storm that had followed.

What she felt for Maximus still shocked her.

And now she knew he felt the same way. Once Iain left Dunnottar—and he would eventually—they could make a future together. She would talk to Father Finlay—surely there was a way to get the marriage annulled. She and Iain had been estranged for a while now.

Lowering herself into a chair opposite her mother, Heather picked up her embroidery. She needed something to busy herself with, but all the same, it was difficult to concentrate.

She kept remembering what had happened in the guard room, how Maximus had taken her. Images rushed back of the way he'd yanked down her kirtle before feasting on her sensitized nipples, and of how he'd lost control as he plowed her.

Heat blossomed between her thighs at the memory, and Heather clamped them tightly together. Now wasn't the time for such thoughts.

"Is the laird still in a foul mood over Irvine's warmongering?" Heather asked, in an attempt to steer their focus away from herself.

"I assume so," her father replied. His grey eyes were shadowed. "We left just after ye did."

Of course, they had. In her urgency to catch up with Cassian—and with the events that had followed—Heather had forgotten.

"Irvine is a weasel." Her mother sniffed, stabbing her needle into the lèine she was sewing. "His father forged peace with us, and now he's breaking it."

"Surely he won't attack us though?" Heather asked, worry clouding the euphoria that had carried her down from the tower and back to her parents' chambers. "Lady Gavina's his sister ... he wouldn't want to put her in danger."

Heather had grown fond of Gavina since her return to Dunnottar; the lady would understandably be upset by her brother's actions.

"Shaw Irvine was against his sister's marriage from the outset, and he isn't the man his father was," Donnan De Keith replied. He was frowning now. "I'm afraid it isn't only the English we've got to worry about."

XXXVII

YE WILL PAY

LADY GAVINA HEAVED a sigh and put down her shuttle. Upon the loom before her, the scene of Dunnottar was slowly growing, although Gavina appeared to get little pleasure from her talent.

"My Lady?" Heather lowered the spindle she was winding wool onto, her gaze settling upon the blue-clad figure seated by the window. "Is something amiss?"

Dusk was falling over Dunnottar. It was rare for Heather to join Lady Gavina in her solar at this hour, yet it had been the warmest day of the year so far, and her mistress had called for her after supper.

Despite the lateness of the hour, the hammering of iron and the sound of men's grunts and shouts intruded through the open window. Irvine's missive had caused a flurry of activity in Dunnottar. The laird was determined that his brother-by-marriage wouldn't best him. As such, he'd put the Guard to work shoring up the castle's defenses. Naturally, the Wallace's men were assisting.

Heather had been happy to go to Lady Gavina this eve, for she enjoyed her company. It was hard to keep a smile off her face, for now that she knew how Maximus felt, and that he wanted to be with her, she had a clearer idea about what her future held.

The events of the day before had given her hope.

However, something wasn't right with her mistress this evening. Although she'd often sensed Gavina's melancholy at unguarded moments, it had never been quite as evident as now.

"I worry about relations between the De Keiths and the Irvines," Gavina murmured. She shifted her gaze to the view beyond the window, to where the last rays of sunlight had set the sky ablaze. "I fear my brother is on the verge of ruining everything."

"Shaw must be put in his place, Gavina," the woman across the room spoke up. Lady Elizabeth had joined them. Heather rarely saw her during the day as she spent much of her time with her young son, Robbie. "His behavior is outrageous."

"I've sent word to him," Gavina replied, her face growing taut, "pleading with him to honor the peace our father worked so hard to achieve."

Lady Elizabeth didn't reply, although she watched Lady Gavina, a furrow between her eyebrows.

"What does our laird have to say about the situation?" Heather asked when the silence drew out.

Lady Gavina's gaze guttered. "He blames me," she whispered. "This morning he accused me of being in league with my brother ... he thinks our match was all part of an elaborate plan to bring down the De Keiths."

"That's preposterous!" Lady Elizabeth halted her sewing. "Ye wed him in good faith."

Lady Gavina's throat bobbed. "Aye ... but David felt pressured ... by both Robert and my father. I was never his choice of bride."

Heather sucked in a surprised breath at the woman's candor.

"Robert was acting in the best interests of his clan, as was yer father," Elizabeth said after a pause, her tone sharpening. "But Shaw and David can't see past the old hate."

Lady Gavina sighed. "Aye, with the English threatening us again, ye'd think we Scots would band together."

Lady Elizabeth's full lips pursed. "Wallace has done his best to rally us under one banner," she replied. "But while Scots fight Scots, invaders will always best us."

Darkness had fallen when Heather finally left Lady Gavina's solar. Usually, she enjoyed her mistress's company, but the subject of this eve's conversation had left her mood subdued.

She hadn't realized just how unhappy the laird and his wife were together, and Shaw Irvine's betrayal had succeeded in making things even more difficult.

No wonder her mistress seemed subdued these days.

Outdoors, the sounds of industry had faded with the setting of the sun.

Passing through the gallery that led from Lady Gavina's rooms toward the tower stairs, Heather reflected on the importance of finding the right partner in life.

Lady Gavina hadn't chosen her match—but Heather had no such excuse.

And if it wasn't for Iain, she and Maximus could be open with others about their feelings for each other. They could have asked the chaplain to wed them yesterday eve.

But she was still a wedded woman, and she hadn't been able to slip out of the keep to talk to Father Finlay.

This was all because she'd thrown herself into a relationship with Iain Galbraith without a thought to who he really was. She'd been taken in by his arrogance, his charm. She'd been such a fool that she'd even liked his dominance, for it had made her feel wanted, protected in the beginning.

How she wished she could travel back in time and tell her old self to stay away from that man.

But would she have listened?

She'd been so willful then, so sure of herself.

Lost in her thoughts, she didn't see the large figure step out from behind one of the thick stone columns.

An instant later, Iain Galbraith loomed before her.

Heather skidded to a halt, a scream rising in her throat.

However, Iain lunged forward and grabbed her by the upper arm, his fingers digging painfully into her flesh. "Call for help, and I'll go upstairs and slit yer Da's neck ... like I should have done a week ago."

Fear clamped across Heather's throat, and she swallowed the scream. The menace in Iain's voice was real. She believed his threat.

Reassured that she'd do as bid, Iain towed her back the way she'd come before hauling her down a narrow stairwell. Only the guards used these stairs, as they led to the upper ward ramparts.

Halfway down the steps, Heather started to struggle. She wasn't sure where he was taking her, but her instincts screamed danger. She had to get free of him.

A swift elbow to the belly caused her struggles to cease. He grabbed her by the hair, dragging her after him. Heather's gasp of pain echoed against damp stone.

Reaching the bottom of the stairwell, Iain shouldered the door open and yanked her out onto the wall.

The moon was rising, a bright silver shell in the black sky, and a crisp, briny wind blew in from the sea.

Heather started struggling again, fear overcoming the pain in her belly and scalp. She couldn't see why he'd bring her out here—other than to throw her off the walls to her death.

She kicked him hard in the shin, wriggling like a hooked eel as she tried to get free of him.

"Bitch!" Iain grunted. "Ye will pay for that." Ignoring her struggles, he towed her after him along the wall. "A man goes off to fight for Scotland, and ye can't wait to spread yer legs for others," he continued, his voice flat and hard.

"I didn't," Heather gasped. "I was faithful to ye after ye left ... ask anyone in Fintry."

"Liar!" He shook her like a dog. "My brother saw ye with that *cèin*. Ye have been letting him hump ye... with yer rightful husband under the same roof!"

Terror clawed its way up Heather's throat. If he knew about her and Maximus, she was doomed. However, she wouldn't give up. She had to make him see sense.

"It was over between us, Iain ... even before ye left Fintry," she gasped out the words, oblivious to the fact that her scalp felt as if it were aflame. "We weren't happy together. That's why ye never let me know ye were alive. Ye only want me now because I've wounded yer pride."

Iain ground out a curse and slapped her across the face. Heather's head snapped to one side, her ears ringing. But still she persisted. "Leave it be, Iain ... or ye shall hang for this."

Draco Vulcan stepped out onto the walls and inhaled the tang of the sea. Agitated, he flexed his hands at his sides. He hadn't been at Dunnottar long, and already he could feel restlessness rising within him like a spring tide. Even a day of toil, helping clear ditches before the western walls, hadn't eased it.

We're so close to solving that riddle ... just one more line.

They just had to discover the identity of the White Hawk and the Dragon.

Whenever he had a spare moment over the last few days, Draco had immersed himself in the books Cassian had taken from the laird's library, searching for clues. Yet nothing they'd read so far was helpful.

Draco wasn't a patient man. Already, the search frustrated him.

Glancing up, his gaze alighted upon the silver-tailed Broom-star.

As always, the sight of it made him tense. He hated having his fate in the hands of that curse. That witch had made them all her slaves. Right now, the bitch was probably looking down from the heavens, laughing at their hope.

But this time, they'd foil her.

Mouth thinning, Draco walked to the edge of the walls, his gaze sweeping over the lower ward and the sea beyond.

I just want an end to all of this. The thought was bleak, but it was one that visited Draco often. After so long alive, even throwing himself into the Scottish cause couldn't fill the void within.

Only death would do that.

A noise drew Draco from his dark thoughts—a faint, muffled cry.

Turning from the view, he surveyed the ramparts of the upper ward. The walls lay in shadow, save for the areas where torches burned. Yet Draco had a hawk's gaze. He'd always been able to see things in the darkness that others couldn't.

And so, he easily picked out the tall, broad-shouldered man with wild hair who dragged a woman along the far wall.

Draco watched them, his gaze narrowing. He recognized them both.

And as he looked on, the man silenced the woman's protests with a swift punch to the belly.

Draco tensed. His first instinct was to go to the woman's aid—a foolish urge that had gotten him in trouble more than once over the past centuries—but the wall on which he stood was cut off from the pair of them.

He'd have to go back indoors and find the stairwell to the northern ramparts.

And if he was going to do that, he might as well fetch the man who was largely responsible for the scene unfolding before him.

Draco spun on his heel and made for the stairs leading down into the lower ward.

He needed to find Maximus.

XXXVIII

UPON THE TOWER

"MAXIMUS!"

EMERGING FROM the guard hall with Cassian, Maximus glanced up at his name. The pair had shared supper together, and he was about to start his evening shift on the watch.

Draco strode toward them, purpose emanating off his lean frame.

"You need to get up onto the northern ramparts ... now," Draco announced, without preamble. "Galbraith's got Heather up there ... and I'd wager he plans to throw her off."

For an instant, Maximus merely stared at his friend, shock sweeping over him in an icy wave.

And then he moved.

Not bothering to thank Draco, or to farewell Cassian, he took off. He sprinted across the lower ward bailey and up the steps into the keep.

Neither of his friends said a word.

Maximus flew through the hallways of the keep to the narrow stairwell that led up to the northern ramparts. All the while, panic thundered through his chest.

What if I'm too late?

If he was, he'd rip Galbraith to pieces with his bare hands.

"Stop, Iain!" Heather heard the pleading sound of her own voice, but was past caring, past having any pride at all. Iain was now dragging her up the steps of one of the smaller watchtowers that lined the ramparts. "Please!"

He ignored her, pulling her the rest of the way and throwing her up against a battlement. The air gusted out of Heather's lungs as her back hit solid stone. Gasping for breath, she looked up at the enraged man that loomed over her.

She'd tried to calm him, to change his mind—but every word she'd uttered had just served to anger him further.

The Galbraith rage was legendary in Fintry. It hadn't taken her long before she'd discovered what a terrible temper her husband possessed, or that he wouldn't be contradicted.

She should have left him then, should have made her way back alone to Dunnottar and admitted her mistake to her family.

But she hadn't, and now it had come to this.

"Cheating *whore*." Iain grabbed her by the throat and lifted her up. "How many have there been over the years?"

He clearly didn't expect her to answer, for the iron grip on her windpipe prevented Heather from making any response. She clawed at his fingers, yet they didn't budge. She was no match for his strength.

"Whore or not, I'm going to have ye, one last time," Iain growled as he grasped at her skirts with his free hand. "And then ye are going over the wall."

Terror slammed into Heather, and despite that she couldn't breathe, she resumed her struggles. She'd fight him to the end; she had to. She tried to kick him, but he merely shoved her legs apart with his knee and began to unlace his braies.

What an awful irony this was.

She'd once been dizzy with desire for this man, had once craved his touch. But now the feel of his hands upon her skin made her bile rise.

And still she fought him—even as her lungs started to burn from lack of air and her vision swam. Iain cursed while he struggled with the laces on his braies. Even half-dead, she was still thwarting him.

But in the end, it would be all for nothing.

He didn't need to throw her over the walls to end her life. He was going to strangle her first.

Chill darkness closed in on Heather, as if she'd just been plunged into deep, cold water, and her struggles started to fade.

Maximus. Grief surged up within her. Consciousness began to slip from her grip. *I'll never see him again.*

Suddenly, the pressure on her throat lifted. No longer held up, Heather slid down the wall, choking and gasping for breath.

For a moment, she merely lay there, sucking in great lungfuls of air. But as her vision cleared, she saw two men fighting on the top of the guard tower.

Iain and Maximus.

She wasn't sure how her lover had discovered she was here, but the relief at seeing him slug Iain across the face and send him reeling back against the battlements made her choke back a sob. *He found me.*

However, while she lay there struggling to regain her breath, her gaze never leaving them, she saw that the men were evenly matched.

She'd thought Cory could handle himself in a fight—but Iain's ferocity was something to behold. He was taller, broader, and stronger than his opponent. Yet Maximus was quicker, lighter on his feet. And he fought with a savagery that equaled Iain's.

Steel flashed in the hallowed light of the single torch that burned atop the watchtower.

Iain had drawn his dirk.

A moment later, the scrape of steel against leather warned her Maximus had done the same. The two men lunged and stabbed at each other, circling the top of the tower like alpha-wolves.

I need to help him. Clutching her throat, Heather tried to scramble to her feet. But her legs had turned to porridge, and she was shaking so violently they wouldn't cooperate.

A hiss of pain echoed across the tower, yet Heather wasn't sure which man had just been injured. They fought in a blur now, blades flashing, grunts and curses cutting through the cool night air.

And then, as she stared at them, her heart thundering in her ears, she saw the fight turn in one man's favor.

Maximus slammed his knife into Iain's shoulder. An instant later, he punched him in the stomach with his free hand.

The impact sent the pair of them reeling back against the northern wall, just a few feet from where Heather sat.

Iain snarled a litany of curses, struggling against his opponent. And then Maximus yanked the blade from his shoulder and stabbed it into Iain's throat, cutting off his tirade.

All of a sudden, it went silent upon the tower top.

A choking sound intruded as Maximus withdrew his blade and sheathed it at his hip. He then grabbed the struggling man and attempted to haul him over the edge of the wall.

But despite that he was mortally injured, Iain Galbraith was a big, strong man—and he fought his opponent with everything he had left.

Heather could see that Maximus wasn't going to be able to cast him over the edge on his own.

But then, he wasn't alone.

Two figures emerged from the shadowy stairwell leading down to the wall. They moved fast, reaching Maximus's side in just a few strides. Together the three of them picked Iain up and hauled him onto the crenelated edge of the tower.

Heather's breathing stopped while Iain balanced there, still struggling weakly.

Then he was gone.

Breathing hard, Maximus turned, staggered, and slumped against the wall.

Heather let out a whimper. *He's injured.*

Maximus Cato was immortal, but she knew he could feel pain as keenly as any man. She didn't like to see him suffer.

Muttering a curse under his breath, Maximus pushed himself off the battlements and moved to her.

"Heather, carissima." His voice was rough, broken. "I'm so sorry I didn't come earlier. Did he hurt you?"

Iain had, although not as badly as he'd intended. Her struggles had been so frantic that he hadn't been able to rape her. And her throat, although badly bruised, didn't feel permanently damaged.

Heather opened her mouth to speak, but only a rasping sound escaped. The full realization of how close she'd come to dying hit her then, and tears spilled over, coursing down her face. Despite her blurred vision, she spied the other two men draw near behind Maximus, their faces recognizable in the guttering torchlight: Cassian and Draco.

Maximus sank to his knees before her, muttered a string of words in his own tongue, and hauled her into his embrace.

And when his arms fastened around her, the last strands of Heather's courage snapped. She sank into the wall of his chest, a sob convulsing her aching throat.

Maximus gathered Heather in his arms and heaved himself to his feet. His left flank throbbed, for Iain had stuck him twice there with his dirk. The wounds would heal soon enough, yet right now they hurt so much he felt bile sting the back of his throat.

Holding Heather against his chest while she trembled and wept, Maximus turned to his friends.

Both Cassian and Draco were watching him. "We'll go down to the rocks and deal with Iain," Cassian informed him, his gaze dropping to Heather's tear-streaked face. "You'd better get her back to her family."

Maximus nodded, grateful that his friend knew what needed to be done. "I'll join you as soon as I can."

Cassian and Draco both nodded, and then the pair of them turned and disappeared down the stairs. A moment later, Maximus followed with Heather.

Iona gasped at the sight of the bloodied man who carried her daughter into the solar. Seated next to her mother near the window, Aila cried out, "Heather!"

Donnan De Keith slammed down the cup of wine he'd been enjoying in front of the fire and hauled himself to his feet. "What have ye done to her?"

"Nothing," Maximus grunted, carrying Heather over to a chair and lowering her gently into it. "Iain Galbraith attacked Heather ... dragged her up onto the walls ... and tried to kill her."

The baldness of the guard's words made a chill steal over Donnan. "Where's he now?"

"Dead."

The word fell dully in the now silent solar.

Iona and Aila were staring at Maximus wide-eyed and pale faced, while Heather struggled to sit up straight. Her neck was reddened, her face tear-streaked.

Something twisted deep in Donnan's chest. He'd never seen his strong, proud daughter in such a state.

"Maximus saved my life," she rasped, wincing, for speaking hurt her. "I left Lady Gavina ... and was on my way back here ... but Iain was waiting for me in the gallery."

"Lass!" Iona rose to her feet and hurried over to her daughter. Kneeling before Heather, she grasped her shaking hands, eyes glittering with tears. "Thank the Lord ye are still with us."

Donnan watched his wife and daughter together, warmth seeping into the icy shock and anger that still pulsed through him. Heather's departure from Dunnottar years earlier had caused a rift between mother and daughter that he'd feared would never heal. And since Heather's return, there had remained a reserve between the two of them—but not now.

"I'll get ye some wine, Heather." Aila hurried to the sideboard and poured a cup of bramble wine before carrying it to her sister. "Ye need something to calm yer nerves."

Donnan turned back to the guard. "So, ye killed the swine?"

Maximus nodded. "Stabbed him through the throat and threw him over the walls." He grimaced then, and Donnan raked his gaze down the length of him to see that the left side of his vest was wet with blood.

"Ye are injured."

"It's not as bad as it looks." Maximus waved off his concern. "For Heather's sake ... no one in this keep can know of what happened tonight. I'm going to make sure Galbraith's body is never found ... but I need ye and yer family to keep this secret."

Donnan held the man's eye, his own never wavering. "Aye ... none of us will speak a word."

XXXIX

ALLIES AND ENEMIES

"THE LAIRD WILL see ye now." Donnan De Keith stepped out of the clan-chief's solar, and his gaze settled upon Maximus. A silent look passed between the two men, one that needed no words. "The Wallace is with him."

Maximus nodded. He wasn't surprised. Three long days had passed since Iain Galbraith's death—and the Wallace's men had been out searching for him.

They'd never find him though.

After leaving Heather with her kin, Maximus had left the castle and skirted the rocks below. He'd found Cassian and Draco—with Iain Galbraith's broken body.

The man was now buried under a pile of rocks five furlongs farther up the coast. No one would ever find him.

Stepping inside the solar, Maximus's gaze swept the large, comfortable chamber. It was a masculine space: a deerskin covered the flagstone floor, and a stag's head loomed above the hearth at one end of the solar, while a sword hung upon the opposite wall under the De Keith banner.

Maximus glanced at the motto embroidered there. Veritas Vincit—*Truth conquers*. His belly tightened. Sometimes telling the truth wasn't in one's best interests.

Two men stood by an open window. Outdoors, it was a fine spring morning, balmy with the promise of summer. The bellows of warriors at combat practice drifted into the chamber, a reminder that Dunnottar was preparing itself for battle.

"Good morning, Cato," David De Keith greeted him. Dressed in fine chamois braies and a crisp white lèine, the laird leaned against the window frame, silver goblet of wine in hand. Although the man's expression was genial enough, his brown eyes were hard, assessing.

Hearing how the man had raged for days after the threatening missive from his neighbor, Maximus knew his relaxed posture was a ruse.

A few feet from the laird, William Wallace remained silent. A thick, dark beard hid most of his lower face, and his brown eyes were inscrutable when they settled upon Maximus.

Wallace was a warrior. Maximus had met few men with his size and presence. Unlike De Keith, he didn't cradle a goblet of wine. He was dressed in a mail shirt and thick leather braies, as if he expected to go into battle at a moment's notice.

"You called for me, De Keith?" Maximus greeted the laird. He then acknowledged the Wallace with a respectful nod.

"Aye ... we're hoping ye will be able to clear something up for us," David De Keith replied. He swirled the wine in his goblet before shifting his attention to his companion. "Wallace ..."

William Wallace cleared his throat and pushed himself up off the window ledge. He then took a step toward Maximus. At his full height, and this close, the man was truly a giant. "One of my men has gone missing," he rumbled.

"I know," Maximus replied coolly. "We've all been out looking for him."

"Well ... his brother believes ye are responsible."

Maximus cocked an eyebrow. He knew he had to be careful how he played this scene. Wallace wasn't a fool. "His brother?"

"Aye ... Blair Galbraith is our smith," De Keith interjected. "Surely, ye have met him?"

Maximus shook his head. "I haven't been at Dunnottar long."

"So, ye didn't have anything to do with Iain Galbraith's disappearance?" Wallace pressed, his gaze never leaving Maximus's face.

"No."

Silence fell in the solar, broken only by the gentle crackling of a lump of peat in the hearth.

"Galbraith's estranged wife lives here, does she not?" Wallace asked finally. When Maximus remained silent, he pressed on. "There are rumors that ye are her lover."

Maximus drew in a slow, steadying breath. This was it—the moment that the meeting could turn against him. After a pause, he answered. "I love Heather De Keith."

The laird snorted at this admission, and Maximus tore his attention from the Wallace to look at him. David De Keith wore a sour expression.

Deciding to ignore his rude response, Maximus focused on Wallace once more. "This has nothing to do with Galbraith's disappearance. I don't know what happened to the man."

"Come now, Cato," De Keith snapped. "Why else would the warrior vanish?"

"David's right," Wallace said, his voice held a note of hardness to it now. "Galbraith didn't hide his rage at discovering that his wife had left him. If he found out ye had been swiving her, I imagine he'd have been incensed."

Maximus held the Wallace's eye. He didn't like lying to the man, for he respected him. The Wallace wasn't someone you crossed.

"We've been discreet," Maximus said after a pause. It was another falsehood—he and Heather had taken foolish risks.

"I'm not fond of liars," Wallace replied, his voice hardening further still. "But ye and I both know that I can't condemn ye without proof."

"Ye have proof," David De Keith cut in. "The man is plowing Galbraith's woman. It's clear what happened: they fought and Cato killed him. Somehow, he's managed to dispose of the body."

"And how would I do that?" Maximus countered, defending himself properly for the first time. "Would someone not have seen?"

"I don't know how ye managed it." The laird glared at him now. "But ye are the only one in this keep with a reason to kill him."

"That's not entirely true," Wallace cut in. "Galbraith wasn't popular among my men." He heaved a weary sigh then, as if this conversation was becoming tedious. Reaching up, he nipped the skin between his dark eyebrows.

Watching him, Maximus sensed the Wallace was now making up his mind about something. "Iain Galbraith was good in a fight ... but he was a troublemaker," he said finally. "Few besides his brother will miss him."

"It doesn't matter." David De Keith was scowling now, his fingers clenched around the stem of his goblet. "If this man killed him, he must be punished. I won't have murderers in my Guard."

William Wallace swung his dark gaze to the laird, pinning him to the spot.

The atmosphere in the solar changed then. Despite that De Keith ruled here, he was clearly wary of the big man standing a few feet from him. They'd all heard tales about what the Wallace was capable of when riled. His temper was different to Galbraith's—slower to kindle and far more dangerous.

The English garrison he'd burned in the chapel here at Dunnottar had learned just how little mercy he had.

But now, Maximus was seeing a different side to him. Wallace was also a practical man.

"Then I shall invite Cato to join *my* force," he said softly, his gaze boring into De Keith's. A beat of silence passed, one that De Keith didn't dare fill.

Maximus's breathing slowed. Had he heard right?

Wallace shifted his attention back to Maximus then. "Draco tells me ye fought together in the past ... that ye are a man of courage and honor ... that ye have commanded warriors and led them into battle."

Maximus swallowed. He wondered what tales Draco had spun this man. How would the Wallace react if he knew the man before him had previously commanded the first cohort of the Ninth—and that he'd once slain many of Wallace's countrymen for the glory of Rome.

"Will ye join us?" Wallace asked.

Maximus stared back at him. The question both humbled and surprised him. He'd enjoyed being part of the Dunnottar Guard, yet the thought of joining something bigger, of fighting to protect this land, made his chest constrict. Now that he'd given his heart to Heather, he could also give his loyalty to a cause beyond breaking the curse that bound him.

"I would be honored," he replied. He then shifted his gaze to the man who still stood by the window. David De Keith glared back at him. His eyes were narrowed, and a muscle flexed in his bearded jaw.

It was just as well that Maximus had gained an ally in William Wallace today, for he'd certainly made an enemy of the laird of Dunnottar.

"I'm going to ask Heather to become my wife."

Maximus's assertion caused both Cassian and Draco to cease eating. The three of them sat at the captain's table at the far end of the guard's mess. Around them, loud male voices boomed off the stone walls; the noise was almost deafening, yet Maximus had raised his voice so that his friends could hear him.

Cassian swallowed a mouthful of boar stew and reached for the cup of wine before him. "You're making a mistake."

Maximus met his friend's steady hazel gaze. "Am I?"

"Cassian's right. There's a reason none of us form attachments," Draco spoke up. He was watching Maximus with a veiled expression. He shifted into Latin then, as he continued. "We're on the cusp of breaking the curse ... a woman will only distract you."

Maximus shook his head. "A month ago, I'd have agreed with you," he replied, also transitioning into his native tongue, "but meeting Heather changed everything for me."

"That's exactly it," Cassian cut in. "You've known her less than a month, and you're about to propose. You're love-struck, and it's turned you into a half-wit."

The words were harsh, uncharacteristically so from Cassian.

Taken aback, Maximus held his friend's eye, while Draco wisely held his tongue. They all knew what had prompted Cassian's comment.

"Lilla has been dead three hundred years, Cass," Maximus said finally. "Yet you still carry her shade with you. Isn't it time you let her go?"

Cassian scowled, a muscle bunching in his jaw. "It's easy for you to say such things now," he growled. "*Everything* is easy in the beginning. She's still young, and it feels as if nothing will ever change. But wait for the years to pass ... watch the woman you love wither before your eyes while you're powerless to do anything to stop the march of time. And then, one day the Grim Reaper comes for her ... and you're powerless to stop him too."

A heavy silence fell between them. The noise in the mess hall was as loud as ever, yet Maximus was oblivious to it.

All these years later, and he could still feel Cassian's pain.

Next to him, Draco was swirling his cup of wine, his sharp-featured face unreadable. This wasn't a discussion that the Moor was going to get into.

Maximus understood his reticence. After seeing how he'd hurt Evanna all those years ago, and after her violent reckoning upon him, he'd done his best to wall up his heart. He'd spent years outrunning love, but in the end, it had hunted him down.

He hadn't wanted to fall for Heather, but now he had, his life finally had meaning again.

"I'll not deny anything you've just said," Maximus answered when the silence drew out. "If we don't break this curse, I'll be doomed to watch Heather grow old and die … if illness or injury don't take her first. But I'd rather suffer the pain of loss than walk through the centuries alone." His gaze swept from Cassian's stony face to Draco's impassive one. "Let the pain come when it must," he concluded. "It's time for me to move on in life … perhaps we all need to."

XL

YER BLESSING

MAXIMUS EMERGED FROM the chapel to see the steward outside the nearby storehouses. Donnan De Keith stood, a thick ledger under one arm, talking to one of the servants.

A tight smile stretched Maximus's face. *Just the man I need to see.*

He'd just spoken to Father Finlay, and was about to go in search of Heather's father—but Donnan had made it easy for him.

Seeing Maximus descend the stairs, the steward sent the servant off and limped across the bailey toward him.

"Strange time of day for prayers?" Donnan greeted him, gesturing to the chapel.

Maximus shrugged. He hadn't visited the chapel to pray, but to have a quiet word with the chaplain. There was something he'd needed to be sure of before he took the next step.

"Ye shouldn't venture down this end of the lower ward," the steward continued, his voice low. "Galbraith's forge is right behind me."

That fact hadn't escaped Maximus. He'd smelled the tang of hot iron and heard the ring of steel being beaten as he approached the storehouses. However, he had more important things on his mind right now than the belligerent smith.

"It went well with Wallace and De Keith earlier," he replied. "I'm no longer under suspicion. The laird isn't happy about it though, so I'm not with the Guard anymore ... Wallace has invited me to join his men instead."

Donnan's gaze widened. "Ye've joined the cause?"

"Aye ... and not before time."

The steward favored him with a long, assessing look. "Still ... his brother will want yer guts."

Maximus's mouth curved at the steward's concern for his hide. "Blair Galbraith messes with me at his peril."

Donnan huffed. "Why is it that my daughter always loses her heart to arrogant men?"

Maximus tensed at these words. Was that what the steward thought of him? "I admit I'm arrogant," he said after a pause. The pair of them turned and walked away from the storehouses and the forge. "But I hope you don't think I'm cut of the same cloth as Iain Galbraith ... that will make things ... awkward."

Donnan cut him a sharp look. "Awkward ... why?"

Maximus drew in a deep breath. "Because I wish to ask for your daughter's hand."

The steward halted, turning to face him. Maximus did likewise, their gazes fusing. Fortunately, although the man's face had gone slack with shock, there was no anger kindling in his eyes.

"Ye wish to wed Heather?"

"I do."

"And she wants to be yer wife?"

"I think so ... once you give me your blessing, I will go and ask her formally."

The two men stared at each other for a long moment before Donnan murmured a curse under his breath. "Her husband's only been dead three days," he reminded Maximus, deliberately lowering his voice. There was no one about, yet the steward was wise to be cautious.

Caution had made Maximus visit Father Finlay. Of course, a handful of them here knew that Iain Galbraith was dead, but there was no corpse to prove it. That being the case, Maximus had been concerned the chaplain would refuse to wed him and Heather. Once he'd told Father Finlay his intentions, the man had held his gaze for a long moment. Maximus's pulse had quickened when he spied a shrewd glint in the man's eye.

He suspects the truth.

"There isn't a body ... but I think we both know Iain Galbraith is dead," the chaplain had finally answered when the silence drew out. "The Galbraith brothers were always a mean pair ... some might consider Iain's disappearance a mercy. Ye seem like a good man, Maximus. Ye are free to wed Heather De Keith ... if she wishes it."

Those words had caused a wave of giddying relief to crash over Maximus. Now, the only obstacle to his happiness was the man standing before him.

"Heather and Iain were estranged for over two years ... and he treated her badly before that," Maximus pointed out. "Your daughter deserves to be cherished by a man who loves her."

Donnan pursed his lips. "And that man is ye, is it?"

"It is."

The steward stared at him for a heartbeat longer before he snorted and raked a hand through his greying brown hair. "I suppose I shouldn't tar ye with the same brush as Galbraith," he muttered. "*He* never asked my permission before he wed Heather in Stonehaven kirk."

Maximus didn't answer.

Donnan scowled then. "And I suppose ye plan to take her away from here too?"

"No ... I'm happy here, and once the conflict is over, I wish to stay." As Maximus spoke the words, he realized they were the truth. When peace settled upon Scotland again—and it always did, even after years of strife—he wanted to make this fortress or nearby Stonehaven his home.

A nomadic life no longer held any appeal.

Donnan raised his eyebrows. "Ye do?"

Maximus nodded. "I adore yer daughter ... her fire, her courage," he said finally. His chest constricted as he admitted this. It wasn't easy for him to say such things before another man. "And I know I'll never meet anyone like her again. She is the other part of me I never knew was missing. Dunnottar is her home ... and so it is mine as well."

He would have said that he'd lay down his life for Heather—but such a gesture wasn't possible for an immortal.

Donnan watched him a little longer, and then his mouth curved in the hint of a smile. "Fine words, lad. Let's see if ye mean them."

Maximus inclined his head, his pulse accelerating. "Does that mean I have yer blessing?"

"The roses are bonny this year." Gavina De Keith bent over the rosebush and sniffed. "Have ye smelled these pink ones?"

"No." Heather smiled as she approached the Lady of Dunnottar. She then stooped and inhaled the sweet perfume. "Heavens ... that is lovely."

"I think we should use those ones to make soap and perfume, My Lady," Aila piped up from where she was weeding around a bed of primroses. "Since they are so well scented."

Lady Gavina's face lit up at this suggestion. It warmed Heather to see the lady smile; she'd been so pale and withdrawn of late. Outdoors, in the small garden in the castle's upper ward, Lady Gavina's cares appeared to lift from her.

Maybe we should spend more afternoons together in the garden, Heather reflected. *The sunlight and fresh air are good for her.*

It was another bright day, with a robin's-egg blue sky stretching above them. A warm breeze fluttered in from the south-west, bringing with it the scent of grass and wildflowers.

Heather breathed it all in, aware that the happiness within her made the day seem even more beautiful. The only shadow over it all was that she hadn't seen Maximus since that awful night on the tower top.

She ached to lay eyes on him again, to touch him. She wished he were with her right now.

The night before, she'd voiced her frustration to Aila as they readied themselves for bed, but her sister had merely smiled. "He'll be keeping away until this all blows over ... the whole castle is in an uproar over Galbraith's disappearance, and Iain's brother is pointing the finger at Maximus."

Remembering her sister's words, Heather's belly clenched, her joy dimming. Of course, Blair would do such a thing. He was a mean-spirited man who'd been looking for a chance to get even with her for years.

And it was him who saw us together, she thought, her gaze traveling to the watchtower where she and Maximus had given their hearts to each other, and their bodies. *Maximus was right to be cautious.* As always, her impetuous character had gotten her into trouble.

Only this time, she was more worried for Maximus than herself.

"Can ye hold this for me, Heather?" Lady Gavina's soft voice intruded then. "While I cut some lavender."

Heather nodded, taking hold of the wicker basket her mistress passed her. She then followed Lady Gavina to where a profusion of lavender grew against a wall. Another pleasant, yet sharper scent, filled her nostrils. The smell of lavender was a perfume she'd always associate with her mother.

Heather's mouth curved when she thought of Iona De Keith. Ever since Iain's attack, her mother's attitude toward her had softened. Gone were the judgmental glances and snide comments. Gone was the aloof shield she'd worn around Heather since her return.

Her mother had even wept when Heather told her and Aila what had actually happened on the tower top—of what Iain had tried to do.

"Beast," Iona had choked, a tear trickling down her cheek. "I'm glad he's dead."

And so was Heather. Only, she didn't want Maximus to pay for it.

Holding out the basket, she watched as Lady Gavina delicately snipped off lavender heads. The lady was in a much lighter mood today; she even hummed to herself as she worked.

A short while later, Aila cleared her throat behind them. "Ye have a visitor, Heather."

Both Lady Gavina and Heather glanced up. Aila had just risen to her feet after weeding and was brushing soil off her hands. Yet her attention was upon the gateway that led out of the walled garden into the upper ward bailey. Heather followed her sister's gaze to a tall, dark-haired man.

Maximus leaned against the stone arch, where rambling roses were just coming into bloom.

Heather's heart leaped against her ribs at the sight of him, and her fingers clenched around the basket handle.

Lord, how she'd longed for him over these past few days—how she'd ached to seek him out. But after all the problems her rashness had caused, she hadn't dared. Aila, ever more prudent and patient, had been right.

Better to wait till the storm passed, till he was free to come to her.

"Who's this?" Lady Gavina asked, raising a finely arched eyebrow.

"Maximus Cato," Heather whispered, her voice catching as she said his name. "He's one of the Dunnottar Guard ... and the man I love."

Tearing her gaze from Maximus, Heather glanced over at Lady Gavina and saw that her cornflower-blue eyes had gone huge. Heather offered her mistress a nervous smile. "There are one or two things I haven't shared with ye, My Lady. But I'm happy to."

Lady Gavina watched her for a long moment before her lips curved into a smile of her own. "I look forward to hearing yer news, Heather," she replied softly, "but it can wait." Lady Gavina motioned to Aila. "Come ... let's carry our flowers indoors."

And with that, Lady Gavina took the basket from Heather and glided out of the garden, Aila hurrying behind her.

On her way out, Aila cast Heather a wide smile over her shoulder.

Maximus stepped aside to let Lady Gavina and her maid pass, nodding respectfully to them both.

The Lady of Dunnottar acknowledged him with a nod of her own, and then she and Aila disappeared, leaving Heather and Maximus together alone.

XLI

ETERNITY BECKONS

HEATHER TRACKED HIS path across the garden toward her.

Maximus walked slowly between the beds of thyme and rosemary. However, his gaze never left her face—not for an instant.

By the time he stopped around three feet from Heather, her heart was pounding so loudly in her ears that she felt a little queasy.

This man made her feel every emotion keenly. She didn't know why the sight of him made her so nervous, only that his nearness now caused a wave of dizziness to descend upon her.

Dressed in hunting leathers, with no sign of the injuries he'd taken three days earlier, Maximus watched her with an intensity that made Heather start to sweat.

"Yer uniform," she murmured. "Why aren't ye wearing it?"

He smiled. "I'm no longer a member of the Guard."

Heather's breathing quickened as alarm fluttered up under her ribcage. "Ye aren't? Is it safe for ye to be here?" Her voice trembled slightly, betraying her worry.

She resisted the urge to wipe her damp palms upon the skirts of her kirtle.

He nodded. "The Wallace has invited me to join his men, and I've accepted ... but that's not why I've come to find you."

Heather swallowed, her thoughts reeling. Her throat tightened, pride swelling within her. She couldn't believe it. He'd joined the cause.

His gaze roamed over her face, his dark eyes shadowing. "Are you well, Heather? I've wanted to check on you over the past days ... but it hasn't been safe to do so."

"I am well," she assured him. Iain's brutality had terrified her, as had her brush with death, but with each passing day, the shadow he'd cast over her pulled back. She offered Maximus a smile then, in an attempt to mask her nervousness. "Ye know I'm tough."

"You are," he murmured. "But everyone has their limits." He broke off there, moving a little closer. "I've just talked with your father," he continued, his face so serious that Heather's breathing constricted. Was there something amiss? Her worry increased when he cleared his throat. The man was clearly on edge. "I've asked for his blessing ... that is ... if you wish to wed me." He paused once more. "Father Finlay has also assured me that he's happy to conduct the ceremony."

Silence fell. For a few moments, Heather merely stared at Maximus. Incredulous, she took a step toward him. "Ye asked Da for my hand?"

"I did."

Her gaze roamed over him. "And I see no blackened eye or broken nose as a result?"

A smile crept over Maximus's handsome face. "That's because the request didn't anger him. Donnan has agreed."

Heather gasped. "He has?"

"Aye, I told him I love his daughter to distraction ... and wish to wed her."

A moment later, she flew into his arms, raining kisses over his face.

Maximus laughed, holding her tightly. She felt the thunder of his heart against her and realized that, although he hid it well, he was as nervous as she was.

"Does this mean you will be my wife, Heather?" he asked, the husky edge to his voice betraying him. "You know who I am ... and you understand what it would mean to bind yourself to me?"

She stared up into his dark eyes, which now gleamed with emotion. "Aye," she said, her own voice catching. "I love you, and I choose to bind myself to ye without hesitation. I want nothing more than to spend the rest of my life with ye, Maximus ... whatever fate deals us."

His throat bobbed. "There's something else, Heather ... I have news."

Heather tensed, for she could feel the urgency vibrating off him. "What is it?" she breathed, worry shadowing her joy. "Is something wrong?"

Maximus shook his head. Reaching out, he took her hands, drawing her against him. "We've solved another line of the riddle."

Heather stood before Maximus in the doorway of Dunnottar chapel, a posy of purple blooming heather in her hands. Dressed in a lilac kirtle over a gold-hued lèine—one of her mother's garments that she and Iona had spent all night adjusting so it fitted properly—Heather couldn't stop smiling.

Maximus grinned back while Father Finlay wound a ribbon of turquoise and sea-blue De Keith plaid about their joined hands.

Her husband-to-be was dressed in chamois braies and a black lèine, his Roman sword hanging from one hip, his dagger strapped to the other. He was so handsome that it hurt Heather to look upon him, yet she did. Her gaze drank him in.

The chaplain led them through their vows, and when Maximus said his, Heather's vision blurred.

"I take you, Heather De Keith, to be my wedded wife," he began, his gaze riveted upon hers. "To have and to hold from this day forward, for better for worse, for richer for poorer, for fairer or fouler, in sickness and in health ...to love and to cherish, till death us part ... according to God's holy ordinance ... and thereunto I pledge you my troth."

Till death us part.

One day it would—whether or not Maximus broke his curse. The wheel of time couldn't be stopped. Just as summer couldn't last forever, neither could life—not for her at least. Meeting Maximus had made Heather determined to grasp every last bit of happiness while she could, for one never knew what lay around the corner.

When the Hammer strikes the fort upon the Shelving Slope.

Excitement quickened Heather's pulse. She was delighted they'd solved more of the riddle—no wonder Maximus had been so eager to share the news with her. Of course, she should have realized what the 'Battle Hammer' signified. But when the laird read out the missive from Shaw Irvine, she'd been distracted. Maximus had dominated her thoughts that evening.

And yet, one more line of the riddle remained unanswered. Until they deciphered it, her husband would remain immortal, and she needed to ready herself in case the Broom-star faded from the sky without the final piece in the puzzle being solved.

If the curse remained, one day she and Maximus would be forced to leave De Keith lands—for folk here would wonder why he never aged—but for now, this was their home.

Whatever happened, she had no regrets binding herself to this man.

When their vows were done and Father Finlay had untied the plaid ribbon, Maximus pulled her into his arms for a kiss. It was searing, possessive. The embrace went on and on, and soon Cassian and Draco were wolf-whistling and calling out to them.

Breathless, Maximus and Heather drew apart. However, their gazes were still locked.

Holding hands, they turned to face the group gathered on the steps beneath the chapel. Heather's mother and sister were both weeping. Her father and Maximus's friends were all grinning like fools.

The wedding banquet was a sedate one—the seven of them dined in the steward's solar. Servants had dragged in a long table, and Iona had ordered the cooks to prepare a feast of roast goose stuffed with chestnuts and pork, a range of breads studded with nuts, and kale braised in butter.

Donnan De Keith had a barrel of his best plum wine brought up from the cellars. Aila poured them all large cups before passing them around. Heather noted that her sister blushed as she handed Cassian his cup.

With all the excitement, she'd forgotten about her sister's infatuation with the handsome captain.

A little of Heather's happiness dimmed then. The curse was on Cassian too; and unlike Heather, Aila would never learn of it. Not only that, but she glimpsed no interest in Cassian's eyes as he took the cup and thanked Aila with a smile.

Her sister pined for a man who didn't feel as she did.

"A toast to the newlyweds!" Donnan De Keith climbed to his feet and raised his cup high into the air. He then cleared his throat and began a blessing. It was an old one that had been passed down through the ages of this land. "May the road rise to meet ye ... may the wind be always at yer back ... may the sun shine warm upon yer face ... the rains fall soft upon yer fields. And when eternity beckons, at the end of a life heaped high with love, may the good Lord embrace ye with the arms that have nurtured ye."

"May the road rise to meet ye!" Everyone at the table raised their cups in unison.

Heather took a sip of wine and turned to Maximus. He was watching her with that intense look that made her limbs feel as if they were melting.

"And when eternity beckons?" he asked softly.

"I will be waiting," she whispered back.

They ate and drank late into the afternoon, and then finally, when Cassian and Draco staggered away to their quarters and Heather's parents dozed in their chairs before the fire, Aila ushered the newlyweds off.

"Go on." She waved Heather away when she started clearing the table. "A bride doesn't do any chores on her wedding day. I'll get the servants to help me with these." Her grey eyes gleamed, her mouth curving at the corners. Get going before Da wakes up and pours ye more wine."

Maximus and Heather needed no further encouragement. Taking his wife by the hand, Maximus led her out of the keep and across the lower ward bailey to the guard tower.

"Cassian has given us our own quarters on the top floor," he announced with a grin. "It'll make a nice change from sleeping in the barracks ... the snoring in there was awful."

Heather laughed. "Aye ... but maybe *I* snore."

His grin turned wicked. "You don't ... I've spent nights sleeping by your side, remember?"

Warmth filtered through Heather. Aye, he had—and it had all started that night at *The Bogside Tavern*, a night when they'd been strangers. How long ago it seemed now—even if a full turn of the moon hadn't yet passed.

Reaching the top floor landing, they stopped before a large oaken door. Then, without warning, Maximus scooped her up into his arms.

Heather squealed in surprise. "What are ye doing?"

"Among my people, we have a tradition," Maximus told her, still grinning. "A man carries his bride across the threshold into their new home."

With that, he shouldered the door open and walked inside, kicking it closed behind him.

"I like this tradition," Heather admitted. There was something special about being carried in like a lady. She couldn't stop smiling as she gazed around the small chamber that would be their home from now on. A hearth burned at one end of the space, where two chairs sat awaiting them. A scrubbed wooden table dominated the room, while a door led through into what Heather supposed was their bed-chamber.

"I know it's small, but it's ours," Maximus murmured.

"It's perfect," she answered.

And it was. One day, when peace reigned once more, she hoped they'd have a home of their own in Stonehaven. Until then, these rooms and his company were all she needed.

He carried her across the living space then and into the bed-chamber. A bed dominated the far corner, near a small shuttered window, while a heavy curtain shielded the privy in the opposite corner.

Someone had scattered rose petals over the floor and the coverlet of the bed.

"God's teeth ... I didn't realize Cassian was the romantic sort," Heather said, her gaze shifting from the rose petals to the spray of spring flowers in a pot next to the bed.

Maximus laughed. "I doubt he's responsible for these touches ... I'd say your sister is the culprit."

Setting her down upon the sheepskin before the bed, Maximus leaned in for a kiss. It was soft, deep, and achingly sensual. Heather swayed against him, a groan rising in her throat.

His mouth moved over hers, and his fingers went to the laces of her kirtle. Unlacing them, he pushed the dress and the lèine underneath off her shoulders. He then stood back. His gaze raked over her while her clothing pooled around her ankles, leaving the rest of her bare.

His look was scorching, and Heather's heart began to pound wildly. Finally, they could be together without worry of discovery. They were man and wife now.

"Look at you, bonny Heather," he murmured. "Risen from the ashes."

Heather's mouth curved as she remembered their conversation back at *The Bogside Tavern*. So much had happened since that night. "Aye," she whispered. "It seems that I'm a phoenix after all."

Maximus smiled. "I'm going to take my time over this," he said, his voice husky. He then reached down and began to unbuckle his sword, dropping it to the ground before he pulled his lèine over his head. "A woman as beautiful as you needs to be loved *slowly*."

Heat built in the pit of Heather's belly at these words. Standing naked before him, she felt powerful, cherished.

He stripped off the rest of his clothes. His arousal was achingly evident, his shaft thrust up against his belly. Heather swallowed hard while excitement reared up within her; how she longed to touch him, taste him.

Heather's gaze returned to his face. He watched her, his eyes alive with hunger.

"I'm not sure I want ye to go slowly," she gasped as her breathing quickened. "It'll be torture."

His mouth curved, a wicked light catching in his dark eyes. Then he stepped close, his hands cupping her face. The heat of his body, so close and not quite touching, enveloped her. "It will," he murmured, his voice full of promise. "And we shall enjoy every moment of it."

EPILOGUE

NEWS FROM THE SOUTH

A fortnight later ...

MAXIMUS STEPPED UP onto the wall and breathed in the warm afternoon air. This was his favorite spot, this corner that looked south-east across the North Sea.

As he was no longer part of the Dunnottar Guard, he didn't have to stand watch on the ramparts. But he still liked to come up here, to admire the view and be alone with his thoughts for a while.

Maximus hadn't expected to see anyone, and so he was surprised to discover two familiar figures standing near the southern guard tower.

Cassian and Draco.

Frowning, he headed toward them. "What are you doing up here?" he greeted his friends.

"Waiting for you," Draco replied.

Maximus halted next to them and leaned against one of the crenellations. He noted that Cassian was frowning, and Maximus knew why. They'd been poring over those volumes, but were still no closer to solving that last line.

"The Broom-star only remains in the sky for two to three moons at most before it passes from sight," Cassian pointed out, "yet we still don't know who the White Hawk and the Dragon are."

Maximus heaved a sigh, raking a hand through his hair. He didn't need reminding. Despite the joy he'd found with Heather—or maybe because of it—the curse had been on his mind often over the past days.

"Well, we know the 'Battle Hammer' will strike at some point," he said finally. "Maybe the riddle will solve itself then." Maximus shifted his attention to Draco. "The Wallace has friends everywhere ... has he heard anything about Irvine's intentions?"

"Don't look at me for answers," Draco replied with a frown. "If I knew anything, I'd tell you."

"But you have the Wallace's ear, do you not?"

Draco grunted. "As much as anyone can ... the man keeps his counsel close, even with his most trusted warriors." Draco paused there. "He's suffered betrayal in the past ... and it's made him wary."

Maximus nodded. He knew something of William Wallace's history—of how he'd once been in love with a woman called Marion Braidfute. Their story had ended in tragedy when Marion was murdered in the Scottish town of Lanark. Fueled by rage and grief, Wallace attacked Lanark and took revenge by killing its English sheriff, Sir William Heselrig.

"Wallace is more focused on the English than on clan Irvine," Draco admitted after a pause. "He's determined to see the Balliol family on the Scottish throne once more."

"I do have some good news though," Cassian spoke up once more, favoring his friends with a tight smile. "De Keith wants a spy placed at Drum Castle ... and I've agreed to make the arrangements."

Grins spread across Maximus and Draco's faces in response. This was good news indeed. They had their own reasons for wanting to know the moment Irvine moved, but De Keith's paranoia served them well.

"And he's increased the Guard, I see," Maximus said, raising an eyebrow.

"Thirty new men," Cassian confirmed. "Even with the Wallace's force here, he's not taking any chances."

The three men fell silent then, letting the sigh of the wind eddy around them atop the wall. Below, the clang of metal from the forge echoed against the stone. Galbraith had wisely kept his mouth shut ever since Wallace decided to let the mystery of his brother's disappearance go. However, Maximus had seen Blair a handful of times since—the man had a glare to curdle milk.

All of a sudden, a shout from below intruded. "Captain! There's a man at the gates. He brings word!"

Cassian pushed himself off the wall and strode past Maximus and Draco, heading toward the stairs that led down to the lower ward.

His friends followed him. There was an urgency in the guard's voice that alerted Maximus's instincts. Something of note had happened.

They approached the main gates, where a courier stood next to a lathered courser. Clad in dusty leathers, his broad face flushed, the messenger watched Cassian approach.

"Captain Gaius," the man gasped, still out of breath from the ride. "I have news for the laird ... and it's not good I'm afraid."

"What is it?" Cassian greeted him. "You can tell me first."

"The English have attacked. They have taken most of the Lowlands. And as I speak, Stirling is under siege."

Behind them, Maximus heard the gathering crowd of guards and warriors start to mutter amongst themselves. Curses and oaths rang against the walls. They all knew that the English had been raiding north of the border, but no one thought they'd be so bold as to launch another full-scale assault—not this soon, at least.

Cassian ignored them. "Will Stirling hold?"

The man's throat bobbed. "I doubt it ... Edward's forces far outnumber ours ... the castle is likely to fall, if it hasn't already."

This news caused a chill to filter across the bailey. The angry mutters of the men behind them quietened to an ominous rumble.

"Come." Cassian beckoned to the man. "De Keith and Wallace need to hear about this. I'll take you to them."

Maximus watched the two men walk off; they clove a path through the crowd to the steps leading into the keep. Once they'd disappeared, he turned to Draco. As often, his friend's expression was impossible to read.

"Well ... things are changing," Maximus said in Latin. "Maybe that bodes well for us."

Draco nodded, his mouth compressing. "Not for Scotland though," he reminded him.

Maximus frowned. Draco was right. The people of this land had repelled a number of invaders over the years, including the might of the Roman Empire. King Edward of England wanted dominion over Scotland, and it appeared he wasn't going to give up easily. Bloody years lay ahead for all of them.

But this time, Maximus would be fighting on the side of the Scots, and he was proud to do so.

Turning, he spied a woman emerge from the guard tower behind them. As always, the sight of his wife warmed his soul. Heather stood on the top step, brow furrowed as she watched the milling crowd. Maximus left Draco with a nod and made his way up to her.

"Edward has attacked," he greeted her without preamble. "Stirling is under siege."

Her throat bobbed, even as her grey-green eyes hardened. "So soon?"

Maximus nodded. Stepping close, he gazed down at her. "Honestly, Dunnottar is the safest place to be in Scotland right now."

"But the English have taken this fortress before," she reminded him, "and don't forget Irvine and his 'Battle Hammer'."

There was little chance of that.

"And yet we have the Wallace," he said after a pause. "A host of loyal men follow him, me among them."

Heather held his gaze, her jaw firming. "The English hate Wallace, ye know? If Edward Longshanks discovers his greatest foe is here, he'll pull down this fort, stone by stone."

Maximus smiled, his fingers catching her by the chin. "And we'll be ready for him."

She stared back at him, her lips parting. "Ye are the bravest man I've ever met, Maximus Cato," she murmured. "Does anything scare ye?"

"Not much," he admitted sincerely, "not anymore." He hesitated then, his fingers tracing the line of her jaw. "Just the thought of living on without you, carissima."

The End

FROM THE AUTHOR

Well ... where to begin.

MAXIMUS was the book of my heart. I enjoy writing all my stories, yet I've never loved writing one as much as I did this novel. I actually started typing slower ... just to prolong it!

Maximus and Heather stole my soul. I don't usually start stories with a 'one-night stand', but it felt right for these two passionate characters. The adventure that follows had me awake at night thinking about how I was going to get them out of the trouble I'd written them into! On The Road Romance is so much fun to write!

I loved being able to blend two eras with a little bit of fantasy. Those of you who've read a few of my books know that I have a passion for the Dark Ages, and after writing about three sexy centurions, I definitely have a hankering to set some novels in Roman Britain ... so watch this space.

There's quite a bit of historical background that went into this novel (read my historical notes below for details on it), and it was great fun to weave some real events and characters into the plot. But for me, the story is everything, and I hope Maximus and Heather's HEA left you as breathless as it did me.

Get ready for Cassian's story!

Jayne x

HISTORICAL NOTES

These notes are quite long—but if you like to know where my ideas come from, you should find them really interesting!

This tale hinges around the legend of the Ninth legion—an army of around five thousand men who marched into the wilds of Caledonia in around 118 AD and were never seen again.

The Ninth legion was also called 'the Hispana', or Spanish legion. The commanders would have all been Roman (hence Maximus coming from Ostia near Rome), but most of the legion was made up of soldiers from Hispania (Spain). Hence why my next two heroes come from there: Cassian comes from the north of Spain, and Draco is a Spanish Moor from the southern coast of the Iberian Peninsula.

There are many stories and theories about what may have happened to all those men. The most likely (posed by the author Rosemary Sutcliffe in her amazing book, *The Eagle of the Ninth*) is that the soldiers were slowly picked off by Pictish war bands on their way north and then ambushed when their numbers dwindled. The book has been made into the movie *The Eagle*, which is good (although the storyline has been altered a little!). The movie *Centurion* is also about the fate of a group of Roman centurions from the Ninth who survive a massacre and try to return to their garrison in the south. Both movies are worth watching if the legend fascinates you, as it does me.

Of course, my story where our three survivors are cursed by a Pictish bandrúi, is pure fantasy ... but who knows ...

Halley's Comet is a prominent feature in the whole series. Back in the Dark Ages and Medieval period it didn't go by that name (as it was named after the scientist who 'discovered' it in 1758). Instead, there are references to it being called 'the fire-tailed star'. Maximus calls it 'the Broom-star', which was actually a name that Chinese astronomers attached to the comet. Halley's Comet appears in our skies every 75-76 years, and in ancient times it was often heralded as an ill omen. The comet actually appeared in the night-sky in the months preceding the Norman invasion of England, something which the English blamed for their defeat. The Bayeux tapestry even shows the comet! The year that Maximus and Heather meet, 1301, was a year in which the comet was sighted.

Dunnottar (pronounced *Doonotter*) does mean 'fort on the shelving slope' in Scottish Gaelic: Dùn Fhoithear. The castle is a mighty stronghold perched upon cliffs on the north-eastern coast of Scotland. As I mention in my story, the castle was taken by the English in the final years of the 13th Century and then liberated by William Wallace and his men. When the English garrison realized they were doomed, they locked themselves inside the chapel, hoping to find sanctuary there. However, Wallace showed them no mercy and burned the lot of them to death inside it.

William Wallace, of course, is the famous Scottish freedom fighter. He has a small role in MAXIMUS, but as you might have guessed will be appearing in the next two books as well. History records him as a huge, giant of a man with thick dark hair and beard. He was also reputed to have a terrible temper. Not a man to mess with!

The year 1301, when our story starts in earnest, is also in the midst of the First Scottish Wars of Independence (although the conflict wasn't called that at the time). This was a politically complex time, and as such, I have deliberately simplified aspects of it. When MAXIMUS begins, the English have started raiding again after a period of uneasy peace. Later that year, Edward 'Longshanks' of England resumes his campaign in earnest—as we discover in the Epilogue. The laird of Dunnottar, Robert De Keith was an English prisoner, as I describe, and he did have a wife named Elizabeth. However, his brother David, is fictitious, as is Lady Gavina.

Apparently, the De Keith and the Irvine clans did feud over the years, although Shaw Irvine and his 'Battle Hammer' are pure fiction.

When Maximus and Heather arrive in Stirling, I mention The Battle of Stirling Bridge. This occurred in September 1297, when the forces of William Wallace and Andrew Moray defeated the English there. I also mention the church of the Holy Rude. The kirk does exist, although (to my knowledge) there is no temple of Mithras underneath it!

I got the idea for the temple from a church in Rome, Italy. The Catholic church of San Clemente al Laterano (near the Colosseum) stands atop a 2nd Century mithraeum, a temple to the ancient Roman god Mithras. I visited the church and temple many years ago (I lived in Rome for a decade in my twenties), but can still remember descending to the dark, damp, cave-like vault, and seeing the altar where a relief depicts Mithras slaying a bull. In the pre-Christian era of the Roman Empire, Mithras was a very popular god worshipped mainly by soldiers.

This idea was so cool, I've been dying to use it in a story for years!

Of course, as with all my novels, I bend and shape historical fact to suit the story I'm telling. As much as I love research and incorporating fascinating details, they can never overshadow the love story.

CHARACTER GLOSSARY

The three immortal centurions:
Maximus—from Ostia, Italia
Cassian—from Brigantium, Hispania
Draco—from Valentia, Hispania

William Wallace—Scottish freedom fighter

The De Keiths
Robert De Keith (former laird of Dunnottar, currently imprisoned by the English)
Elizabeth De Keith (Robert's wife)
Robbie De Keith (Robert and Elizabeth's young son)
David De Keith (Robert's younger brother—current laird of Dunnottar Castle)
Gavina De Keith (David's wife, née Ivine)
Donnan De Keith (Steward of Dunnottar)
Iona De Keith (Donnan's wife)
Heather De Keith (Donnan and Iona's eldest daughter)
Aila De Keith (Heather's younger sister)

The Irvines
Shaw Irvine (laird of Drum Castle—brother to Gavina De Keith)

The Galbraiths
Logan Galbraith (laird of Culcreuch Castle)
Lena Galbraith (Logan's wife)
Cory Galbraith (Logan and Lena's son—the eldest of four sons: Rory, Aran, and Duglas)
Iain Galbraith (cousin to Cory, former blacksmith of Fintry)
Blair Galbraith (Iain's younger brother, smith at Dunnottar)

ACKNOWLEDGEMENTS

Thanks so much to my wonderful readers. Your emails and social media messages mean the world to me—it's such a thrill to know that my stories touch you.

I'd also like to thank the wonderful Otago/Southland Chapter of RWNZ (Romance Writers of New Zealand). You're such a supportive and encouraging group of writers. Among the group, special thanks goes to Laura H, for her suggestion that Halley's Comet would be a cool inclusion in this book. You were so right, Laura!

And a huge thank you to my husband, Tim, who works as hard as I do on these books! You're amazing, Timbo.

ABOUT THE AUTHOR

Award-winning author Jayne Castel writes epic Historical and Fantasy Romance. Her vibrant characters, richly researched historical settings and action-packed adventure romance transport readers to forgotten times and imaginary worlds.

Jayne is the author of the Amazon bestselling BRIDES OF SKYE series—a Medieval Scottish Romance trilogy about three strong-willed sisters and the men who love them. An exciting spin-off series set in the same story-world, THE SISTERS OF KILBRIDE, is now available as well. In love with all things Scottish, Jayne also writes romances set in Dark Ages Scotland ... sexy Pict warriors anyone?

When she's not writing, Jayne is reading (and re-reading) her favorite authors, cooking Italian feasts, and taking her dog, Juno, for walks. She lives in New Zealand's beautiful South Island.

Connect with Jayne online:
www.jaynecastel.com
Email: contact@jaynecastel.com

CPSIA information can be obtained
at www.ICGtesting.com
Printed in the USA
BVHW031006140221
600081BV00005B/88

9 780473 532932